Haines Junction

Haines Junction

a novel

David Thompson

CAITLIN PRESS

01 02 03 04 05 06 18 17 16 15 14 13

Caitlin Press Inc.
8100 Alderwood Road,
Halfmoon Bay, BC V0N 1Y1
www.caitlin-press.com

Text design by Kathleen Fraser.
Cover design by Vici Johnstone.
Edited by Susan Mayse and Kathleen Fraser.
Printed in Canada

Caitlin Press Inc. acknowledges financial support from the Government of Canada through the Canada Book Fund and the Canada Council for the Arts, and from the Province of British Columbia through the British Columbia Arts Council and the Book Publisher's Tax Credit.

Canada Council   Conseil des Arts
for the Arts   du Canada

BRITISH COLUMBIA
ARTS COUNCIL
An agency of the Province of British Columbia

Library and Archives Canada Cataloguing in Publication
Thompson, David (David William)
Haines Junction / David Thompson.

ISBN 978-1-927575-04-8

I. Title.

PS8639.H62673H25 2013   C813'.6   C2013-900323-1

Contents

Roswell

My name is Joshua Waldo Lake Shackelton. I was born after the Great War in 1946 in New Mexico in a small town called Artesia, south of Roswell, the world-famous site of alien research. Artesia was named after the artesian wells that once irrigated the thirsty peach orchards until they were pumped dry in the 1920s.

My friend Greg and I were adventurers. The desert and hills were ours to explore, and our imaginations carried us wherever we wanted to go. I loved the outdoors.

We built a fort about a mile from our homes out of construction salvage. With my dad's binoculars we scanned the desert for signs of aliens and wildlife.

Greg stood on a small rise, his thin arms poking out of his striped T-shirt and his skinny legs sticking out of baggy short pants. Holding the binoculars tightly to his eyes, he made the sound of a radio. "Aaawk, Gila Monster One to Gila Monster Two. Armadillo preparing for attack. Take evasive action."

Then we would race across the sand, ray guns in hand, to where the animal was lurking, only to discover it was a clump of bushes.

"Come in, Gila Monster One. This is Gila Monster Two. False alarm, I repeat, false alarm. Return to base. Over and out."

We would run back to the fort and once again secure it against invasion.

The flying disc recovered by the army's 509th Bomber Wing in 1947 was known to everyone. We spent days scanning the skies for bright, shiny cigar-shaped objects and theorizing about the life of an alien. Greg asked the questions. I had all the answers.

"Do you think they know algebra?" Greg asked thoughtfully, scratching his brush cut.

"They do square roots in their heads," I said.

"What if they attack us like in *Creature from the Black Lagoon*?" Greg shuddered.

We had just seen the movie, and he was still terrified.

"Don't worry, we can outrun them. They have different gravity on their planet, so their bodies are weaker," I said. "Charles Atlas could probably take them all on himself."

"What do you think their planet is called?" Greg asked.

"Zots."

"I think you're right."

With the help of the G.I. Bill, my parents bought a house on the banks of the Pecos River three dusty miles from town. My life in Artesia was unremarkable. My mother stayed home and cared for Dad and me. She came from a large family, and her mother, her sisters and their many kids visited nearly every day. My grandmother couldn't seem to hug me enough.

"Come here, you little boy, come see your grandmother," she would say, holding out her arms.

My father was a skilled electrician, and when he was sober, a good father and husband. He had a warm heart, but life got the better of him. He liked to drink and gamble more than anything. He would come home and sway back and forth in the middle of the living room with a smile on his face—he was a happy drunk—and make excuses for losing his paycheque. Apparently he wasn't a very good gambler, because we never had any money.

"Why don't you just cash your cheque, stand on the street corner and give the money away?" my mother asked.

Funny thing about Mom. No matter how angry she was, she never raised her voice. Not like Joy and Richard Wallace next door, who fought so the whole neighbourhood could hear them. "Self first and self last, Richard, and if there's anything left over it's Richard again," Joy screamed.

I didn't like to see Dad drunk or hear my parents argue. I would leave the house and find refuge in the fort; sometimes I would sleep over in it. It was calm and quiet, and I could look to the skies for spaceships.

I was good in school, always the top of the class. Greg and I won first prize at a science fair with our "soybean in a jar" growth display. We wrapped blotting paper around the inside of four wide-mouthed Mason jars and slipped a soybean between the glass and the paper. One bean had water and sunlight, the next water but no sunlight and the third no water and no sunlight. The fourth we painted red and purple, glued coloured thread on it for roots and called it "a bean influenced by an alien spaceship crash site."

It was a popular display, with the doctored bean getting all the attention. It was easy as pie to convince the younger kids that it really was an alien bean worth a million dollars.

"That's not true. There is no such thing as an alien bean," a second-grade boy argued. "There are alien beings but not alien beans."

"Yes, it is true. Do you know the story about Jack and the beanstalk?" I asked.

"Yes," he said.

"Well, that was an alien bean!"

"Nooo," he said, and ran off calling for his mother.

In the bottom of a bedroom closet I found a battered cardboard box full of papers, photographs and a flight diary. They were from the glory days when my father flew B-25 Mitchell bombers out of Northern England and rained vengeance and death down upon German men, women and children.

The pages of the diary were written in blue ink from a fountain pen, while the cities bombed were highlighted in red. Baden-Baden, Cologne, Düsseldorf and Hamburg were a few of them. There was also a hand-tinted picture of Dad with a note on the back saying it had been taken before he was shipped overseas. He wore his aircrew hat and uniform. He looked off into the distance with a soft smile on his young face.

On lazy Saturday afternoons Greg and I watched war documentaries on television. I fried a mound of egg sandwiches, and we dipped them in ketchup and washed them down with glasses of cold milk. The grainy black and white movies showed a continuous stream of violence against man, beast and property. When the narrator said, "Dresden was firebombed," I would respond, "My dad did that."

I hate to say it, but Greg was impressed with my dad's bombing.

"Bull's eye," he would scream as demolished buildings toppled over into the street in a cloud of dust.

When I had the box out, Dad would happen by and pick up a picture or letter. He would turn them over in his hands, front to back, then toss them back in the box and walk away. Later he would sit in his chair, deep in thought. After a while, he would get up and mutter to himself, "What's done is done," and go about his business.

When he went out, my mother would send me along, hoping I would prevent him from going to the bar. It never worked.

"I have to go down to the hardware store to pick up a thingamabob. I'll be back shortly."

"Take Waldo with you."

Mom always called me Waldo.

"Aww, Ma," I would protest.

I was sentenced to countless hours of waiting in the 1956 Chevrolet convertible while he drank tequila and gambled in Rose's Cantina. He left the roof down in the warm desert nights, so I lay back and watched the shooting stars whisk across the blue-black sky and over the horizon.

From time to time, my father would bring out a bag of chips and a cold Coke. "Is everything okay here, sport?"

"Sure, Dad, everything is just hunky-dory," I would say, never complaining, and then slouch down into the seat and play my marble maze games for the hundredth time.

One night, after waiting for a few hours, I slid over into the driver's seat. The keys were in the ignition, and I thought, "I can drive this thing."

I bunched the car seat blanket under me so I could see over the hood and cautiously turned the key. The Chevy's engine purred to life, and a feeling of power flowed through me. I adjusted the rear-view mirror as I had seen my dad do, disengaged the parking brake, shifted the automatic to R and backed out. I spent the next hour gliding in circles around the parking lot, clutching the steering wheel as tightly as I could.

When I eased the car back into its parking spot, I was covered in sweat. I hadn't realized how nervous I was, but it was exhilarating.

My dad came staggering out soon afterward. "Someone told me you were driving our car."

"No, Dad, how could I? I don't have a licence. They must have been drunk."

"You're right," he said, and weaved his way back into the bar, muttering to himself.

"I bet I could drive him home some night," I thought.

From then on, I was never bored. I learned the pleasures of driving with the ragtop down and rock 'n' roll on the radio. The patrons got used to me. I would put on Dad's aviator sunglasses, prop my elbow on the door and wave to them as I cruised by at barely five miles per hour.

My dad never mentioned it again, drunk or sober, though he did complain about his gas bill.

I dreamed that when I grew up, I would drive in the NASCAR races.

One Saturday afternoon I invited Greg along for the ride. He was thrilled, and we played intergalactic spaceships for a couple of hours. We shot everyone arriving in or leaving the parking lot with our ray guns and we even transported a few of them to Zots.

"This is the best afternoon of my life," Greg said.

"Mine too."

"How did you learn to drive like that?"

"I read the manual and watched my dad," I said.

Late one night the piano playing abruptly stopped, and I heard a ruckus from Rose's Cantina. My father crashed out through the swinging doors, clutching a handful of bills to his chest with one hand and holding onto his hat with the other. A group of men, shouting obscenities and waving their fists in the air, chased him. One brandished a rusty machete. Dad dumped the bills in the back seat and jumped in over the door. We sped away, leaving everyone in a cloud of dust.

Dad careened down the dirt road and hit the highway, scattering gravel over the asphalt. He then gunned it for home much faster than I would have driven. He laughed like a madman. "That was close."

I was terrified and had crouched down in front of the seat.

Worried about my father's sudden unpopularity, I asked, "What happened?"

"They were dealing off the bottom of the deck, so I clubbed one with a tequila bottle. The only problem was I was sitting at a table with all five Santiago brothers."

"Which one did you hit, Dad?"

"I think it was Esteban, the one with the machete. He seemed to be the maddest." He laughed and reached for the car's lighter to light his cigarette.

Dad went back to Rose's the next weekend and bought a few rounds for the brothers. Soon all was forgiven. He'd been correct; Esteban had a bandaged head.

"*Si*, we cheat," Eloy said. "Please accept out humble apologizes." Rodolfo, Noe and Alfonzo apologized too. Then all five brothers sat back and laughed the uproarious belly laugh of the don't-give-a-damns.

For some reason that run-in with the Santiago brothers cemented my father's relationship with them. They started turning up en masse—kids, wives, uncles, aunts and grandparents—to our house for the biggest Sunday barbecues the neighbourhood had ever seen. We roasted whole sheep on spits and washed down mounds of corn, rice and beans with gallons of iced tea and tequila.

"Here's to my new flight crew," my father would announce toward the end of the evening, standing on a picnic table, swaying back and forth as he raised his drink in a toast.

The brothers would raise their glasses and respond in unison, "We are your wingmen, Richard." Then they would laugh their belly laugh.

My mother made no pretense about her feelings and would stay in the kitchen. She didn't like drinking at her house. The Santiago women raised their eyebrows to each other but if my mother saw she didn't care. That's one thing I loved about Mom: she didn't pretend for anyone.

The summer before I was to enter grade ten, my mother took ill and spent a month in the hospital. It was only then I learned she had been dealing with cancer for a long time. My parents had thought it best to keep this news from me.

I visited her almost every day. She lay propped up in bed, weak and pale. Her hair had turned white.

"Waldo, my dear," she would softly say, "come sit down."

She would pat the bed where her hand lay; she was too weak to move it.

I tried not to cry, but I was frantic with worry. What if she died? Who was going to be home when I came in from school? Who would look after the house?

Eloy Santiago told me not to worry. "The angels will look after your mom, and all the popes from all of history will be there to welcome her into heaven."

I believed the angel part but not about the popes.

My father couldn't handle it. He sat by the bed without speaking, holding his head in his hands and crying.

Mom died in late August. The Santiago family was a great help during the funeral, acting as pallbearers, cooking the food and providing a mariachi band for the graveside.

After her burial, my father drank even more, and we both decided it would be best if I went to live with my grandparents, Winslow and Angela, in California.

The night before I left, Dad and I sat in the darkened living room talking. My father opened a bottle of rum and poured himself a glass. I brought ice from the fridge whenever he asked.

"I'm going to tell you a bit of history about me and your grandparents," he said.

"When my mother was just eighteen, she fell in love with my dad, Winslow. He was a ranch hand from California. On a summer's eve they packed their bags, skedaddled from the ranch and eloped. Her father—my grandfather, your great-grandfather Alexander—called the sheriff, and they were caught just as the train was leaving the station. It must have been an anxious moment for them, watching the lawmen run and board the train as it pulled out from the loading platform.

"'Two more minutes and we would have made it,' my mother told me. 'Winslow spent the night in jail.'

"They kept him locked up for three days, and the police officers threatened a beating for what he did. They were no doubt influenced by Alexander's rage," Dad said.

"Dad was no pushover either, and he shook the bars and dared them to try. But being the character that he was, by the next evening he had the jailer playing crib through the bars and feeding him an extra helping of chicken and biscuits.

"Your great-grandfather was a weather-beaten, hard-nosed businessman whose size and personality towered over most men's. He had clawed and fought his way from cowpuncher to one of the biggest beef producers in the western United States. He owned land and railroads." Dad poured another drink.

"When the truth came out that Mom was pregnant, Alexander gave the order to release Dad. A marriage was hastily arranged and took place in the sheriff's office at night to avert prying eyes from the family embarrassment. A reluctant and complaining Justice of the Peace, who didn't bother to put on a shirt but wore pants and suspenders over his long johns, was dragged out of bed to complete the paperwork. One deputy acting as a witness actually held a shotgun.

"'It was the most embarrassing moment of my life,' Mother told me.

"Months later, Mother miscarried twins. The stress did it. The family proceeded to shun my parents for the rest of their days. I'm sure this shunning influenced the lives of me and my four siblings. My mom and dad were devoted to each other. Money, wealth and power weren't going to change that. I swore to God that I would never abandon my family. Grandfather Alexander disowned my mother, his daughter, and broke her heart. How could he do that? She is the sweetest person you ever met. And he abandoned his grandchildren. We all wanted to visit our grandparents but we never could."

That was the end of Dad's story. We sat in silence for a few minutes. Then I went over and hugged him.

"I'm sorry to hear that, Dad," I said.

I went to the kitchen for more ice, and when I returned, he had fallen asleep. I took the glass from his hand, placed it on the coffee table and covered him with a blanket.

The next morning, Dad gave me the price of a ticket and travelling money, then dropped me off at the Greyhound bus depot. Instead I decided to see the world, and walked out to the highway.

As I waited for a ride, a flatbed Ford came down the road in the opposite direction. The cab was packed, and two men sat on the back among tools and lumber. It was the Santiago brothers. They came to a screeching halt when they recognized me.

Esteban, the eldest, ran over, grabbed me by the shoulder and hugged me. "Hey, little man, you're headed in the wrong direction. Where are you going?"

"I'm heading to California to live with my grandparents. I'm hitchhiking to save my money," I said.

"Okay," Rodolfo said.

All five men reached into their pockets, pulled out bills and coins and pushed them into my cupped hands. Noe said, "You can pay us back, if we need it, when we meet again."

"See you again!" Esteban said. They ran back to their truck, jumped in and, with more waves and shouts of good luck, sped away.

"Don't tell my dad you saw me hitchhiking," I yelled after them. "And take care of him for me, please!"

"Don't worry," one hollered back.

I hoped that someday I'd meet the Santiago brothers again so I could pay back their good wishes and generosity.

It took me six days, sleeping under the stars and taking numerous rides, to cross Arizona and reach Visalia.

My grandparents' well-kept bungalow was at the end of a lane, surrounded by olive groves. My grandmother came to the screen door, wiping dough from her hands onto her apron. She gasped when she saw me. "Joshua! What has happened? You are such a sight."

Later she scolded me for not buying a bus ticket. "You could have gotten kidnapped or worse."

Visalia was a classic California small town. As I walked down the wide streets filled with bustling stores, crowded restaurants and places of business, I could feel the energy and prosperity in the air. The fruit and vegetable stands overflowed onto the sidewalks with produce as fresh and ripe as could be.

On Main Street people greeted each other with a friendly smile, and I could sense the excitement at the corner hardware store, where people could buy anything on earth and their credit was trusted. In the town's centre stood a towering red-brick schoolhouse with a silver bell that rang at the start and end of each school day. There was an honesty and hope about the place; everything seemed possible, and life was good.

At school I played football and joined the drama club. My grandmother and I would sit for hours at the kitchen table while she helped with my homework. She was a bright woman who had gone back to school after her children were raised and worked for the City of Visalia as a planner for many years.

I was worried about my dad and phoned him often. I would say, "Hi. How are you doing?"

"Fine, fine," he would slur.

There wasn't much I could say when he was drunk, so after some small talk, I hung up.

More then two years went by. I was on the honour roll and looking forward to graduating when the unexpected happened. Early one morning, before anyone else had gotten out of bed, my grandfather rose and bathed before breakfast. He cooked his own bacon and eggs and made toast and coffee. My grandmother said later, "He never did that before in fifty years of marriage." Then he lay down on the parlour couch and passed away. My grandmother was crushed. Unable to live in the house, she sold it and moved into an apartment. I boarded with family friends for a few months until I graduated, and shortly afterward my grandmother also passed away. I believe she died of grief.

My dad had come up for his father's funeral but was too heartbroken for his mother's; he stayed home.

"I'll come up to put flowers on her grave when I can," he said.

The day after I graduated, I received a notice from the draft board to report to Fort Jackson in Southern Carolina. Two weeks later I was discharged for being colour-blind.

"You might shoot your own men in the jungle if you cannot tell the difference between a Vietcong and an American," the drill instructor said.

Thank God I don't have to shoot anyone, I thought.

The army kicked me out and set me free. My life was now my own. I could go anywhere I wanted. I'd often thought the Canadian forest would be a great place to hike. I could work my way up to Alaska.

I phoned Dad to tell him I was going to Canada.

"You're not dodging the draft, are you, son?"

"No, Pa, I'm colour-blind."

"Okay." He sounded relieved. "Watch out for those pesky blackflies and dress warm."

The phone went silent for a few seconds.

"You know they're all communists up there, don't you?" he said.

"I'll be careful of the blackflies and the communists, Dad."

"Good," he said.

"Goodbye," I said, and hung up the phone.

Winter Harbour

Canadians are so trusting. When I arrived at the bus station in downtown Vancouver, I answered an ad at Canada Manpower and was given directions, ten dollars and a ferry ticket over to Vancouver Island. No one asked my nationality.

The logging camp was asleep when I arrived, having walked and hitchhiked all night from the ferry terminal at Departure Bay. I dozed off on the cook shack steps next to the garbage cans. A while later someone poked me in the ribs. I looked up at an elderly worker clad in kitchen whites from his cap to his sneakers.

"You shouldn't be sleeping beside the garbage. The bears will think you're their next meal," he said. "Are you the kitchen help?"

"I am," I mumbled.

"Good. I'm Bob, the bullcook," he said, holding out his hand for me to shake. "You'd better come inside to get dressed and drink some coffee. Your shift starts in half an hour."

Bob turned out to be an okay guy and treated me well. He told a hundred stories about cooking in camps. Most of them involved bears in the garbage, and all of them ended with the exclamation, "I'll never forget that bear as long as I live! It scared the hell out of me." He wouldn't have made a good stand-up comedian, because he laughed at his own stories.

I barely got through the first day of work. I was exhausted. I gratefully threw myself into the bed I was given in the bunkhouse. From then on I worked six days a week, ten hours a day, for the next eight months. Scrubbing pots was good for me; it was an easy job without stress.

"You're the best damn pearl diver we ever had," Bob said.

The kitchen was run like the army. A troop of cooks, bakers, dishwashers and flunkies, all dressed in starched whites, danced and slid on the linoleum floor around cauldrons of soup and huge grills covered with steaks, eggs, hash browns and hotcakes.

The loggers lined up to fill their plates and every chair in the mess hall. God help the cook who served runny eggs—they'd be tossed back at him— and God help the logger who dared to complain. The cooks had their own ways of getting back.

"Where's my damn medium-rare steak? I've gotten well done three times in a row," a logger said, pulling off his hard hat and sprinkling sawdust on his tray.

"We're sorry. We'll try another," the grill cook said, winking at the baker, who was stuffing trays of buns into the oven.

On my day off, I hiked into the forest. I was surprised to find that solitude appealed to me and at how calm I felt when I was alone in the woods. It was a spiritual experience; I found myself thinking about God more than usual, which had been hardly ever.

In June I gave and finished two weeks' notice, packed my knapsack and headed for the wilderness. I kept on walking and never looked back.

I found a spot I liked and decided to build a log home. At that time I wasn't skilled and didn't have tools. I checked my map and made a three-day hike into Winter Harbour, the nearest settlement, and purchased a saw, axe, file and chisels. Winter Harbour had been a haven for sailing ships two hundred years before. Now it served recreational and commercial fishing boats. I liked the people in Winter Harbour. They were friendly, and over time I got to know all fifty of them.

I visited the library, which was an impressive private collection in the crowded bungalow of Mrs. Hoppel and her husband, Mervin. She was a retired schoolteacher and librarian. Teacher Jane, as she liked to be called, had taught at a Montessori school in Vancouver for years. She was a big woman who set her hair in tight, bouncy curls and wore cotton sack dresses down to her ankles. Rummaging among the books on the shelves and stacked in boxes, she breathed heavily.

"I've got to get back to walking for exercise," she wheezed.

Teacher Jane had an encyclopedic memory for authors and books but not for where she put things. She would invite me in for tea and cookies, and in a motherly way, ask about my health and well-being. Halfway through a cup, she would jump up and start rummaging.

"Here it is, Joshua. I knew I had *Moby Dick*. Next time you visit, I'm going to find you *Mutiny on the Bounty* for sure. I know I have it."

Teacher Jane's husband, Mervin, owned the village's general store and boat rental, which he ran alone. Mervin was small and pale and looked like he had been born to own a store. His striped apron showed a hundred marks from coloured pens he'd stuffed into the chest pocket. He wore a button with the universal "no" sign over the word "nukes." He was outraged by the senseless testing of nuclear weapons on Amchitka Island.

"What's a man doing all alone in the bush like that? He should have a wife," he said when I was in for supplies.

Mervin never spoke directly when he wanted to make his opinion known but spoke of some other person.

I played along with him. "Well, Mervin, if that man did find a woman he could marry, I would advise him to tie the knot. It's lonely out there."

Mervin gave me a studied look and said, "Yes, I believe you're right. It can be lonely.

I chose to build on a rocky ledge and set to work following instructions from a book on building with logs. I made everything from cedar and fir. My swede saw and broadaxe felled trees up to two feet across and one hundred feet tall. I scraped the bark, carefully scribed the logs and fitted them together to create joints that kept out the wind and rain. My first attempts were rough, and I had to stuff the chinks with moss, but as I got the hang of it, the rest turned out pretty good. I had a natural skill for carpentry.

I split the soft cedar into shakes for the roof and gable ends. I salvaged some weather-worn one-by-eight boards from an abandoned building to add a floor and made it draft-proof with building paper. After three months of working long days, I had a snug cabin, eight feet by eight feet and ten feet to the roof ridge. It was small enough that the logs looked oddly out of proportion but it was large enough for a bed, table, several chairs and shelves. I was particularly proud of the door latch and hinges I built from the book's instructions. I had a small stove that I lit on the dampest days, but I did most of my cooking outside over an open fire.

A nearby stream provided crystal-clear water for all my needs. At times I felt like Robinson Crusoe.

I decorated the trees around the cabin with rocks and wood chimes that I spent considerable time balancing. I dyed them red and blue with berry juice. On windy days the intermittent sound of rock on wood was pleasant.

I was reading in my chair when there was a hard knock at the door. It made me jump. I hadn't heard footsteps.

"Who's there?" I shouted.

There was no answer. I sat back, closed my book and reached from where I sat to open the door. Standing on the second step was a tall, thin man whose age was difficult to determine. He wore a multicoloured English footballer's scarf around his neck and a Mao cap with a faded red star. His pea jacket was buttoned tightly around his chest and he'd tucked his baggy pants into his boots. His face was narrow; he had a high forehead, pale blue eyes and a nose that had been broken at some time.

"Polo," he later explained.

His aggressive knocking had thrown me off, and I didn't know what to say. We stood staring for the longest uncomfortable moment.

Breaking the silence and looking at his hat, I asked, "Are you a communist?" I felt stupid as soon as I'd said it.

The question seemed to annoy him. Observing me intently, he answered indignantly in a clear, cultured voice, enunciating every letter. "No, I am not a communist. My name is Cosmopolitan Matisse. I have broken bread with Picasso, explored the Roman ruins of Alexandria, sat with scholars in Timbuktu debating the existence of self, combed the endless Casbah of Marrakesh for treasures and worshipped with the Buddhists in Ceylon."

He then lowered his head and looked over his glasses. In an authoritative voice he asked, "And who, may I ask, are you?"

I had nothing to compare with his pedigree but I started to answer, "I'm from California—"

He interrupted me by raising his palm and said, "I am completely surprised to see that you are here. This is totally unexpected. I never knew that anyone else lived in this part of the forest."

"My name is Joshua Shackelton, and I have been here for a while," I said.

He raised his eyebrows higher than I had ever seen anyone do before. "Joshua Shackelton. That is an unlikely name. Is it an alias? Are you hiding from something or someone?"

Why he would think I was hiding, I didn't know. Unnerved by his questioning, I started to answer, but he interrupted again. I thought he was damned rude.

"I know how long you have been here. If you had been here longer, I would have paid you and your humble abode a visit earlier." He stuck his head farther into the doorway and swivelled it around to get a better look.

"I was unaware that there was a restriction on who could live here," I said.

"No excuses, no excuses," Cosmopolitan said, closing his eyes and waving an unusually long index finger in the air.

Then, using the same finger, he jabbed in the direction he came from, saying, "I live just over there. Everyone knows the code of the forest."

His know-it-all attitude was starting to annoy me. I said, "I have never heard of the code of the forest."

I could see his mind was racing to make up an answer. "The code of the forest is…" he said slowly, stalling for time. Then, getting an idea, he quickly finished, "…that neighbours should be seen and not heard."

"That saying is 'Children should be seen and not heard,'" I said. My confidence shot up once I'd answered him back.

"Whatever," Cosmopolitan said with another wave of his hand.

It turned out he lived inland, ten miles deeper into the forest.

"I thought I was living here alone. That was my intention," I said.

"Well, you are not alone. I am here, and that's that. I guess we're neighbours," he said.

I realized then that what he wanted most was a neighbour. He had his head turned away but looked at me sideways, and his expression told me that he was glad I was here. Later I learned that Cosmopolitan, like Mervin, always beat around the bush and never said directly what he meant or wanted. He was also more argumentative than I could sometimes bear. I accepted him for his sake, not my own; I thought he needed companionship and a friend. I never asked him why he was in the forest. It was none of my business.

On his first visit I invited him in for tea, and he accepted eagerly. Cosmopolitan glanced at the stack of books and papers piled on the shelves, and as his eyes brightened, he let out a snort. "I see you have discovered Teacher Jane's stash of books."

Cosmopolitan visited for two days. He would sit and talk, then jump up and walk off in a different direction each time. Where he was going, I didn't ask. I thought his nervous energy kept him hopping. He preferred to sleep under the stars in a worn canvas sleeping bag that warded off rain showers. He enjoyed the meals I cooked and hungrily scraped the pots clean. Another time he invited me to his place and led the way through valleys, over mountains and across torrents of streams.

His home was crude and disorganized. It was basically a smoke-stained blue tarp stretched between trees. On two sides wooden crates made do as shelves and a windbreak. An open firepit, ringed with rocks, sat in the middle of the camp. On the rocks rested a metal grate scrounged off a boiler from an old shipwreck, and on the grate sat various pots and pans blackened from years of use and filled with rainwater in his absence. A heavy canvas hammock stamped US ARMY hung beneath the tarp, and a faded Hudson's Bay Company blanket lay in it. Everything smelled of cooking grease.

Cosmopolitan and I became friends, but it was a strained relationship. He argued about everything and corrected me constantly. I became a listener only. It was tiresome, but he weighed my response and found it wanting every time. Annoying as it was, I kept my feelings to myself and let him lead the way in all conversations. I wouldn't get drawn into an argument.

After a while he sensed my reluctance to talk and changed his manner. He started asking my opinion, which I gave in moderation, not wanting to get him going on any subject.

Unfortunately we got into a heated argument that almost put an end to our visits. We were sitting under his tarp out of the sun, reading and sipping tea, when Cosmopolitan looked up and announced, "The Atlantic Ocean is far greater than the Pacific and all the other bodies of water put together, including the Great Lakes."

"Oh?" I said.

"Yes, without a doubt. The Atlantic is colder, more people have drowned in it than in any other ocean and more people make their living from it than any other body of water," he said.

Never had it crossed my mind that one ocean could be greater than the others, since each had its own qualities. They were all joined anyway. And I knew he was wrong about size. I sensed that he was setting up an argument, and against my better judgment, I was dragged into it.

"A grade five geography class would argue with you, Cosmopolitan," I said. "The Pacific Ocean is larger."

That was all he needed to start a tirade. I listened for about ten minutes, then picked up my belongings and said, "I have to go."

That argument cemented my feelings that Cosmopolitan was not going to change, and I would never get satisfaction from our relationship.

I didn't visit Cosmopolitan for the longest time, nor did he visit me. Eventually we met in Winter Harbour, going through books at Teacher Jane's house. He was glad to see me. "I'll come and visit you soon, Joshua, within the next month." He seemed to have forgotten our argument, or maybe he didn't realize it was an argument.

Four weeks later I knew the knock at the door was his. He stuck his head inside, happy to see me. We spent a few days catching up and reading. The day before he planned to leave, we walked down to the ocean.

A warm breeze swept through the air. The sun was high in the sky, the water sparkled and waves washed up on the shore with a gentle whoosh, then receded back into the ocean.

"This is the Pacific, Cosmopolitan," I said. "Isn't it great? How could we argue over something as wonderful as this?"

I kicked off my shoes and, yelling with exuberance, I ran and dove into the surf. Treading water, I looked for Cosmopolitan. He hadn't moved from where we'd stood.

I waved and called, "Come in, Cosmopolitan! Come in, it's lovely!"

But Cosmopolitan didn't move. He was rooted in his spot like the trees behind him.

I waved and shouted once again, "Cosmopolitan! Cosmopolitan! Come in, it's beautiful!"

He walked closer but stayed out of range of the lapping waves.

"I cannot!" he yelled. "I'm not sure."

He turned to leave.

"Forget about your opinions," I called. "Come in."

But it was to no avail. Cosmopolitan walked away and disappeared into the woods.

I was enjoying the ocean and wasn't sad about Cosmopolitan. I finished swimming and gathered shells and a few pieces of wood to hang around the house. After that day I rarely saw Cosmopolitan, and I started to spend more time at the beach and in the ocean.

Then Cosmopolitan showed up. He looked haggard and tired.

"Are you okay?" I asked.

"Yes, I'm okay. I've come to say goodbye, Joshua. I'm leaving. I've brought you these." He handed me two of his burned and dented cooking pots.

I accepted them graciously.

"Joshua, you live here because you choose to. I live here because I'm fearful and I have to have things my way because of that. I have to be right and in control, even in the forest."

I didn't ask him what he was fearful of. I thought if he wanted to tell me he would.

Looking out at the ocean, he said, "But I realize there are some things I cannot control. I'm going to have to learn which things I can control and which I can't. Remember when I told you I knew Picasso? Well, I did, and he told me the people in his paintings looked normal to him. Who would have figured? Maybe my life looks normal to me."

We shook hands. I wished him happiness, and he left. I watched him disappear among the trees and wondered if I would ever see him again.

Later that week I went into Winter Harbour and bought a second-hand wetsuit from Mervin. I asked about Cosmopolitan, but no one had seen him. I went back to the beach and swam out to the kelp beds to join the otters. I floated on my back with a flat stone balanced on my stomach, cracking open sea urchins that I dived for. The otters learned that I would open urchins for them and piled my chest high with the spiny creatures. People on tourist yachts seemed unable to take enough pictures.

A few months after Cosmopolitan's departure, Lennon and Angst walked into my life.

I was basking on the hot sand, welcoming the cool breeze, when I heard clanging pots and laboured breathing coming my way.

Bopping along the top of a dune, a head of bristly hair preceded a sun-burned, bearded face that wore tightly strapped welder's goggles. It looked like two black olives on a pink plate. Next a round torso emerged, dressed in army surplus khaki with woollen puttees wrapped loosely to the bottom of short pants.

Bells, pots and pans hung off the sides of the little man's backpack and clattered randomly like an out-of-tune wind chime.

"Keeps the bears away," he later explained.

In his left hand he clutched a gnarled shillelagh, and on his right walked a nervous black and white border collie. When the dog spotted me, it stopped in its tracks and let out a woof. It looked anxiously back and forth between me and its master, who trudged on oblivious to the dog's warning.

Lennon, as I later learned, was almost blind. He saw only shapes and colours.

He asked the dog, "What is it, boy? Another marmot?"

He would have stepped on me if I hadn't spoken out, "Whoa there, partner."

Lennon stopped and held out a hand, trying to touch the person who'd spoken. He pulled the goggles off his head, squinting hard and breathing heavily. Sweat covered his face. Later he explained that he'd had absolutely no expectation that anyone would be in this neck of the woods. When I spoke, he nearly jumped out of his skin. He said, "Who goes there?"

"Joshua, the keeper of the surf and sand," I said.

Lennon laughed with relief and replied, "That is a fine title. It sounds like you should brandish a trident." He told his dog, "It's okay, Angst. It's only the keeper of the surf and sand."

The dog sat down and gave me a rolling-eyed look of concern—was I friend or foe?—but when I scratched his head, he relaxed and wagged his tail. Lennon dropped his heavy pack, and it landed with a thud behind him. He groaned and sat down, stretching out his hand for me to shake, but because of his bad eyesight, he was off the mark. I shifted over and shook his hand, which had the grip of someone who was used to hard work.

Lennon introduced himself and his dog. "This is Angst, and I'm Lennon."

"Pleased to meet you," I said. I thought the dog's name was interesting; wherever Lennon went he would have angst with him.

"What month is it?"

"July."

"What are you doing here?"

"I live here."

"With whom?"

"Myself."

"Have you extra food?"

"Lots."

"Can we go eat?"

"Yeah, sure," I said, and helped him up.

A pot of salmon and brown rice soup simmered on the stove—it was one of Cosmopolitan's old pots, which I'd scoured clean with sand—and

I'd baked whole-grain bread in a Dutch oven beside the open fire. Lennon helped himself to both until he was full. The dog sat patiently, occasionally licking his lips, until Lennon dipped a chunk of bread into the soup and fed him. The dog took the food gently from his hand, and when he was full, went to lie in the shade.

"One thing I know, Joshua," Lennon said between mouthfuls, "is that this wilderness is crawling with men like you and me who live out their lives in self-prescribed solitude."

"What makes you think I'm living in self-prescribed solitude?" I asked.

"Well, aren't you?" he said.

"No, I like it here. I'm not running from anything," I said.

Lennon stopped his spoon midway between the bowl and his mouth and looked at me. "Mostly women sent us here, Joshua. Just about every damn one of us had a woman," he said.

"I didn't," I said.

"You're young. Give it time." Then he looked at his dog and laughed. "Give it time, right, Angst?"

Angst's ears perked up at the sound of his name.

Lennon visited for two days. I was glad of the company. He was a melancholy type, obviously well read, and perhaps in his sixties.

As he ate, Lennon made a number of toasts:

"Here's to rice and salmon."

"Here's to the Toronto Maple Leafs. May they crush the Habs and win the Stanley Cup."

"Who are the Habs?" I asked.

"Les Habitants is the nickname of the Montreal Canadiens hockey team," Lennon said.

"What is the Stanley Cup?"

"Forget it. All you have to do is hope the Habs are crushed by the Maple Leafs," Lennon said.

"Canada!" I said.

"Americans!" Lennon snorted.

"Here's to Yoko Ono. May she pose for *Playboy*."

On the evening of the second day he told me, "We will be leaving in the morning, Joshua. But I tell you, each one of us in his own time and in his own way comes to grips with the past and leaves this life."

I didn't bother explaining that I wasn't living the life he described, but I knew he was. I asked him, "What are your plans now?"

Pausing for a moment, Lennon pondered his own condition, then said in a tired voice, "In my own time, in my own way, I will make it out of this wilderness." He raised his coffee cup in a toast and said, "Here's to freedom."

I thought, no, you won't go back, Lennon. You've travelled too far on this road, and besides, time is running out on you. One day your bones will bleach in the sun, and Angst will lie down beside you until his bones do the same. Just like Anthony Quinn in *The Hunchback of Notre Dame*, but it will be Angst beside you, not the woman you loved.

Pushing his empty soup bowl aside and leaning out of his chair, Lennon brought his face close to mine and said, "Let me tell you about happiness, Joshua. We are all born the same, but everyone at some point in his life loses his happiness. And once it's gone, poof! It's a hell of a thing to get it back. Ha! If we could just keep our happiness and innocence, what would life be like then?"

"I don't think keeping your innocence is possible," I said.

"Paul Tillich, the theologian, agrees with you," he said, "but I never had much use for theologians. They struck me as being in love with the sound of their own voices."

That evening we returned to the beach to watch the sunset. I had carved a bench from a salt-bleached driftwood log with a tangle of roots. The three of us—Lennon, Angst and I—jumped up onto the bench and sat in silence to watch the sun sink into the ocean. It was so dramatic that I wouldn't have been surprised if the water started to boil. We sat for the longest time until darkness blanketed the land and the stars and moon came out. The moon cast a line of light upon the water that seemed to point directly at us.

Lennon broke the silence. "God, that was good soup!"

You never know what someone is thinking, I thought.

More silence followed. Then he said, "I am looking forward to my death."

You really never know what someone is thinking, I thought. I didn't answer him, since I couldn't understand how anyone could look forward to his death.

"Yes, sincerely I do," he went on. "The natural one, the one everyone has coming."

"What do you mean?"

"If you think about it, everything of this world comes to a complete halt. Finis, kaput, done. Everything is left behind. You don't pay taxes or alimony in the next world."

"That would be a relief," I said.

"Were you ever married?" he asked.

"No, but I paid taxes." I'd worked in the logging camp long enough for the Canadian government to collect its share.

We sat for a while longer, then slid off the log and headed back to the camp.

The next morning I made breakfast of the leftover soup and packed the remainder of the bread in his packsack.

Lennon ate his breakfast with as much relish as he'd eaten his supper the evening before.

"Do you know the past and present answer for angst?" he asked.

"Do you mean the dog?"

"No," he said. "Angst, sorrow, torment, worries."

"No," I said.

"I'm not sure that I do either, but I'm working in the direction of free will accepting divine guidance. There's so much angst around us, we might as well start paying more attention to both."

Lennon swung his pack onto his back, picked up his walking stick and called for Angst. He warmly shook my hand and said, "Goodbye."

I watched them go; the dog stopped after a short distance and looked back as if he wanted to say something. Then he turned and ran to catch Lennon, his feet sending spurts of sand flying in the air.

Then, to my surprise, Lennon stopped, turned and walked briskly back. He said, "Everything must pass, Joshua. See if you cannot find your way out of this wilderness."

He turned and I watched them disappear into the early morning fog farther down the beach. I called after them, "Thanks for the visit."

For the next few days I pondered my situation. Maybe I needed to leave and seek a life among people. I decided I would. I could always come back if I wanted. It took a month to close up the log cabin. I cleaned it from top to bottom and made all necessary repairs. On the shelves I left pots, pans, tools and books. I was sad to leave but sure that someone would move in. I hoped they would find the place as happy a home as I did.

I took a final trip into Winter Harbour, lugging my gear. I set it up on the boardwalk and sold it at a discount.

"Headed out, are you?" Mervin asked, counting out twenty bucks for the wetsuit I'd bought from him a year ago for eighty dollars.

"How much do you want for the knapsack?" asked a store customer, oblivious to the fact I was stuffing it full of groceries.

"It's not for sale," I said, and jammed more into it.

I visited Teacher Jane and returned my books. She wasn't very well and lay back in her chair clutching a handkerchief to her mouth. She wheezed and coughed when she talked. Mervin catered to her every need. He had the same kindness as she did. They made a lovely couple.

"Take good care of yourself, Joshua, and drop us a line to let us know where you are."

I shook their hands and kissed Teacher Jane on the forehead.

The next day I caught a bus that took me across the island to Port Hardy. I purchased a second-hand sea kayak and took it out for a trial run in the bay. It handled beautifully, and I felt comfortable in it. A few days later I headed south along the coast until I reached Telegraph Cove. From there I wound my way through the islands of the Broughton Archipelago, avoiding the strong whirlpools and tide rips, and landed at Sullivan Bay.

I followed the ways of the Kwakwaka'wakw and gathered herring, salmon, shellfish, berries and camas to eat. I explored the inlets and rivers and drew the boat up on the beach. Then I camped and hiked deep into the forest. I explored old cannery camps, shipwrecks and buildings, taking pictures all the time. Scattered up and down the coast were fishing lodges and Kwakwaka'wakw villages where I stopped to visit and purchase food.

I loved the challenge and revelled in my ability to trek over great distances. There was no place I couldn't go, and there was no one to tell me not to.

I climbed mountains and walked along razor ridges. I was on a particularly steep one with a drop of a thousand feet on either side when a helicopter swooped in. It scared the hell out of me, and I kneeled down, straddling the mountain and hanging on for dear life. The wash from the prop tore my hat from my head, and I watched it disappear. The pilot realized his mistake and backed off to a safe distance. Obviously he was excited to see someone so far out and so high on a mountain.

The person next to the pilot raised both arms in a gesture to ask if things were all right. I gave them my biggest grin and a thumbs-up. They took pictures, talked between themselves, waved and flew away.

I headed up the Burke Channel to Kimsquit. I camped on a beautiful stretch of beach and roasted salmon Nuxalk-style, spread open on sticks and propped up beside a roaring fire. I stood sipping tea and watched the light from the fire cast a long reflection over the water. I glanced across the clearing; propped against a tree was a stick that looked familiar. I studied it for a moment, then realized what it was. I put my tea down and ran over to Lennon's shillelagh. I stared at it in disbelief, but I was happy to see something of my old friend.

Just off the sand in a thicket lay a bundle of clothing and a packsack. I walked closer and recognized Lennon. He'd been dead for some time. His bones were bleached, and his clothing was in tatters. He must have dropped in his tracks; the pack was still on his back.

Scattered on his chest I saw a sprinkling of wilted flower petals. If some-one knew he was here, why hadn't they buried him?

"How did you get here?" I asked out loud.

I sat down about five feet away to think. That's when I noticed the large, bare footprints leading out of the woods and across the sand to where Lennon lay. I could even make out the imprint of two large knees where someone had kneeled beside him. A cold shiver went up my spine. I didn't want to think about sasquatches, but what else could I do?

I remembered Angst and tried to whistle for him, but my lips were dry. I half-expected him to leap out of the woods, but no dog appeared.

I didn't sleep that night.

It took the better part of a day to dig a grave, neatly arrange Lennon's bones and pile a mound of rocks over him. I laid his walking stick and his pots and pans on the stones. I spent one more night and drifted off into a restless sleep. I awoke hearing a rustling of branches moving away from camp. I built up the fire and sat near it, my knees pulled up and a blanket over my shoulders. In the far distance I heard a whistle, and in response, another whistle even farther away.

Lennon had friends other than me, it seemed. In the morning there were two pairs of footprints, one set bigger than the other, and fresh wild rose petals on the grave.

You're Not My Son

Months earlier Lennon and Angst had hiked down the beach toward the north end of Vancouver Island when Angst stopped dead in his tracks and let out a woof. He'd been trained to give that signal when another person came into view.

A tall, thin man knelt behind a cedar drift log bleached by the sun and worn smooth by the sand and sea. At a small fire he roasted black-shelled mussels he'd gathered from the tide pools. He flicked the mussels out of the fire and waited for them to cool. For the last fifteen minutes he'd heard clanging pots and bells. When Lennon came within earshot, he called out, "Ahoy! Who goes there?"

"It is I, Lennon, and my faithful companion, Angst," Lennon answered.

"Angst isn't a faithful companion," the man yelled back.

"Angst is my dog's name," Lennon said wearily. He'd heard that comment too many times. Guided by his walking stick and the man's voice, he flopped down beside the fire and dropped the pack off his shoulders.

"Good name," said the man.

"Do you have extra food? I'm starving." Lennon patted his stomach and squinted to see better.

"Help yourself to these mussels. I've more than enough. Are you all right? You don't look too well." He hopped a couple of hot mussels from hand to hand and passed them to Lennon, who hopped them the same way.

"Who are you?" Lennon asked, feeding Angst one of the mussels.

"My name is Vincent Rembrandt. I have travelled the world, broken bread with Matisse at his home in France, explored the catacombs of Paris, studied the Torah with the rabbis of Jerusalem, answered the call to prayer in Medina, searched for the lost city of Atlantis, exported Persian rugs from Iran and twice attempted the north slope of Mount Everest."

"You don't say," Lennon said. "Well, as I said, I'm Lennon the astronomer and stargazer, and this is my dog, Angst. I rescued him from the streets of Vancouver about a year ago on my way to pick up my unemployment cheque."

"I see," said Vincent.

"What did Matisse have to say?" Lennon pulled another mussel from its shell. "These are delicious. A little tomato sauce with vinegar and olive oil would be perfect."

"Pass the salt, *s'il vous plait*," Vincent said.

"Salt?" said Lennon. "Why? These don't need salt."

"Matisse said, 'Pass the salt,'" Vincent said.

"I thought he might have mentioned the influence the painter John Peter Russell had on his work."

"He never mentioned anything of the sort. We had much more important things to talk about," Vincent said. He stood, brushed the sand off his trousers and walked down to the water.

"Can we finish off these mussels?" Lennon called after him.

"Do what you want. I don't care."

Lennon ignored Vincent's sullen tone. He ate the last of the mussels, giving some to Angst, then gathered firewood and set up camp for himself between two drift logs a little farther down the beach. Then he returned to Vincent's fire.

Vincent came back and sat down. A breeze stirred up sparks, and the coals in the fire glowed brighter.

"Damn smoke." Lennon rubbed his eyes and squinted. "So how long have you been out here, Vincent?"

"Years," said Vincent. "I've been hiking and living in different parts by myself."

"Did you meet anyone on the way?" Lennon poked a stick in the fire. Angst lay with his head on Lennon's lap, having had his fill of mussels.

"No, hardly anyone," Vincent said.

"Not even Joshua? He lives a few days south of here," Lennon said, pointing in that direction with his stick.

"Oh, him. Is that his name, Joshua? I met him briefly passing through. He sold me some food. Charged way too much for it."

"Nice guy, that Joshua. We stayed a few days, and he fed both of us, didn't he, Angst? We had some fine soup. Damn, that was good soup."

"I can make a soup," Vincent said, not looking at Lennon.

"Hmm," said Lennon.

The sun was setting, and the moon and the stars were brightening the inky blue sky. The breeze was warm, and the only sound was the waves on the beach. Lennon sighed and relaxed against a log.

"Why are you here?" Lennon asked, no longer able to mute his curiosity.

"What?"

"Why are you out here alone, living under the stars?" Lennon said, waving a hand at the sky.

Angst sat up and looked at Vincent as if he too wanted an answer.

"I'm just out tripping about, that's all," Vincent said.

"I've seen a hundred men like you in my travels," Lennon said. "They don't just trip about."

"You don't know my business," Vincent said.

"And why are you making things up about Matisse? Anyone would have known about John Peter Russell if they met Matisse. That's all he ever talked about."

"You're being a little nosy, aren't you?" Vincent said.

"I haven't time to beat around the bush. Time is short for all of us. If you had really talked to the rabbis of Jerusalem, they would have taught you that too," Lennon said.

Vincent had been sitting cross-legged in front of the fire, and Lennon thought for a moment he was going to walk down to the beach again or start an argument. He didn't. He appeared ready to talk, but he seemed to want to hear Lennon's story first.

"So what about you? Why are you out here living under the stars?" Vincent said.

Lennon knew if he was ever going to get Vincent to talk, the price would be his own disclosure.

"I was in love and I lost the woman I loved," Lennon said. "Simple as that."

"Did she die?" Vincent said.

"No, that would have been too easy. She fell in love with another man right under my nose. I had no idea. She told me she loved me but she was courting another fellow at the same time. It's hard to describe what goes through your head when these things happen."

"What was her name?" Vincent asked.

Lennon looked at the ground. Dusk was falling, and the firelight flickered off his forehead. After a while he said quietly, "Her name is Judy, and this is the first time I've mentioned her name since the day she said goodbye."

"What did you do when she left?"

"I tried everything—denial, anger, rewriting history—but I never begged or threatened and I never took a drink. I left it alone, let her go her own way and chose this life."

"A life on the run," Vincent said.

"Do you know what I feel most of all?"

"No."

"I feel stupid."

Vincent got up and went off to gather firewood.

Lennon took out a package of sunflower seeds and sprinkled them on a flat rock to toast. Vincent returned and built up the fire. He lay on his side facing the flames and chewed on a sliver of wood.

After a while he flicked his toothpick into the fire and said, "My name isn't Vincent. It's Paul, and I'm a printer by trade. I was born and brought up in Kelowna. My dad worked and my mom took care of the house. I was the third of six children."

"Why are you here?" Lennon asked.

Paul looked into the fire. "I was slandered."

"That's bad."

"I was disowned. My father said to me, 'You're not my son.' I lost my friends, I was shunned and I was let go from my job. No one believed me. I never took their Salvation Army money. I never touched it. But I was blamed for it."

"How much?"

"Thousands of dollars. I couldn't believe it happened. I never took a dime in my life."

"It's shameful to treat an innocent man like that," Lennon said.

"I'm an honest man. I don't steal, especially from a church. Do you know what a slandered person becomes? I became a walking, talking zombie. One of the living dead."

"Is that why you changed your name and live these made-up lives?" Lennon asked.

Paul nodded. "I'm fearful of being recognized. I can't take the pain of knowing people think I'm a thief. Do you know what the worst thing is, Lennon?"

"No, what?"

"I lost friends and family that I loved."

The conversation went quiet. Both men did what they had done countless times before, looked into the fire and became lost in their thoughts. When the fire died down and the last sunflower seed had been picked off the rock, they rolled out their sleeping bags and turned in for the night. Paul could hear Lennon saying his prayers.

In the morning a light fog drifted over the beach. There was dew on the ground, and both men pulled the covers over their heads to keep off the chill.

"My ears are cold," Lennon said.

"Bit of a chill this morning," Paul agreed.

The men made breakfast of dry cereal and black coffee and stood near the fire to eat.

"Someday I'm going home," Paul said, "even if it's just to have a hot plate of bacon and eggs for once."

"I think of food all the time. I liked scrambled eggs on toast and bacon for breakfast," Lennon said.

Both men laughed, and Lennon raised his cup. "Here's to White Spot restaurants."

Lennon was going north, and Paul made a decision to go south.

"Do you know what we have in common?" Lennon said. "We both ran. We fled from our fate. Maybe we should have faced it differently. Now I wish I had."

"You think we should have sat in the fire and burned like the Mohawk in Pauline Johnson's poem?"

"Yes, something like that. We should have seen our problems through to the end," Lennon said, "instead of fleeing."

"I wish I had been braver," Paul said.

"Well, let's part on that thought. I wish you well, Paul. May the slander end for you. I'll keep you in my prayers."

"And may you find happiness every day of your life," Paul said.

Lennon walked inland and found a road. After a week of hiking and thumbing rides, he and Angst arrived in the industrial seaside town of Port Hardy exhausted and undernourished. After a few days' rest and a hot bath in a bargain motel, they hitched a ride with a gillnetter captain bound for the cannery at Namu, a small village on the mainland coast of the Inside Passage.

"Come on, Angst. Let's go take a look at Burke Channel. Some people say sasquatches be there."

At Namu, Lennon walked around the cannery buildings and introduced himself to the residents. He met two families of California tourists and got a ride to the eastern bank of Kwatna Inlet.

"If you could drop me off, I'd appreciate it. I'm going to hike into Bella Coola."

"We've been coming here for the past five years. The kids love it, and so do we," said Pat, one of the boat's owners. The other was his brother-in-law Ron.

The Americans were travelling in a fifty-foot steel-hulled sailing yacht with a 115 hp Perkins diesel engine. The families were skilled and avid sailors.

"This is a beautiful boat," Lennon said.

"Do you ever get lonely out there, walking all by yourself with just your dog?" Pat's ten-year-old son wanted to know.

"I've never had a lonely day in my life. There's too much to see and do," Lennon said.

After a long day of cruising on the channel, Pat eased the boat toward a short beach and Ron rowed Lennon ashore in the ten-foot inflatable Zodiac.

"Goodbye, Mr. Lennon! Goodbye, Angst!" The kids yelled and waved from the bow of the boat. Angst wagged his tail wildly. He liked the kids and their attention.

"Thanks for the ride," Lennon yelled back, waving the small Stars and Stripes they'd given him. "Have a good holiday."

"You also," they shouted. The boat drifted out into the channel, and the inboard motor coughed to life. They were still waving as they motored across the water, leaving waves that washed up on the shore.

Angst and Lennon watched the boat until it went out of sight. When the silence returned, Lennon walked eastward along the beach, then deeper into the forest.

"Come on, boy, we have to make camp before dark."

The next minutes were Lennon's last upon this earth. He started to think of his mother, who'd passed away when he was a child, and a strong sense of her presence came over him. He saw her clearly in his mind and he was aware of her love for him.

He looked across the channel to where the mountains swept down and joined the water.

For the first time he understood the mystery of that union.

"The finite meets the infinite, Angst," he said, pointing across the water, "Right there before our very eyes. Strange, I hadn't noticed that before."

Everywhere he looked, the universe appeared in perfect order.

"My eyesight must be improving," he said out loud.

As he walked along, the crunch of his feet on the gravel was louder than he had ever heard it before. Angst walked close beside him so that they touched.

Lennon stopped for a moment. A searing pain bolted across his chest; he propped his walking stick against a tree, grabbed his shirt with both hands and ripped it open. His eyes went wide and slowly shut and he fell on his back. His spirit had flown before he hit the ground.

For two days and nights Angst sat beside the body. In the darkness, shadowy figures came out of the forest and poked Lennon with their fingers. They whistled quietly among themselves and faded back whence they came. Angst had no fear of them and accepted their pats on his head.

On the third day the American tourists returned, and Angst ran barking along the shore for a mile before they spotted him.

"Look, isn't that Lennon's dog?" one of the older kids said. "Where's Lennon? Maybe the dog is lost. Maybe Lennon's lost too."

Pat and Ron found Angst's behaviour strange, so they drew the boat close, dropped anchor and went ashore in the Zodiac. Angst was glad to see them and ran in front as they walked along. For over two hours they hiked up and down the shoreline, calling Lennon's name. There was no response.

"That's strange," Ron said. "I figured that dog and Lennon were inseparable."

"Let's take the dog with us. We can't leave him here in case something has happened to Lennon," Pat said.

"Can we keep him, Dad?" the youngest asked, helping Angst onto the boat.

"We can't keep him, but the folks in Namu will care for him until we find Lennon," Pat said.

The families docked in Namu and left Angst with the store owner. "We'll pay for his food until Lennon shows up."

"That won't be necessary. We can look after him," the store owner's wife said. "I remember this dog. His owner was a pleasant fellow. I hope he's all right."

The store owner called the RCMP in Bella Coola, and they filed a missing persons report.

"Thanks for this," the officer radioed, "we will get on it."

Four hours later a de Havilland Beaver float plane touched down in the area where Lennon was last seen. It taxied to the shore, and two officers got out and hiked for most of the day. They found nothing. A telex was sent to all coastal detachments, but other pressing matters came up, and after a week Lennon's case was set aside.

While Lennon was being searched for, Paul took the ferry from Departure Bay to Horseshoe Bay north of Vancouver. From there he took the bus to Kelowna and arrived at his parents' home early in the morning. Everyone in the house was asleep, so he lay on a lawn chair in the backyard. He woke when Kate, his younger sister, shook his shoulder.

"Paul! Paul! Is it really you?"

"It's me."

Kate bent over and hugged him in the chair. "Come inside. Mom and Dad will be so glad to see you."

"Will they?"

"Yes." Kate pulled him out of the chair and led him into the warm kitchen, which smelled of freshly brewed coffee and toast. She ran up the stairs, calling, "Mom! Dad! Paul's home."

Paul stood in the middle of the kitchen; he hadn't expected this welcome. He'd thought there would be arguments and accusations, and he'd be turned out again. But Lennon had believed in him, and that had given him confidence to face his accusers.

The sound of footsteps came down the stairs. Paul's white-haired father, Paul Sr., had dressed quickly in his Salvation Army uniform, but the tunic was unbuttoned and the suspenders hung at his hips. He rushed into the room, followed by Paul's mother in her robe and pincurls.

His father grabbed him and wrapped his arms around him. "Paul, my child, thank God you have returned. We didn't know how to find you. We found the money last year behind a filing cabinet when we renovated the office. It was the treasurer who misplaced the funds, not you. I was wrong. I am so sorry."

His father cupped Paul's face in his hands and tearfully asked, "Can you ever forgive me?"

Paul felt relief. The past eight years of his life had been hell, and for what? A weight was lifted from his shoulders, and he felt as if he would float off the floor.

"I'm dizzy," he said. "I have to sit down."

His mother helped him to a chair and stood over him. She put her arm around his shoulder and kissed his forehead.

"I'm so glad you're home. It broke my heart to lose you," she said, and hugged him again.

Paul Sr. sat down opposite him. "It's not your fault, Paul, it's mine. I'm supposed to be a man of God. How could I accuse my own flesh and blood?"

The pain in his father's face was almost more than Paul could bear. "Dad, Dad, don't worry about it. It was nothing, just a misunderstanding. These things happen. As long as everything turns out okay in the end, I'm happy."

It wasn't easy, but over time the family grew strong again. Paul moved back into his bedroom, which held not a scrap of his belongings.

Kate stood behind him as he looked at the new furniture. "They wanted to forget."

Paul was saddened at the evidence of his shunning. "Let's not talk about that again."

For the next month Paul Sr. paraded Paul Jr. around town, introducing him to old and new acquaintances. The news spread quickly that Paul was home and the missing money had been found.

"Here is my son Paul, home from the forest," Paul Sr. tried to joke.

"Damnedest thing, that money went missing and you got blamed. It's a terrible shame to ruin a young man's life," Stu the pharmacist said, giving Paul Sr. a hard look.

Paul Sr.'s face went red.

"Glad to have you back, son," said the Salvation Army treasurer. "I hope my misplacing that money didn't inconvenience you."

"No, not at all," Paul said, and shook his hand. He wouldn't tell anyone what he'd gone through; it was almost impossible to describe anyway.

There wasn't anything else to say about the last eight years. Paul knew his life before, during and after slander. He liked the before and after much better.

A year later, at the age of forty, Paul fell in love and married an older divorcée named Judy. When they settled into their new home, Judy bought a cat. She called it Angst.

"I always wanted to call a pet Angst," she said, cuddling the purring long-haired Persian in her arms.

She also liked to toast sunflower seeds on a rock placed on the barbecue grill. "Paul, dear, would you sprinkle a bit more salt on those? I think they're ready."

Paul never mentioned Lennon and his dog named Angst.

The DC-3

The forwarded letter from my dad caught up with me before I paddled out of Namu. It was fat, and when I opened it, I found a scrawled note, two hundred dollars in American bills and two official-looking deeds.

"Dear Joshua," the note started. "I thought you might be interested in these deeds I found tucked away in your dresser drawer. Vancouver is in the Yukon, right? You might be able to look these up and make a fortune, ha! Much love, Dad. PS: Are you still keeping an eye out for those commies in Canada? We're bombing the hell out of them in Vietnam."

The two gold-embossed deeds had been issued by the Klondike Big Inch Company in 1955. One came from a box of Quaker Oats Puffed Rice, and the other from a box of Quaker Oats Puffed Wheat. The deeds stated that I owned two gold claims, one square inch apiece—C 314998 and B 194915 on Group Two in Lot 243—on 19.11 acres lying three miles upstream from Dawson City.

I remembered dumping the cereal to find the deeds at the bottom of the box and how excited I'd been to own gold claims in the Yukon. Greg, my best friend, owned a couple, and we spent hours poring over the atlas and planning our trip to the Yukon.

"You're Sourdough Sam, and I'll be Sergeant Preston of the Royal Canadian Mounted Police," I said.

"Okay, but Buck is my dog," he said.

It had been one of the greatest advertising promotions anyone had ever seen. After the Klondike Gold Rush, it must have been the biggest event in

40

the history of the Yukon. I felt good that my dad had sent the deeds; it gave me some direction. Maybe I would go to the Yukon and claim my land.

Wealth was not a goal in my life. In fact I wasn't a good businessman at all. In hindsight I could have sold my cabin on Vancouver Island; instead I left it for whoever wanted it. I'm sure I didn't have a capitalistic bone in my body. My dad must have sensed this, warning me again about communists. Since I thought Stalin was one of the greatest betrayers of mankind, he worried needlessly.

It was time to make new plans. I didn't feel badly about Lennon dying. He'd told me, "Joshua, I'm looking forward to my death." Lennon was a smart man; he knew about the beyond. I was sorry he'd died alone but I did bury him, and his other unusual friends visited his grave. All in all it was peaceful and dignified. What could be better than having the great forest of Canada as your final resting place?

I was more worried about Angst, Lennon's dog. I hoped he was well and had found his way to safety.

As I paddled northward, I searched the shore and beaches for flotsam and jetsam. I found hatch covers, fishnets, pairs of running shoes tied together, a nylon suitcase full of technical books and maps, and one time, a cooler packed with beer and soda. I never liked the taste of beer, so I drank the soda and left the beer to float away. I hoped that some happy beer drinker would find it and think he was the luckiest guy on the planet. I could imagine him saying, "Fishing and free beer! It doesn't get any better than this."

I remembered reading about a scientific mini-submarine that broke its moorings and was now floating around in the Pacific Ocean. I daydreamed about salvaging it and kept my ears peeled for the clang of metal being driven up on the rocks. If I did find it, I would scratch my name and date on the conning tower to lay my salvage claim, then inform the authorities at the next town. The finder's fee would be tens of thousands of dollars.

One evening, after a long day of paddling, I glided into a bay at the northern tip of Hunter Island and found the remains of an ancient village. Stately longhouses had fallen in on themselves, and totem poles now lay among the bushes. No one lived here today. Long ago the villagers had fallen to the ravages of smallpox.

I made camp beside a longhouse and had a meal of tea and buttered bread toasted over the fire. Then I fell asleep. I woke with a fever raging through my body. My skin felt as though it were on fire. I moaned and tried to stand but I couldn't. I staggered about and fell on all fours. With my last strength I crawled to the shallow creek and lay in it, trying to find relief from the burning. I rolled on my back and let the water wash over me. I've caught the pox, I thought.

I became aware of shadowy forms gliding around me. I struggled to focus and recognized three women dancing and chanting with baskets in their arms. Each woman's face was painted from above the tip of her nose to her hairline. One was painted red, another blue and the last violet. All three wore their hair combed back with a topknot tied over the forehead. Furs hung around their shoulders, and they wore long coats with tassels. They had piercings through their noses, below their bottom lips and in their ears.

They sang in melodious, soothing voices. The woman decorated in red stepped forward to dip her cedar basket into the stream and poured the water over my head and chest. The blue-faced woman stepped forward and did the same thing. Then the third woman, who looked older, also poured water from her basket over me.

They stood for a moment, singing, then turned and left. I propped myself up unsteadily on my elbows and watched as they walked along the stream's edge away from the ocean and disappeared into the forest.

I fell back and lay in the creek. A while later my fever was gone, and the water had chilled me. I staggered back to my camp, removed my clothes and fell asleep on the sleeping bag. When I awoke, the sun was high in the sky. The mosquitoes had feasted on my naked body and I was covered in bites. Aside from that, I felt strong and refreshed.

The next day I paddled up Fitzhugh Sound into Bella Bella. It was late fall, and I decided to winter there. I rented a cabin, and when word got around that I was a carpenter, there was no end to the work people offered me. It was as if folks had been waiting for someone to drop out of the sky to do their backlog of renovations and repairs.

"Can you hang my screen door?" Mrs. Caldwell, the village nurse, asked. "My husband, Jake, has told me for the past year that he'd do it. He said it would take special tools and two days of work."

"Sure," I said, and hung it in two hours with a hammer and a screwdriver.

The local eatery, owned for the past thirty years by Moe Stone, was in need of a renovation.

"I have to do something. The counters and flooring haven't been changed since I took over the business," he said.

Moe (or Stoner, as the locals called him) bought the material, and I spent most of the winter renovating the restaurant.

I was installing the counters when I felt someone staring at my back. I turned, and there sat Angst with his head cocked to one side and, I swear, a smile on his lips. He ran and leaped into my arms, licking my face.

At that moment Moe walked in and asked, "Is that your dog? He's been hanging around here for ages. I was feeding him. The store manager at Namu sent him over hoping to find the owner."

"Yes, Angst is mine," I said. "Thanks for looking after him."

"Is that his name, Angst? We called him Mojo because he always seemed to be running around getting his mojo going and making friends with everyone. A boatload of American tourists on their way to Alaska dropped him off. They were thinking of keeping him but said an old fellow lost him, and they figured the best place for the dog to run into the owner was Bella Bella."

I put Angst down and told Moe and the cook, "You'll have to shut the grill down. This place will be a mess when the sawdust starts flying."

"That's okay by me. How long are we shut down for?" Moe asked.

"Two months," I said.

The cook wiped his hands, untied his apron and threw it on the stovetop. "That's great. I'm going to visit my aunt Maggie and uncle Sidney and my cousins Roberto and Roberta in New Mexico."

"Could you make me a couple of hamburgers before you go?"

"Sure thing." He tied the apron back on, twisted a dial and popped the gas on to heat the grill. "You want cheese on those?"

"Just on one. The dog doesn't like cheese," I said.

When the snow left and the rivers opened up, I finished the restaurant renovation, said goodbye to my new friends and got ready to head out.

Moe came to see us off. "If you come back this way, drop in. I'm sure I'll have more work for you, Joshua. You did a hell of a beautiful job on those counters."

"You're welcome," I said, shaking his hand warmly. "Thanks for the work and thanks again for taking care of my dog."

It was always exhilarating to be moving on in the spring. I was pleased to have Angst as a travelling companion. He sat in front of me on the kayak like the bulldog hood ornament on a Mack truck, barking at everything that sailed above or on the water.

I travelled north up Finlayson Channel to Butedale, then up Grenville Channel to Prince Rupert. On one occasion I took a week to hike into the Coast Mountains. With Angst I worried less about bears. One night we heard the whistling again. Angst sat up and looked in that direction, wagging his tail a hundred miles an hour and barking happily. More whistling answered his response, but I saw no one.

I paddled up Revillagigedo Channel past Ketchikan, Alaska, then along Clarence Strait to the fishing village of Wrangell. I had decided by this time to head inland through northern BC rather than paddle up the Stikine River. The Tlingit and prospectors travelled up and down the river, but I was tired of paddling and wanted to get my feet on the ground.

Wrangell had an all-purpose sporting goods store perched above the boat-filled harbour. Decorated with old fishing equipment, it was also the post office, grocery store, ticket office and gas station. The owner was Spike Nickel, a tall, thin, distracted-looking man with sparse blonde hair and a freckled face. A long scar crossed his nose.

"I was good at volleyball back in high school," he told me when I asked about his name.

Spike had more than his fair share of second-hand fishing boats, nets and crab traps, and he also flew charter flights in his 1952 Cessna 170B.

"Give me a hundred dollars and your kayak, and I'll fly you into Telegraph Creek first thing tomorrow morning," he offered between mouthfuls of a mashed potato, boiled cabbage and mayonnaise sandwich. It was black with pepper.

Angst looked at him hungrily.

"Do you have any more sandwiches?" I asked.

"Sure do. Come on in." He held open the swinging gate at the back of the store, and I followed him down a passageway into his living room and kitchen.

"This is my wife, Penny, and the rug rats are all ours," he said.

Penny jumped up and started picking up toys, bikes and a crawling baby, and with loaded arms attempted to straighten the faded, tasselled slipcovers over the worn furniture.

"Why didn't you tell me we were having guests?" Penny asked. She had a red paisley bandana tied on her head, and her hair was coming unbraided. She looked tired.

"I'm Joshua, and this here is my dog, Angst."

"Good name. I'll have to remember that," Penny said, walking down the hall to a room full of noisy kids.

Between running out to help in the store and making sandwiches and coffee, Spike managed to give me some information about hiking across northern BC.

"Telegraph Creek is a good place to start. The valleys are flat, and there are a lot of beautiful places to visit—lakes, rivers, mountains and so on," he said. "Penny and I hiked it years ago. Then the kids started coming, and that was the end of that. My good friend Hoot lives down that way."

I slept on their couch that night, and in the morning Spike nudged me awake as the sun was rising over the mountains. The house was silent.

"Let's go, Joshua. The round trip is going to take me all day."

He put on a pot of coffee and made more potato and cabbage sandwiches for breakfast. "No use letting the cabbage go to waste," he said.

The only thing that made the cold sandwiches palatable was the hot coffee we drank to wash them down.

The air was cool at Wrangell's small airport. Before we got into the plane, a 150-pound motor block was manhandled in behind the front seats.

"I've been meaning to get that thing over to Telegraph for the past six months." Spike pulled on a leather aviator's helmet and snapped a pair of goggles on his forehead.

"I'm curious," I said. "How did you get that scar on your nose?"

"I cracked up a few years back taking the same trip into Telegraph Creek. That airstrip gets strong crosswinds once in a while. I smacked my nose when the plane stood right up on its nose and ruined the prop. But we fixed it. It's surprising what a little haywire and duct tape will do," he said with a wink and a toothy grin. He had a piece of cabbage stuck between his teeth.

We bounced down the gravel runway, throwing up clouds of dust, then lifted into the air. Angst, sitting on my lap, looked up with his brow furrowed and a worried expression in his eyes.

"I like your dog's name," Spike shouted over the engine's noise. "I've had lots of angst in my life. The next dog I get, I'll call him that to remind me."

"You don't want to be reminded of your angst," I shouted back.

"You're right there. What the hell am I thinking?"

As we headed through the mountains, the plane seemed so small that I felt like a mosquito flying among giants. Spike set a course up the Stikine

River valley at three thousand feet. We had flown for about an hour when he spotted a small herd of moose feeding in a pond alongside the river.

"Yahoo," he yelled, and circled back, flying lower and lower in an ever-tightening circle to get a better look. When I felt the block shift into the back of my seat, I was going to say something, but at that moment Spike had seen enough and straightened out the plane. We continued on our way.

"That was something, eh? All those moose, but come hunting season, you'll never see one of them."

The rest of the trip was uneventful, and both Angst and I fell asleep to the drone of the engine. I woke when Spike yelled, "We're almost there. I've got to buzz the lodge."

"What?"

"The block is for Hoot, the owner of the hunting lodge at Glenora. I buzz the house, and they know to come and pick it up at Telegraph Creek. There it is," he said, pointing ahead.

Suddenly the atmosphere changed. I was no longer in a Cessna 170B but in a British Sopwith Camel on a World War I strafing mission of the enemy trenches. Spike pulled his goggles down over his face and aimed at the lodge at the end of the valley. He dropped out of the sky, levelled off at a hundred feet and, with all the speed he could muster, screamed over the buildings. I looked back. The horses in the corrals were bucking, chickens flew everywhere and someone who was hanging out laundry had dropped the basket of clothes and was running for the house. I had a feeling that if they'd had the chance, they'd have shot us out of the sky.

"That should get their attention," Spike yelled.

"No kidding."

We landed on the gravel runway in clouds of dust. I again helped move the engine block and set it beside the plane.

"Hoot's going to be happy to finally get this," Spike said.

I got my pack, and Angst and I sat in the shade of the bushes away from the plane. A while later a battered pickup bounced off the road, raced down the runway and came to a sliding stop just inches from the plane. A man jumped out furiously waving his arms. He looked like an older version of Tom Mix, the silent screen cowboy, with a battered ten-gallon hat and his pants tucked into cowboy boots. He ran over and stood on his tiptoes inches from Spike's face, his head going back and forth like a metronome cussing him out. When the wind shifted I caught snatches of the conversation. It wasn't kind.

Spike stood with his arms out and his palms up, brows raised and shoulders shrugged. He looked apologetic, but the man was having none of it. He finally turned, kicked gravel at the plane and walked over to where I stood.

"Who the hell are you?" he asked.

Angst growled at his tone.

"I'm Joshua. I just flew in with your friend there."

The man gave me a hard look, "Today, Spike is not my friend. I'm Hoot. I own the lodge down the way. Are you looking for work?" He held out his hand and shook mine.

"I wasn't, but what did you have in mind? I can do carpentry."

"Great! Let's go."

I helped muscle the block into the back of the truck and threw my pack in after it. I shook Spike's hand goodbye and wished him luck. Hoot's dressing down didn't seem to faze him at all, and he gave me a hug and a warm goodbye.

"Goodbye, Hoot," he said, but Hoot ignored him.

As we drove down the winding single-track road to the lodge, Hoot filled me in on his personal history and his family's history and was starting on just about everyone's history in Telegraph Creek when we came to the lodge. A woman stood in the middle of the road with a broom as if waiting to use it on someone.

"That's my wife, Abby," Hoot said. "She's still mad as hell."

"Is this the culprit?" she asked, waving the broom as we got out of the truck.

"No, no," Hoot said. "That one flew out of here already."

He had hardly gotten the words out of his mouth when Spike flew over at a respectable thousand feet.

"There goes the idiot, but don't worry, dear, I told him off real good. He won't go scaring the hell out of us again."

"Made me drop my clean laundry in the dirt," she said, "and those chickens won't be laying for months."

Abby and Hoot were hospitable, and while I was staying at the lodge, I sat up late listening to the dozens of stories Hoot had to offer. Abby fell asleep and snored quietly as the evening wore on.

Over a week I repaired the tin roof on the main lodge. Angst would follow me up the ladder and sit in the sun while I worked. He couldn't climb down, though, so I carried him. After I finished the roof, I told Hoot I wanted to be on my way. He paid me, and I caught a ride into Telegraph Creek with him and from there set out overland north to the Yukon Territory.

"You take care, young fellow," said Hoot with a toothless laugh. "I hear there are wild rabbits out there that will get you for darn sure."

I had become adaptable to my environment, having researched or discovered most of the edible plants and berries. I could navigate for a hundred miles with compass and map and come out within yards of my destination. I was confident of my strength and travelled with ease through the forests and across lakes, rivers and mountains. I was an adventurer.

As I hiked north, the landscape changed. The trees were smaller, and the air was drier. Ancient glaciers had scraped the sparse broad valleys clean and left the rock slab exposed. The mountains were not as formidable as they had been farther south, and this made the going easier.

After hiking for ten days, I was between Telegraph Creek and the Nakina River. A ravine ahead narrowed sharply among the stunted spruce trees. Thick green streaks smeared the grey rock and flaked off when I touched them. It was paint. My eyes traced it up to the tail section and fuselage of a large airplane. At first I wasn't sure what I was seeing, it was so surreal. I asked out loud, "What the hell is this?"

I dropped my pack, and Angst sat down beside it. I found other deep scour marks and oil stains on the ground. I looked around and surmised that the plane must have come in at a shallow angle, maybe even trying to land, and struck with great force. I found the wheel assemblies farther away with the tires blown out. I thought this supported my theory.

The plane's fuselage appeared intact. Its wings and engines were folded back and jammed along each side of the ravine. Other bits of wreckage lay scattered about, but for the most part the plane was in one piece.

Small poplar trees had grown up around it. If I'd been hiking a hundred yards on either side, I might have missed it.

I sat down and marvelled at what was before me. I cannot describe the excitement at coming across such wreckage.

That night I camped next to the plane and spent hours picking up pieces of bent and twisted metal. I examined them closely. All the printing I could find was in English, and the plane's colour, shape and size told me it was an army DC-3. I'd often seen them as a kid growing up near Roswell in Arizona.

Searchers must have found and catalogued this crash years ago. I guessed the crew hadn't survived, and their bodies had been removed. I didn't expect anything significant to remain. When I tried to enter the fuselage, I found it sealed shut with no point of entry. Now my curiosity was piqued. Ice packed the cabin halfway up the windows, and I began to suspect this was an undiscovered crash site.

"What a find," I said to Angst.

It took two days, using a log and rocks, to pry a section of the wing back and open the rear cargo door just enough to let me squeeze through. As the door opened, a gush of water poured out and soaked my boots and pants. With the water came the distinctive, sickly odour of rot and decay.

For the first time I was concerned about what I might find.

A weak light filtered through the side windows, so I lit a torch of grass and branches. I got down flat on my stomach and slid over ice that lay three feet below the ceiling.

As I moved toward the cockpit, my light flickered off a body sitting upright in a seat. Its head was thrown back at a twisted angle and rested on the window. I couldn't see the man's face and was just as glad. His tunic was shredded, exposing a gaping chest cavity. There were rodent tooth marks on the bones; weasels or something had eaten him. His legs and buttocks were firmly encased in ice. I called him the Colonel because of all the ribbons and stripes on his tunic. A brown leather briefcase was handcuffed to his shrivelled wrist.

The pilot and co-pilot had taken the brunt of the crash, and the cockpit was reduced to compacted rubble. Their broken bodies were frozen solid. The co-pilot's arms were up over his head as if he'd tried to shield himself from the impact, and the pilot sat bent over, his head on his knees. They wore uniforms.

I took what looked like a logbook from an overhead pouch and retreated. I stopped near the Colonel and slipped the handcuff off his hand to take the briefcase.

I sat by the fire, chilled from the DC-3 freezer, and opened the book. The most recent entry—a flight out of Anchorage, Alaska—was dated November 11, 1963. The destination had been Austin, Texas. There was a fuel stop at Whitehorse in the Yukon Territory, and it looked as though the plane was flying the quickest route down the coast. Earlier entries listed flights in and out of Dallas.

A quick twist of my Swiss Army knife, and the briefcase opened. The contents spilled on the ground. It was full of papers, some stamped Top Secret and For Your Eyes Only. Most were frozen together. I spread them out, anchored with rocks, to prevent the wind from blowing them away.

In the thickest file, a black and white picture of a young man was stapled to the inside cover; the name A. Hidell was written in India ink across the bottom of the photo. Other pictures showed a different young man holding a rifle, then the same picture but with Hidell's head on the other man's body. There was even a rough paste-up. The file contained pictures and maps marked with grease pencil in blue, green and red. A group of pictures held together with a paper clip showed a tall building labelled Texas School Book Depository and aerial views of Dealey Plaza next to the depository. Lines drawn on the same picture extended from the building to the street and were marked in different colours as options #1, #2 and #3. One point was labelled "grassy knoll #1," a bridge was marked #2 and the book depository was marked #3.

One photograph showed A. Hidell with a tall, thin, blonde woman, and written on that was "Lee and Marina on return from USSR." In other pictures Hidell stood on a street passing out pamphlets; fastened to one was a white label with the words "Mexico, October 1962" written on it.

There were other files and letters typed on thin paper with handwritten comments around the borders. At the bottom of the briefcase I found a small blue jeweller's box containing a gold nugget roughly the shape of Alaska on a gold chain and a note that read, "To Mary, much love, Dad." There was a receipt from a store for two Alaska gold nuggets and chains, but I'd found only one piece of jewellery. I didn't read all of the papers. I stuffed them back into the briefcase and returned it to the Colonel.

"Here you are, sir," I said. "Sorry about your daughter's present."

Some papers blew away, and others I used for fire starters.

I hadn't explored the rear of the plane, so I crawled back in over the ice. The canvas sacks of five-star sleeping bags and other bundles of survival gear were packed into the cargo area.

A lot of good it did these guys, I thought.

I clambered over a mound of jumbled and broken wooden crates with thick manila rope handles attached to their sides. Some were shattered open, and the dim light showed the flash of metal. I pulled on the closest box. It fell apart, and with a musical clink, out slid hundreds of one-ounce gold bars. There were also wads of American hundred-dollar bills frozen into the ice on the floor.

One long crate was harder to open. I chipped it free of the ice, pulled it outside and broke off the rusting metal hasp with a few whacks of my axe. Inside were two rifles wrapped in thick yellow industrial wax paper and packed in heavy grease. Two smaller boxes under the rifles contained hunting scopes and about a hundred rounds of ammunition.

These were definitely surplus rifles. While they appeared to be in good shape, their walnut stocks were worn and scratched. Looking closely, I could make out bold letters on the breech that said "Mannlicher-Carcano," and underneath, in smaller italics, the word "Italia." These were the same as the rifle that A. Hidell and the other man held in the photos. I packed them up and returned them to the plane.

The gold was another matter. I sat and pondered what to do. A fortune lay there, and it was mine if I wanted. But I believed it was blood money, and it would be bad karma to touch it. Also, I believed that if something wasn't mine, I should never take it, no matter how long it had been left. I'd never agreed with Carter looting King Tutankhamen's crypt even though the Boy King had died thousands of years earlier.

I was no fool. I knew exactly what I'd found. I remember being in gym class and hearing the news over the school's public address system that President Kennedy had been assassinated. Everyone remembers where he or she was on November 22, 1963. I didn't expect anyone to find me here, but I was worried. I wasn't going to stick around and take a chance.

I left everything in the plane. The gold, guns and money belonged to the US Army. Let them find it and take it. No one would ever know I'd been here. There must have been a massive search, and they would still be looking. The army would never give up and wouldn't want the briefcase and cargo falling into the wrong hands. Well, they didn't have to worry about that anymore. It had fallen into the wrong hands.

The next morning, satisfied that I'd left no sign of my visit and glad to be leaving the DC-3 to itself, I hiked on northward. I made camp beside a lake halfway between the plane and Atlin, a gold mining town in northern BC where Doctor Banting, one of the discoverers of insulin, used to bring his family for summer vacations. I built a fire and roasted a trout that I'd caught on a Brooks' Montana Stonefly Nymph after two casts. I shared the fish and a pot of rice with Angst, who devoured it hungrily. We had enough food, but on our long hike it seemed we were never full. I think we were burning more calories than we consumed. Whenever we arrived in a town, I stocked up on butter, pasta and especially cakes and pastries. After months in the bush, I could eat an apple pie in one sitting.

I spread my groundsheet on a level spot beneath a tree and lay down in my sleeping bag. The sky was clear, so I didn't put up the rain tarp. Angst curled up by my chest, and we fell asleep.

I dreamed that I got up and stood looking over the lake. Angst sat beside me doing the same. Aware of something behind me, I turned and saw a towering, massive bear, bigger than anything I had ever seen. It was standing upright, and its fur was glossy like silk and rippled in the breeze. The bear looked over my head, stretched out its foreleg and pointed north. Its extended claws were encased in beautiful gems that sparkled in the midnight sunlight. The bear dropped to all fours, and even then it stood taller than my head. Then it turned and vanished into the woods.

I awoke in the morning to the sound of ravens cawing in the tree above me. "What was that all about?" I asked them.

They cawed again.

"I wish you could speak," I shouted up.

Until this dream, I'd been undecided about my destination, but now I knew it was the Yukon.

Angst wouldn't stop sniffing the ground around the camp. He ran back and forth into the woods, huffing and snorting as if a real bear had been there.

I packed up and walked out of the bush at Atlin four weeks later. I hitched a ride into Whitehorse and for the next couple of months worked in the Taku Hotel on Main Street. I washed dishes and did maintenance.

At coffee time I would sit by the window looking out at Fourth Avenue and the RCMP detachment headquarters across the street. Janet—a slight, hardworking waitress with her hair in a net, fancy glasses and a cigarette in her mouth all day long—joined me. She had a sharp tongue and a sense of humour; the customers liked her. We sat together on our breaks, talking, smoking and drinking coffee. I noticed she wore a chain with an oddly shaped gold nugget on it. I asked, "Where did you get that gold nugget?" As soon as the words were out of my mouth, I knew I shouldn't have spoken.

Janet grabbed the chain. "I shouldn't be wearing this." She scooped up her cigarettes and lighter and went back to work.

I knew what I'd done, where she'd gotten that nugget and why she was agitated. The Colonel had had a girl in every port, and this one had absolutely no clue what had happened to their romance.

After that, Janet avoided me, and months later when I left for Haines Junction, she didn't say goodbye.

Copper Johnson

One hundred miles west of Whitehorse, nestled at the base of the St. Elias Mountains where the Alaska Highway swings north and the Haines Highway swings south, is the village of Haines Junction. When I set my eyes on it, I knew I wanted to live there. I was tired of wandering and wished to settle down.

The sun has always shone on me in Haines Junction. I purchased a small cabin on an overgrown half-acre lot at the end of a dusty street in town and set about making renovations. When people learned I was a good carpenter, I never had to look for work again.

The following spring Atco arrived with ten halves of houses perched on trailers, guided and chased by pilot cars. The next day a crew of carpenters showed up from the Union Hall in Whitehorse. Between Haines Junction and Destruction Bay they set up five new double-wide homes for employees of the Kluane Game Preserve.

I was hired, given three meals a day and paid union wages, which gave me more money than I had ever seen before.

"Yeah, we get travel, overtime, meals and room. It pays to be union," one carpenter told me.

Overtime was time and a half, which worked out to an amazing $7.57 an hour.

"And you get the immense pleasure of calling us your brothers," quipped another guy.

I never liked factory-built houses. I preferred log houses, but these were cheap and went together quickly. The game preserve employees moved from cramped apartments to three-bedroom houses in a couple of weeks.

When Atco laid me off, I travelled to Burwash Landing and met with Arnold Joe, a carpenter who hired me to help frame a house.

Burwash, sixty miles north of Haines Junction on the Alaska Highway, overlooks the rocky, windswept shores of Kluane Lake. The Southern Tutchone villagers are generous and friendly people who I'm proud to say befriended me.

Arnold and his cousins took me on fishing trips, guiding me to all the best spots. We hiked into the surrounding mountains, followed ancient trails and found mounds of neatly stacked, black-tarnished .303 rifle shell casings.

"American army," Arnold said.

"What?" I asked.

"The casings belonged to soldiers hunting sheep back in 1943 when the Alaska Highway was going through Destruction Bay. They pretty near shot every last goat and sheep there was on this mountain for food."

When people passed on, I was invited to the potlatches, and a year later I was invited back for the headstone ceremony. I was impressed by the generous gifts that the Tutchone gave on these occasions.

I was pleased when Arnold introduced me to his great-uncle Copper Johnson. The elderly gentleman was a storehouse of knowledge. His family didn't know how old he was, but his appearance and spiritual awareness led me to conclude he was about a hundred years old. From the moment we met, we became like father and son. I respected him greatly.

"I was a young man when the first white men came down Marsh Lake in all kinds of boats with sails on them. They camped on the beaches. One offered me a plate of beans, but I wouldn't take it. I ran away. That was in April of 1898," he said.

At a potlatch I sat beside elders who had known Copper all his life. "In the old days, Copper would strip down and run a moose till the exhausted animal collapsed. You don't see that anymore."

Copper was always asking questions. "Joshua, do you believe there is only one God?"

"Yes, I do."

"That's good."

Copper spoke of the past, describing the hard life his people lived and the freedom they enjoyed.

"We were free from religious and government influences. Those were the good old days. I don't mind sharing with the non-Natives, but I sure as hell don't like things being taken away, especially our kids for residential school."

Copper loved country and western music. When I went to Whitehorse, I picked up a new tape. Patsy Cline and Buck Owen were his favourites. We were having coffee his wife, Mabel, had made, in their snug three-room log cabin, warming ourselves like two cats in the sun and listening to CBC's Saturday afternoon all-request show on the radio.

"Joshua, do you think 'I've Got a Tiger by the Tail' is a good song?"

"It's the best," I said. "One of my favourites of all time."

Copper laughed, slapped his knee and spilled his coffee. "You're right there, young fella."

While the music played in the background, Copper launched into one of his many stories. "Now, I'm going to tell you something, so listen good. Long ago there was a summer as cold as a winter. Life was difficult because nothing had a chance to grow, and newborn animals didn't make it. The ice stayed on the lakes all year round. It was thin so we couldn't walk on it or put our boats out on it. At that same time a trading party that included my relatives from Dawson came over, bringing dried meat to trade for copper. It was a good thing too. They had lots of meat, and we didn't have so much. Among them was a young man named Joseph Copper, who thought he found a big gold nugget on a White River creek."

"How big?" I asked.

"You know the size of bread dough before it's baked? Well, it was that big. But it turned out to be a copper nugget and not gold at all. Joseph thought he had it made. He was planning his wedding and everything. He still got married, but he didn't have as big of a time as he thought he would have."

When he finished, Patsy Cline was singing the last notes of "Leavin' On Your Mind."

Weeks later, listening to the same radio program, Copper told me, "I'm going to tell you another story about one of my relatives. It's almost two hundred years old."

He pulled his chair up until our knees touched; he did this when he wanted to talk seriously. Copper counted back through the years, using his fingers as a guide and starting with his present family. He amazed me by reciting names and their meanings, generation after generation. When he came to the person he wanted to talk about, he stopped and said, "That is about two hundred years."

Copper spoke about a young man who was called Seeing Person because he had visions.

"Seeing Person would leave our people for long periods of time. He travelled great distances to Alaska and down the coast and sometimes down south to Teslin and that area. He travelled alone, and when he returned, he was worn, tired and hungry. He would tell the people his visions but otherwise he rarely spoke. The vision story that came down and meant the most to us is about a time when all things will change. There will be suffering, the weather will not be the same, summer will stop and things will change quickly. Then after a time life will get better. All the people will live in peace and treat others as brothers. That is why, Joshua, you have to believe in one God. When all of us understand it's the same God we believe in, then we'll understand what a big family we are. This man knew about the white man coming and told the people about the big boats full of them. He told us many times that things would change."

"It sounds like he was talking about today," I said.

"One spring Seeing Person went on another journey, but this time the elders gave him gifts in appreciation of his visions. One gift was a walking stick, and another was a gopher-skin cloak to keep him warm. After that trip he never came back. His family waited for years, but he never came back. They had a legend that he would return one day, but we have not seen him since. Maybe someday."

I was touched that after all these years Copper's voice still held a note of sadness when he spoke of his long-ago relative.

"I'm going to tell you something else, and when I do, I'm afraid for my relative Seeing Person. Russians came over here hundreds of years ago, too, and made people slaves. Some were chained and forced to work like animals on gold diggings. Here, I'll show you."

I followed him out to the shed behind his cabin. The walls were slanted to one side—the winds from the lake had pushed them over—and the weather-beaten grey door was off its hinges and propped up against the opening. It would never fit back into its leaning frame.

"Here," Copper said, rummaging in a dark corner among gas cans and boat motors. He pulled out a crudely forged pair of rusted shackles. "I found these in a place where there were old diggings."

Days later Copper came to the job site where we were replacing shingles on a house. He stood on the road and waved me over. I put Angst under my arm and climbed down the ladder to join him.

"That dog can go up but not down, eh?" Copper laughed.

Angst barked at him.

"One thing I forgot to tell you, young fella, is that on one trip Seeing Person brought back a pure white round stone. It came from boat people he met on the coast. They had dark hair and eyes like us but were from far away. It sounded like a pearl."

When Copper finished, he looked at me to make sure I understood what he was saying. I nodded in agreement, though I wasn't sure of the pearl's significance. Was he telling me there were Asian explorers on the West Coast? He nodded and went on his way.

Copper also described traditional Native medicine, how healers blew smoke into a person's ear to cure earache and what plants were good for what ailments. I was always interested in hearing how diligently these hardy people worked to ensure their survival.

"Joshua, I am going to tell you the truth now." Copper often started a serious talk with this statement. "When the people got sick and their lungs filled up and breathing was difficult, they would take a red-hot copper knife and insert it between the back ribs into the lung. Then they would let it drain." He winced and made the sign of a knife thrust.

I shuddered, feeling the pain. Years later, when Copper was infirm, I visited him at the Whitehorse General Hospital. He was sitting up in bed, and the nurses were changing his shirt. There on his back below each lung were two horizontal scars about two inches across, perfectly healed but still red and sore-looking after all those years.

About a month after Copper told me of these treatments, I was back in Burwash delivering plywood that I'd picked up for Arnold in Whitehorse. Arnold was helping his uncle and aunt clean their cabin. I pitched in and loaded an old Ski-Doo onto the back of my truck to take it to the dump.

"That Ski-Doo was a dandy when it was new, but now it's so old that I can't even get parts for it," Copper said.

Their home was neat and tidy, and the furniture was simple, but a large window overlooking the lake made the room bright. In one corner, under a stack of newspapers, sat an oak trunk.

Arnold asked, "Do you want this old trunk, uncle?"

"I was hoping Joshua would take it," Mabel said.

I opened it, looked inside and thought it would be good for storage.

"I'll take it off your hands," I said.

"It's for you," Copper said.

I cleaned the trunk and set a doily on top, and it made a nice coffee table. Its domed lid wasn't the best place to set dishes, but it was great for resting my tired feet after work. I also thought it tied the room together.

Months later, on a freezing day deep in the heart of winter when it was sensible to stay indoors, I decided to sand and refinish the trunk. It was solidly built with dovetail joints and hand-forged metal on the corners and lid. The runners on the bottom indicated it could be dragged over land or snow. It was beaten and bashed and had probably been used as a travelling trunk for clothes and personal belongings. A drop-in drawer straddled the top, and it was about two feet deep. Someone had chiselled the symbols "A3BS" on the inside bottom. Did they represent someone's name?

I sat with my feet up, sipping a cup of coffee and wondering what the letters and numbers meant. Maybe I was a little bushed when I decided I had to visit the Whitehorse library and research this. I wanted the facts.

Although the temperature was still in the minus 30s, I thawed out my truck with my propane Tiger Torch, set inside a stovepipe slid under the oil pan. People walking by—their heads were covered in scarves so I couldn't recognize them—shouted, "Cooking your truck again, eh, Joshua? Keep an eye it doesn't light up on you."

More than one vehicle had burned to the ground before the fire engines could get to it. The firemen would spray down the blaze, and the car would remain on the side of the road like a blackened ice palace until spring thaw.

The truck started on the first try, and three hours later I was thumbing through library books. I found nothing useful, so I gave up. I asked the librarian about that other interesting story Copper had told me. "Do you have anything about the history of Russian miners on the Alaskan coast?"

She guided me to an area where history books crammed the shelves. She said, "But if you really want to know, you should ask Azvolas in Haines Junction. He's somewhat of an expert on the subject."

Azvolas was my neighbour. I did my shopping and headed back to visit him.

"Old Russian Cyrillic numbering, Joshua," said Azvolas when I drew a picture of the carving for him.

His name meant oak, and it suited him to a T. He was a huge oak of a man, six feet eight inches tall and over three hundred pounds. As an industrial electrician, he worked at the Whitehorse Copper and Keno Hill mines. When I met the shift foreman from Whitehorse Copper, he told me, "Azvolas is brilliant at his trade. We're lucky to have him work for us."

Azvolas had emigrated from Lithuania, fleeing the Communists, and moved to Haines Junction in the early 1950s with his wife and children. He was well-read.

Rebecca, his wife, matched him in girth but not height. She was a math professor educated at the University of Prague, but in Haines Junction she taught piano and was a substitute teacher at the St. Elias School.

Visiting Azvolas was an occasion. Not only was the house a complete shambles, buzzing with activity, but he took it upon himself to educate visitors on any subject that came to mind. Azvolas's booming, accented voice kept his guests pinned, while Rebecca seemed happy to produce large quantities of baked goods. Guests were equally happy to devour these with great cups of steaming sweet tea. His son and daughter, who were destined to be as big as their parents, ran in and out of our conversation, clutching homework and asking questions.

Azvolas was opinionated and didn't let others get a word in edgewise, but apart from that, he was a good guy. It was easy to listen to his lectures, and I always enjoyed the food.

He pulled a worn black notebook off the crammed shelf in the living room and made quick calculations. "The numbers say 1726. It's a date. That trunk more than likely came across the Bering Sea and was traded full of merchandise to the people along the Alaska coast. Somehow it found its way into the Yukon's interior. Maybe Skookum Jim packed it over the Chilkoot Pass." He laughed at his own joke.

The symbols were no big mystery after all. They meant nothing except the trunk was old. I thanked Azvolas, ate another piece of poppyseed cake and headed home.

The cold weather stuck, so I kept refinishing. Inside the trunk, a faded and water-stained lining was held in place with tacks. The once bright yellow flower-printed cloth tore off easily, and a folded brown paper fell out.

"What could this be? A map to the Tsar's fortune, perhaps?" I asked Angst, who looked into the trunk with interest.

I carried the brittle paper to the kitchen table and carefully unfolded it. I was right; it was a map. It had mountains and rivers drawn on it, with a red stylized arrow and letter N indicating north. Words were scribbled along the margins, and one place was highlighted with a neat little red star with a blue circle around it.

I studied the map carefully, but since I didn't understand the writing, I visited Arnold and Copper. Together we might be able to unravel the information.

"Look real hard at that, Joshua. Could be important. Show it to Arnold too," Copper said.

The map was crudely drawn and wildly out of scale. Some parts were written in Russian Cyrillic and other parts in Southern Tutchone. The Dezadeash River was labelled Titi'at Man, and we guessed that Aze Chu was the Dusty River. The Bates River was written as Tashal Chu'. The map appeared to centre on an area east of the Alsek River, which the Dezadeash and Dusty run into, but all other references were smudged, faded and hard to read.

Arnold laid it on the kitchen table. He drank two cups of coffee and smoked three cigarettes before announcing, "I give up. I know the Tutchone words, but everything else is Greek to me." He explained the words he knew.

I was glad he gave up. I was worried his cigarette ash would burn a hole in the map and make it even more mysterious.

Next I took it to Azvolas, who explained the Russian but little else. Between the three of us, we couldn't agree what it meant. Frustrated, I stuck the map between the pages of *War and Peace* and left it there.

Over the next year I thought about it occasionally. Azvolas did too. A couple of times he called across the log slab fence when I was in the backyard, "Joshua, what are you going to do about the map? I'd like to see it again. We could go treasure hunting."

"Later," I shouted back.

My curiosity was piqued. Was it a treasure map? Or something else of value? The need to know got the best of me, and in mid-September, when my work was caught up and I had a few weeks to spare, I packed my gear and headed for the Alsek River valley.

I left Angst with Azvolas. "Keep him tied, or he will chase after me no matter how long I've been gone."

"Do you want me to go with you? I can get packed in an hour."

"No thanks," I said. "It's just a quick trip, and I'll travel faster alone." I liked Azvolas, but having that big man lumbering through the bush behind me would have slowed things down.

I travelled along the Dezadeash River to its confluence with the Kaskawulsh River; from there they form the Alsek River. The star on the map indicated a spot downriver from the junction and east of the Alsek. I hiked for four days in a constant rain through tall willows, keeping a lookout for bears. I estimated the distance and felt confident that I was in the right spot. The Bates River reference to the east gave me a helpful bearing.

The place had a strange atmosphere. The last rays of the sun touched the tops of the mountains, giving a forlorn feeling. For the first time I felt uneasy and wished I hadn't travelled alone. I should have brought Angst.

I made camp and cooked an evening meal over a small fire, but my stomach felt queasy and I didn't have much of an appetite. I turned in after placing my handgun on a white canvas for better visibility in the dark. The bear spray I left in the pack; it was only good for gophers if they should attack.

A stirring around camp hours later woke me out of a deep sleep. I raised myself up on an elbow and groped for the gun, straining my eyesight to catch a glimpse of what was there. The smell of roses was everywhere, and a breeze blew across my face as someone passed by. Only when I heard footsteps moving away from the camp did I know for sure it was a person.

I had no idea who it was, but I knew it was unusual. Unable to fall back to sleep, I lay in my sleeping bag and waited for the sun to come up. When it was light enough, I made a close inspection of the ground and found a clear set of moccasin footprints. Next to the prints was the indentation of a walking stick. I was puzzled and couldn't figure out why someone would walk through camp without greeting me. It made me nervous, and for the next while I looked over my shoulder.

After a breakfast of eggs and back bacon, I hiked along the valley, looking for any sign of a human presence. I found a few rotting tree stumps that had been cut with an axe; they fell over when I kicked them, which meant they were more than a hundred years old. I'd hiked far enough to get tired when, through my binoculars, I spotted the faint outline of a pathway up the mountainside above me. The path went south to north, and I thought I could make out the dark shadow of an adit in the face of a large rock outcrop.

The going was steep, but in short order I'd hiked up to a tunnel's entrance. The wind moaned through the opening, and again a feeling of desolation overwhelmed me. I felt strongly that this was the place on the map. I dropped my pack, took out a flashlight and walked into the cool darkness. My eyes adjusted, and I could see fairly well.

The tunnel ceiling was just below a man's height, so I walked stooped over. Water lay on the ground, and drops fell from the ceiling, making a musical sound as they hit the puddles. Old weather-worn timbers lay scattered about, as did rusty metal bands, cut nails and splayed wood-stave barrels. I carefully examined the timber posts for bear fur that might have snagged on them but I saw none.

I found more rusty shovels, holed buckets and a tipped-over ore cart with its metal wheels sticking out like the legs of a dead cow. The tunnel went around a corner, and I followed into the darkness. Everything looked ancient. A lamp with the remnants of a bent and yellowed candle stub hung off a post. I thought for a moment of lighting it but didn't. Then the flashlight picked up something white on the ground against the wall—human remains. In my travels I'd encountered skeletons before; they didn't bother me. At that moment the wind moaned down the tunnel, making the most awful sound and raising the hair on my neck. I calmed myself by thinking there was nothing here to harm me.

It was a complete skeleton. I moved closer for a better look. To my dismay the man bore heavy, rusty chain shackles on his wrists. This must be one of the Russian mines that Copper had spoken of. Was this his relative Seeing Person? I walked out of the tunnel, disturbed by what I'd seen. I couldn't imagine the life that person had lived—cold, hungry, the prisoner of a slave owner here in the Yukon. I was angry with his keepers. "Damn, damn, damn," I swore. They were so blind for gold.

Why he was left to die alone I don't know, but I made up my mind to give him a decent burial. For the next three hours I built a cairn over his bones. Before placing the last rocks, I carefully removed the shackles from his wrists, took them outside and, whirling them over my head, hurled them with all my strength down the mountain. They spun through the air for a few moments, then bounced down the slope, leaving spurts of dust in their path each time they hit the ground. At that moment the sun broke through the clouds as if a curtain were being raised and bathed the entire valley in the brightest of light.

I walked back to camp, enjoying the cool evening. Maybe the map showed a gold mine, but I didn't care. Giving that man a dignified burial was more important. I was glad that I'd found him. The trip was worthwhile.

The next morning I headed home. A curious thing happened on the second night of my journey. I made camp, fell asleep exhausted and slept until dawn. When I awoke, there beside my head lay a bunch of alpine flowers, and tied around them in a little bundle was the most perfect pearl you ever did see.

At that moment a scurrying behind me stopped my heart, but it was Angst, who had gotten loose and followed my trail. He leaped into my arms, his tail beating a hundred times a minute, and licked my face. His joy was irrepressible. I was happy to see him, too, and cooked breakfast for both of us.

A few days after I got back, I bumped into Arnold and Copper. Copper walked with one arm hooked through Arnold's and the other hand holding a cane.

"I'm getting old, Joshua. I've waited a long time for some things, and they have made me old," he said. "But now I'm happy."

"We heard you had a little adventure," Arnold said.

"How did you hear that?"

"We heard, we heard," Copper said quietly, "and we want to thank you for all you have done. I don't know if you understand what it all means, but maybe you should think about it. Now show me the pearl."

I was surprised, because only Angst had seen the pearl, and I'm sure he wasn't talking. I took it out of my pocket. Copper examined it, then passed it to Arnold, who did the same and passed it back to me.

"Yes, that looks the same as the white round stone Seeing Person was given. Keep that, Joshua. It will be good for you. Come and see me soon. Next Saturday would be good. Arnold bought me a new Buck Owens tape, and it's a dandy."

The Wolfbear of Sheep Mountain

One month after my return from the Alsek River I ran into Copper Johnson. He wanted to hear more details of my adventure. We went for coffee and I told him everything. When I finished he sat back, breathed a sigh of relief and said, "You did good, young fella."

Two weeks later a knock came at my door. Angst barked and jumped off the couch to see who it was. It was Copper.

"Can I come in?" he asked politely.

"Yes, come in."

I was pleased to have him visit and I opened the door wide for him. I made coffee and served a plate of Peek Freans shortcake. Angst rested his head on Copper's knee and had it scratched.

"I want to tell you about more things because they fit with your story," Copper said.

He seemed hesitant. Other times, he would jump right in and tell me everything.

"But this one is between you and me, okay?"

"Sure, I won't tell a soul," I said.

"Shake on it," he said.

I shook his outstretched hand, thinking this must be serious.

Once the deal was sealed there was no stopping him telling his story.

"Long ago at the time of the two winters in one year things were bad. People suffered and died. Coldness held the land and my people know when things are bad more bad things happen."

Angst whined and left to curl up by the stove. Copper wiped the hair off his hand.

"The elders back then said they had seen it before. Others said it came from Russia. The Aleut spoke of this. When they heard it was in the territory it was too late to stop it."

"Stop what?" I asked.

I was thinking some kind of influenza had invaded the territory.

"They started to find caribou, sheep, moose and even large grizzly with their throats ripped open and the body left. But there was no blood in the body and little on the ground. Just a carcass was left and the eyes were taken."

Copper stopped. His brow was furrowed. "Do you believe me?"

"Yes, I've seen strange things in my travels and I believe you," I said.

"It was a while before anyone saw who was doing these things. It was near a caribou fence at Kusawa Lake that a family of hunters saw a caribou caught in the fence being taken away. They said the animal that took it stood up like a bear but its head looked like a wolf's and its footprints looked like a bear's, a big bear, maybe four or five hundred pounds. They were worried."

"Sounds like a werewolf," I said.

"I've seen that movie, *Werewolf of London*. The army showed it to us in the '40s when they built the highway. Scared the hell out of the whole village. But that was actors, right?" Copper said.

"Is that the one with Henry Hull?" I asked.

"Yes, the one with Valerie Hobson. Now that was a good-looking gal. All the soldiers hooted and whistled when she came on the screen."

Copper never ceased to amaze me with his memory for details.

"I got to know the cooks in the army camp. They had big tents where they cooked over oil and wood stoves for the five hundred men building the Alaska Highway. They cooked good grub and baked as well. It was all black men. We had never seen them before and at first we were nervous. Some of us took a long time to visit but eventually we found out they were all good guys. We got jobs pearl diving, that's what they called dishwashing, and we ate there all the time. It was the first time we had bananas. One old cook named Booker went up on the mountain with Arnold's grandfather, David Taylor, to hunt sheep. David was older than anyone but he was still strong and climbed those mountains easily. They lay on a ridge spotting when they saw this bear stalking the sheep. David

Taylor told me later he had never seen a bear that high up on the mountain at that time of the year, so he was surprised.

"David told me, 'The bear jumped to its feet, ran on hind legs and grabbed a grown male with a full curl. It scared the hell out of both of them because the creature just kept on running right up the mountain, never stopping, with the sheep in its teeth and arms. Booker never got over it and when he got down the mountain he asked to be transferred out. He had seen the werewolf movie and his imagination was getting the best of him. They didn't transfer him though. He still had to bake and cook.'

"Booker told me later, 'I sleep with my .303 rifle and my helmet on.'

"David told me, 'Copper, you never saw anything like it.'

"I wanted to go see what had happened to the sheep. David wasn't afraid of anything and he was more than willing to go back. We left a few days later and went to the spot where the ram was taken. We found prints and followed the trail for a ways. We came up on an outcrop and there was the sheep. It was dead and besides having its throat ripped apart, its eyes had been taken out (and eaten, I suppose). We were scared. We knew this wasn't man or animal."

"What did you do?" I asked.

"Well, for the longest time David and I told no one about this, then we decided to talk about it with others because it bothered us so much and we didn't know what had happened or what it was.

"'Comes from Russia,' Eliza, David's wife, said. She smoked a pipe and knew everything.

"'It swims across the water from Russia and jumps across the ice—it's that powerful. It is no good. It has been here before. Nothing stops it but the white stone brought to us many years ago by Seeing Person. The men put the stone in their muzzle loaders the Hudson's Bay sold them. They wounded one once and sent him packing back to Russia. That's the only bullet that will hurt him.'"

I was becoming more interested in Copper's story every minute and I knew the white stone was the pearl given to me.

"Do you get it, Joshua? I told this story because you have a pearl, and that pearl is the only thing that can stop the wolfbear. I have heard a report of a large creature being spotted near Sheep Mountain, and the body of a moose was found near Destruction Bay with all the signs of the wolfbear being there."

I started to put two and two together.

"You want me to go hunt this thing with a pearl for a bullet?"

"I think we have to, Joshua, to protect people. If you can overcome your fear and shoot straight you'll be okay," Copper said.

I trusted Copper and I understood what was going on, but I was starting to get a picture of something like a conspiracy swirling around me.

"Remember the three women in the dream you had on the island where there was smallpox?"

"How the hell did you know about them?" I asked. "That was a fever-induced dream."

"I'm like your father, Joshua. I know lots of things. Those women guided you here and made the Junction look beautiful to you so you would settle down. We have a problem and someone with spiritual strength has to take care of it. The pearl was given to you, my friend. There is no doubt in my mind you have a purpose."

I cradled my head in my hands and shook it. I didn't want to get messed up with any four-hundred-pound werewolf vampire that eats caribou and relishes eyeballs.

Copper rubbed my shoulder.

"I have to tell you more. About a year ago other animals were found by Kusawa Lake. The blood is taken, throats ripped out, eyes eaten and bodies left. People have not been attacked but with the modern-day thinning of game and the wolfbear's large appetite we think it is only a matter of time. One family saw such a creature crossing the highway near Burwash.

"When you went to follow your map on the Alsek River we were scared for you because you were alone."

At that moment Azvolas walked in. "Yes," he said, "we were worried so we let Angst go find you but he was too fast and got away from us."

"You're in on this too?" I asked.

"Yes, of course, as are many people in town. As Copper mentioned this animal appeared before when a summer turned to winter and I think it is here because of the damn economic downturn. They appear in troubled times."

"You have to kill the beast and the only way to do it is with the pearl you were given," Copper said.

"I have an old flint lock that will do the job and we will go with you if need be," Azvolas said.

"He can take one person and I have chosen Arnold. He is the most experienced. Come in now, Arnold," Copper called. Arnold walked in from the door leading to the wood shed attached to the house.

"So you really are all in on this," I said.

"Yes, since day one," Arnold said.

"Don't worry. No one is playing you, we all have your best interests at heart," Azvolas said.

"You're not the sacrifice to be thrown into the volcano to appease the lava gods," Arnold said.

"We have to get this thing or I fear we will lose people," Copper said.

"Why don't you talk to the RCMP?" I asked.

"We did, but they asked us what we were smoking and threatened us with jail time if we are growing that wacky weed," Arnold said.

For the next week we made preparations to go into sheep country looking for the wolfbear. Copper told us it was this time of year David and Booker were hunting on the mountain.

Azvolas had a musket in excellent shape and he spent the better part of a day showing me how to use it.

"Hell, Joshua, even my wife, Rebecca, has known how to load and fire this thing since she was a child back in the old country. Her uncle told her it came from Transylvania, where it was used to shoot werewolves with a silver bullet."

"Really," I said.

"No, not really. I picked this up in a pawn shop in Vancouver a few years back. But then this isn't no typical werewolf," he said with a wink and a laugh that didn't bolster my courage at all.

Rebecca packed our food and hugged both Arnold and me goodbye. She seemed worried.

A group of townsfolk assembled outside Azvolas's house as we drove away. They waved. I felt like they were the villagers in *Frankenstein* and we were off to catch Boris Karloff.

Azvolas dropped us off at the base of Sheep Mountain next to the highway and we started our climb. Copper hiked with us for a few hours, then pointed out our direction, shook our hands and left.

"I think you boys are going to do okay. I can feel it in my bones."

"Thanks for that, Copper. I hope your optimism is right," I said.

We hadn't travelled more than a mile when the mist and rain moved in. Then the most blood-curdling scream came from down the valley.

I turned to Arnold. He was pale as a sheet.

"Okay," I said, "I've had enough of this. Let's go back—you look like a white man."

Arnold gathered himself together. "No, Joshua. We have to end this one way or another. I'd hate to see anyone hurt because we didn't do our job."

"I hate this," I said, and we continued on.

I felt like I was in a haunted house movie where everyone in the audience hopes the actors won't go in but they do anyway. Then against all common sense they split up. This gets one or more of the expendable characters, usually the chubby scared guy and his nerdy girlfriend, killed in some gruesome manner.

"We are not splitting up," I yelled at Arnold, who was walking ahead.

"Never think of it," he shouted back.

We climbed higher for the next hour. The path became steeper and the fog became thicker. I could barely see Arnold's packsack bobbing up and down with every step a few feet in front of me.

I was going to say to Arnold how disturbing this all was when suddenly he let out the most horrible high-pitched shriek. It sounded like women had joined us. It was something I never wanted to hear again.

He told me later, "I walked right up on the beast and bumped into its hairy back."

The wolfbear had made a kill. It was feasting and hadn't noticed us. Arnold, acting instinctively, turned and pushed past me, knocking me down on my back. I struggled to aim the gun and frantically tried to pull off the baggie taped over the powder to keep it dry so I could pull back the flint lock.

The wolfbear stood over me, looking just as surprised as we were. It was the most horrifying sight I had ever seen and it smelled. The animal was huge and muscular and its small ears were like a bear's but its face was long like a wolf's. Thick fur covered its massive body and blood dripped off its snarling teeth onto my clothes. I cocked the rifle, aimed and would have pulled the trigger but at that moment Arnold, having regained his courage, decided to play hero. He came running back up, leapt over me and stood poised to challenge the beast, cocking his fists like a boxer.

"Get the hell out of the way and let me shoot this creepy thing," I screamed, still lying on my back.

Arnold jumped out of the way but the beast slashed out and caught him on the chest with its claw. I had seen enough and whether Arnold was out of the way or not I had to shoot. There was a thundering boom, a blinding flash and cloud of smoke and the animal went down with a crash, then just as quickly jumped back up and disappeared into the fog. I'd only wounded it. The gun had gone off in Arnold's ears and he grabbed both of them and hopped back down the trail, cursing with every breath. The shot echoed up and down the valley and I knew Copper would hear it.

Arnold came back, flexing his jaw to get his hearing back. Luckily his wounds were slight but we worried about infection so there on the mountain I tortured him with iodine from the first aid kit.

We grabbed our packsacks and rifle, then stumbled back down the mountain in the dark. When we came out on the highway we could see the dim headlights of a vehicle through the fog. We ran toward it and found Copper and Azvolas leaning up against the car waiting for us.

"Did you get it?" Azvolas asked.

"Yes we did, but I don't know if we killed it," I said breathlessly.

"Someone has to go back up and see if it's dead," Arnold said, hunched over the car's fender trying to catch his breath.

"My family will look for a body tomorrow. Don't say anything to anyone about this. I'll let people know. You must never tell anyone that you shot a wolfbear," Copper said.

We all agreed.

"Arnold, are you okay?" Copper asked.

"It's just a scratch," he said.

"We heard the shot, but what was that screaming afterwards?" Copper wanted to know.

"That was iodine on Arnold's wound," I said.

The next day Copper's grandsons went and looked for a body.

"We had a blood trail but it disappeared high in the mountain. It looks like the animal was headed east to the coast," Mark, the eldest grandson, said.

Copper must have spread the word because the townsfolk seemed greatly relieved that the problem was taken care of, although no one ever spoke directly about it or thanked Arnold or me personally.

I think their secrecy was all about not scaring the tourists away. But then again maybe a wolfbear would attract some.

The next time I was in Burwash I had coffee with Copper. I felt like one of the family after the wolfbear experience.

"Let's go see my wife and see what she thinks of all this," he said.

Mabel was sitting at home with her granddaughter, Liza, beading a pair of men's moccasins. Mabel was short and plump with a round face and snow white hair piled in a bun on her head. She had a wholesome aura about her.

"You wounded it, Joshua?" she asked.

"Yes we did. We were close when I fired the gun and it went down then jumped back up. Your grandson Mark and his brothers saw blood."

"It's just as good if you wound them. He won't come back. That pearl will irritate him until the end of his life," Mabel said.

She then handed the moccasins to me.

"These are for you and I have another pair for Arnold."

"Thank you very much! They're beautiful."

"Look at the beadwork," Copper said.

On the top of each moccasin in the most intricate beadwork was a muzzle loader with a white puff of smoke coming out of the barrel and a pearl coming out of the smoke.

Mabel, Copper and their granddaughter broke out into laughter.

"But Joshua, never shoot the creature that whistles," Mabel said.

"The seven dwarves?" I asked.

"You know what we mean," Copper said, "the Sasquatch."

"Oh, there are Sasquatch, too?"

"Sure, who do you think let us know the wolfbear was in our territory?" Mabel said, hooking more beads on her needle.

"I never would have thought," I said. I tried on the moccasins.

The Raft

If the town of Haines Junction had existed two hundred years ago, it would have been under water. In 1775 the Lowell Glacier surged across the Alsek River, creating Glacial Lake Alsek. It was eighty miles long and four hundred feet deep. When the ice dam broke in 1852, a Tlingit family camping at the junction of the Alsek and Tatshenshini rivers was swept away.

Months before that tragedy, ten men had poled and pulled a raft along the Alsek River shore. The rafters camped with the Tlingit for a few days, exchanging gifts of tools and jewellery before they travelled on northward. Pausing between the Tweedsmuir and Fisher glaciers, they watched as a wall of water, ice and debris roared down on them like a mountain avalanche. The crewmen on the shore threw up their arms—the unbelievers to hold back the flood, the believers to embrace their deaths—but all were swept away. Their brothers clinging to the raft were lifted rapidly up the mountainside and deposited on a rocky outcrop. Then the men watched as the water dropped before their eyes.

After salvaging food and equipment, they blessed the land and prayed for the advancement of their brethren in the next world.

"Leave the bell with the raft," the chief monk said. "They should be together."

The monks hiked single-file along the mountain in their sandals and saffron robes, carrying their begging bowls and chanting as they went. They were never seen again.

Years later the only signs of the glacial lake and the flood were the legends and the high shorelines of driftwood bleaching in the sun.

From my kitchen window I could see the sparkling blue glaciers suspended in the Auriol peaks. I liked living in Haines Junction, one of the prettiest towns in the Yukon. The air was fresh, the people were friendly and I liked my construction work. I also loved hiking in the mountains and forest, and if I had a reason to hike, it was all the more interesting.

Now and then I heard rumours of a large raft with strange carvings that was beached high on a mountain. I read the Bible and other religious books with interest. I believed the story of Noah and his family was allegorical, but I believed the Alsek River raft was true.

When I asked Copper, the Tutchone elder, he said, "I've heard the raft story. I've heard lots of stories, Joshua, and told most of them to you already. Go see Thomas Joe if you want information about this one. I've heard he knows something, maybe more than me. All I can say is, be careful when you look for strange things."

Copper—wise, ancient and a lover of country music—always steered me right.

Thomas was the foreman for the Town of Haines Junction, and no better person could have been hired for the job. There wasn't anything he couldn't fix or wouldn't help you with. He rarely spoke two words, and when he did, they came out in the calmest voice. It seemed he knew exactly what he was going to say and used only the right number of words to say it. I admired him for that.

Thomas was a big man with a round face that reminded me of the smiling statues in the Far East. He was smart and competent, and his extended family of sons, daughters and numerous grandchildren all lived under the sprawling roof of a log home overlooking the Shakwak Valley. He provided generously for all of them.

I visited the town's garage once a week for coffee and to catch up on the news. Sometimes Azvolas, the electrician, would bring baking hot from the oven, and we would sit around the oil-stained plywood table—someone was always using it for a workbench—enjoying each other's company. The mechanics wore their coveralls, and the welders wore their skullcaps with advertisement printed on them. Occasionally a cribbage board would appear, or a good-hearted but competitive game of bridge would go on longer than the coffee break.

We also met in my workshop. Beside my tools, table saw and materials storage I put in a fridge, a couple of old couches and a good black and white

TV. This became a clubhouse where we watched the Grey and Stanley cups on CBC. We accompanied these games with a potluck dinner, and if we were really lucky, Thomas would haul his barbecue over and cook moose steaks and homemade sausage.

These were relaxing times. Our only rule was "work only" from 7:00 a.m. to 6:00 p.m. on weekdays and 8:00 a.m. to noon on weekends. We watched TV after that.

I visited Thomas and his wife, Rose. There was always room for one more at their dinner table.

Rose had her own agenda for feeding me; she never stopped trying to hook me up with one of her unmarried sisters. Marsha would give me a big smile and blush a little when Rose started matchmaking.

When Rose realized I planned to stay a bachelor, she wasn't so pushy. "Too bad," she said. "I could see you and Marsha being really happy together."

After a dinner of roast and garden vegetables, I settled back with Thomas and his eldest son, Elias, to watch *Hockey Night in Canada*. Thomas loved the Montreal Canadiens and wouldn't miss their games for anything. For some reason he liked to watch the Habs in French.

"Seems more authentic," he said.

I couldn't understand a word they said; it also irritated the hell out of Elias. "I wish I knew French. I speak Southern Tutchone, but I doubt if any of the Habs know that," he said.

Elias was named after the Saint Elias Mountains. He was slight like his mother and had a sparse moustache above his lip. He wore glasses and chain-smoked, lighting one cigarette from the other. He was serious and talked more than Thomas.

"Smoking is going to kill you," Thomas warned.

I made sure I was always upwind of the cancer sticks.

Elias and his wife, Annie, lived off the land, hunting and trapping. In the summer the town of Haines Junction hired him and in the winter they moved back to their cabin in the bush.

We kept the sound down so we could talk, but when Jacques Plante made one of his brilliant saves, the cheers would go up.

The Habs were winning a game with the Toronto Maple Leafs, so I steered the conversation toward the raft.

Elias was leaning on the armrest at the end of the couch. Without looking at me, he said, "We know where that is."

Thomas shot him a glance, but the cat was out of the bag.

"What?" said Elias, lifting his head off his hand. "As if nobody had ever known about it."

I couldn't believe what I'd just heard. I thought it was such a big mystery.

"You know where it is?" I asked.

No one answered for a while. Then Thomas said, "I've seen it. My father took me there when I was ten. I took Elias there when he was ten." He cast a glance at Elias. "And I told him to keep quiet about it! If it was common knowledge, people would go up there and cut it up for firewood."

"It's Japanese, Joshua," Elias said, reaching his cigarette to the ashtray.

I'd just gotten over the fact that they knew the location. The raft was Japanese? This really intrigued me.

"How do you know it's Japanese?"

"I took a close look at the characters carved on the logs and I looked it up in *National Geographic* magazine. Those are Japanese carvings," Thomas said.

For months I tried to persuade them that we should visit the raft. They had reservations. "The elders don't like people going up there. And they've warned us about strange things in the night."

I didn't believe any of it.

One afternoon, figuring that I had some bargaining power, I met Thomas at the shop, where he was pulling wrenches on a truck's motor. "If you take me to the raft, I'll share some other information with you."

"What information?"

"DC-3."

Thomas's eyes lit up like hundred-watt light bulbs. He knew right away what I was talking about. He'd heard the rumours about a missing plane.

"Yeah, what do you know about a DC-3?" he asked, keeping his head under the truck's hood and trying not to appear interested.

"Lots."

Thomas said no more. He believed me, and I had caught his interest.

In the fall he agreed to take me to the raft. "It's farther down the Alsek River than where you were before. It's on the Yukon side of the BC–Yukon border. We'll take you there on three conditions. One, we take our cousin Arnold. Two, we hunt moose on the way back. And three, when you see the raft, you tell us about the DC-3."

"Arnold brings us good luck on a hunt," Elias said.

"Okay," I said.

We shook hands to seal the deal.

Arnold was happy to come along. "I need to get away and it's better than hunting werewolves. The wife is after me every day to finish the kitchen. I tell her, who wants to build cabinets on weekends when he's been pounding nails all week? It's only been six months since I tore it apart."

"That's about average for a kitchen renovation. A month for each week you promised—that's fair," I said.

Early in the fall we packed my truck with supplies and equipment, hitched up Arnold's twenty-foot Zodiac on a trailer and drove to the Dezadeash River. After loading the boat and mounting the motor, we said goodbye to Rose and Marsha, and pushed off from shore.

We had two sets of oars and took turns guiding the boat. The motor was for coming back upstream. I observed the other three and felt full confidence in their ability to travel on the river.

On the third day we reached Lowell Glacial Lake, carved out over centuries by the massive Lowell Glacier. We camped on the opposite shore and watched turquoise ice calve into the lake with a thunderous boom. I sat with Arnold, drinking tea and finishing the last of delicious lasagna that Rose had sent along with the warning, "Make sure you eat that lasagna in the next few days before it spoils."

She needn't have worried: we wolfed it down.

The next morning Arnold and Elias wanted to climb the nearby 5,500-foot Goatherd Mountain. Thomas stayed in camp. He said, "I came here to hunt and visit the raft, not waste time and energy by climbing mountains."

The three of us made the climb, and I was glad we did. The scenery was magnificent, especially the view of the glaciers. Arnold and Elias asked about the cave where I'd found the remains of the Russians' slave. I said nothing; I didn't want to disturb that place again. Rest in peace as they say.

On the fifth day we packed up and moved on, but not before discovering a moose had bedded down in the willows just yards from our camp.

"How strange that the moose wasn't spooked by our presence. We must be carrying good spirits with us," I said.

"It's a good sign," Thomas said.

"We should go after it," Elias said.

"On the way back," Thomas said.

Elias's face showed he didn't like being told.

Signs of bear were everywhere. Once a large grizzly crashed out of the bush and ran down the bank to chase the boat, shaking his massive head as he challenged us.

"Must have spooked him at a kill," Thomas said. We moved farther out into midstream.

Two days later, a few miles above Fisher Glacier, Thomas called a halt and instructed Elias and me, "Row onto that beach over there. We're here."

We dragged the boat up onto the shore and packed our backpacks. Thomas and Elias slung rifles over their shoulders, and I had my sidearm holstered on my hip.

Elias looked at my gun with interest and sang a line from the Marty Robbins song "Big Iron": "He's here to do some business with the big iron on his hip."

He didn't sing half badly either.

"If I had my guitar, I could make it sound better and sing the whole song."

From the start the going was tough. The bush was thick, and a light rain soaked us through until we stopped and pulled on our rain gear. It was a relief when we finally broke out above the treeline.

"Things should be easier from now on," Thomas said.

We hiked all day. Then Albert raised his fist, signalling us to stop, and slung his pack to the ground.

"We're here," he said.

I looked around. "I see nothing."

"Can't you see?" Elias asked, pointing to a split in the hill above us.

Then I saw the raft perfectly clearly, but it really wasn't what I'd expected. It was made of large logs, but when it had beached, it had straddled a crevice. As time went on and the bindings rotted, the logs fell in one by one, on top of each other. It was actually a pile of logs and hard to see.

"It's hidden pretty well," I said.

"That's why no one has found it. Planes fly over all the time, but the pilots never see it," Thomas said. "It's protected."

"Let's make camp. Then we'll go and see," Elias said.

Camp couldn't be made fast enough for me. As soon as we were done, I climbed up to get a better look. The logs were about three feet in diameter and over forty feet long. I could tell by the grain pattern that they were Douglas fir.

The logs were in good condition with little rot—the dry Yukon climate tends to be forgiving this way—except where they rested on the ground. There moisture had rotted the wood, and colonies of ants had invaded it.

The workmanship was impressive. The logs were expertly finished and carved. The butt ends were perfectly round, and the holes for the ropes to lash them together ran through the logs straight and square.

We could clearly make out characters carved along the length of the logs, but none of us could read them.

I was amazed at the line of ancient driftwood that stretched from the raft in both directions along the mountainside as far as the eye could see.

"It must have been one hell of a flood when it let go," Thomas said.

As I climbed around the logs, my foot hit something in the gravel that made a metallic sound. I dropped to my knees and scraped until I dug out a heavy hollow metal cylinder that was green with corrosion. The object was about two feet long and about eight inches in diameter. It had a loop as thick as my thumb on the top as if made for hanging. Inscriptions had been cast into it, and on one side a raised flat area bore marks as though it had been struck.

I called out, holding it up, "Hey, look what I found."

Arnold walked up to take a look. After turning it over in his hands and knocking on it with his knuckles, he said, "Ring-a-ding. It's a bell."

After supper we sat by our fire and passed the bell around, examining it and admiring its workmanship.

"Pretty neat, eh? Might be worth a pile of money," Elias said.

"There is no way that's leaving the raft," Thomas said.

Arnold said, "I wonder what it sounds like?"

"Here, let's try it." I held it up by a piece of rope, and Elias struck it once on the flat area with the butt of his hunting knife. The most beautiful musical note resounded, and I felt the vibration up to my elbow. The bell continued to sound for the longest time.

When it stopped, Arnold said, "Wow, that is one hell of a bell. I've never heard anything like it."

The night grew darker. Stars came out, and the moon lit up the mountains. We talked and drank coffee for a while. Then, in a quiet moment, we heard something that brought us to our feet, spilling our coffee, and sent chills down our spines. From across the valley came a sound identical to that of the bell we had just rung. It was as clear as day and lasted about the same time as our bell peal. We stared at each other in disbelief.

Peering into the darkness as hard as I could, I asked, "Did you hear that?"

They all nodded yes. I wished they'd said no.

"That was not an echo," Arnold said. "It's been too long."

We sat back down in silence.

Eventually Elias said with a wave of his hand and a smile, "Naw, can't be. There's no such thing. Is there, Dad? There's no such thing."

"You heard it as well as I did," Thomas said.

"Try it again," I said.

"No, don't," Arnold said. He jumped up, waving both hands to say no. "Let's just pack up in the morning and get back to town."

Elias loaded the fire up, and flames shot into the air, illuminating the mountainside.

"You shouldn't have done that. Now they can really see us," Thomas said with a half-hearted chuckle.

We didn't know who "they" were, but it sounded ominous.

Arnold looked concerned.

"Look," I said, "the only way we're going to know whether or not this was a fluke is to do it again."

Arnold said, "No, not again."

"Let's have a vote."

Thomas, Elias and I voted yes.

"You can do the honours," I told them.

Elias hung the bell. Thomas struck it once and struck it again after the first note faded away. We waited in silence, building up the fire even higher to give us courage. Just when we were beginning to doubt that we'd heard anything before, the sound of the bell came rippling across the valley. We waited anxiously for the second ring. It came as the first one was disappearing into the night.

Arnold kicked the ground with his boot. "This can't be happening."

Thomas looked at me and said, "They're calling you, Joshua." Then he broke into a nervous laugh. It was funny but spooky.

Pointing up the hill, I said, "That raft was beached over two hundred years ago. We should have listened to the elders."

"The elders always know what they're talking about," Arnold said.

"The elders had misgivings about this place. They cautioned people to be careful when they came here and not to be frivolous," Thomas said.

"No one is being frivolous," I said. "We shouldn't tell anyone of this or take any pictures."

"Okay, Joshua. Seeing as the hell has been scared out of us and no one is going to sleep, this is as good a time as any for you to tell us about the DC-3," Thomas said. "It might get our minds off this bell."

I kept my end of the bargain. I told them about how I'd found a crashed plane, how hard it was to find, the uniformed bodies inside, the Kennedy information, the gold, the guns and the stacks of money.

All three of them sat riveted by my every word. No one interrupted until I was done. The sun was rising as I finished.

"That's the DC-3 everyone talks about," Arnold said. "I thought it was a tall tale."

"Did you really not take any of that gold, Joshua?" Thomas asked.

"I'm telling you the truth. I didn't touch a penny. It wasn't mine, so I had no right."

"Most people would think that was crazy, but I respect your honesty," Arnold said.

"Honesty is good, but those guns and Dealey Plaza map—that doesn't sound so good," Thomas said.

"We have to be careful about it. If people knew that we knew, we could be in danger. Some of those agencies in the States are just plain crazy," I said.

We turned in and caught a couple of hours of sleep. In the morning, after coffee and toast, I climbed over the raft and inspected it thoroughly. On one central log there were numerous small carvings set within borders. They were in a line and about the size of a telephone book page. Some were accessible, some were not. I took out my notebook and, with pieces of charcoal from the fire, carefully transferred as many of these images as I could onto its pages. All in all I collected about thirty. I also took an impression of some embossed writing on the bell.

We left that afternoon after reburying the bell. We didn't want to create any bad karma with the unknown bell-ringer.

We loaded the Zodiac at the river. Thomas said, "Each one of you, swear to me not to disclose the location of the raft to anyone or mention anything about the bell."

We all swore.

"And Joshua, sometime soon we're going to sit down and talk about that DC-3."

We arrived back in Haines Junction, bone-tired, twelve days after setting out. I put away the charcoal rubbings and started looking for someone to interpret them. I think I stopped every Japanese tourist that I met in town, but between them not knowing English and their suspicion of me approaching them, I got nowhere.

I even asked my friend Ken Asano, the owner of a local motel and restaurant. He said, "It's not my dialect and it's old. How do you expect me to read this? Do you want coffee?"

I had almost given up when I had a chance encounter with a couple from Japan. As I was having lunch at the restaurant, they greeted Ken, and he responded in the same language.

Ken said something, and they looked over in my direction. He guided the couple to my table, and they sat down.

"My friend Joshua needs help with some Japanese writing. Maybe you can assist him."

We shook hands and introduced ourselves. "Joshua is a very nice name," the man said in perfect English. "We are Gessho and Akina from Okayama. I would be glad to help you in any way I can."

We exchanged polite conversation during a lunch of tomato soup and roast beef sandwiches. Ken's menu was simple and convenient for his wife, who couldn't cook. She told Ken, "I do laundry, make beds, sweep, look after the kids and wash everything, but if you want fancy cooking, go to hell."

The next best thing on the menu was a hamburger, chips and apple pie for desert. The factory pie was frozen, thawed and warmed in the oven. It always tasted like cardboard. I wondered why I ordered it.

I explained what I needed, and that evening Gessho and Akina walked to my house from the motel. I served tea, then laid the charcoal transfers on the Russian trunk that Copper had given me, and Gessho pored over them silently. His hands turned black from the charcoal. After reading a few, he sat back and said something quietly to his wife. She responded, "Ooh!"

"What?" I asked. "What is it?

"This is very curious. This information is very old and may have been written by Buddhist monks. See here." He pointed to a page. "This says Five

Mountain Temple, that is where they lived." He pointed again. "And here is where a ship of sorts was launched from Kamakura." Gessho studied the rubbings some more. Then, without looking up, he asked, "Where did you get this information?"

I couldn't tell him the truth, so I mumbled, "Some old logs."

Gessho looked up and said, "Maybe I should introduce myself more fully. I am Dr. Gessho Suzuki, professor of antiquities at the University of Tokyo. What I am looking at is incredibly important to you and me. Now I will ask you again where you found this information."

I could see how serious he was. I sat back in my chair and told him a condensed account of finding the raft and bell.

He was immensely pleased to hear this and said, "That is good, because what you just told me fits perfectly with these pages of information. I will now tell you the full story of what you have found. It is not complete, because your information is not complete, but I think we can make sense of this anyway. As far as I can see a group of monks had in their possession a bell, which was very ancient and had been in their temple for centuries. Apparently the bell was cast by a faithful follower of the Buddha a short time after his passing. The story attached to the bell is that if monks faithful to the Buddha were to launch a boat upon the seas, it would find a new home for the bell in a place of great spiritual potential. The monks, thinking it was time, launched a raft with the bell on it into the Pacific Ocean. After a time they came to rest where you found it."

Dr. Suzuki pointed to one particular page and said, "This is of great interest. What these letters refer to is a Buddhist legend. The story basically says that the land where the raft comes to rest will be blessed for eternity. The story then describes the way to determine eternity. If a monk of pure heart goes to the raft's mountain every hundred years and drags a silk cloth once over one spot, the time it would take to erode the mountain by this method would be an eternity."

Dr. Suzuki also took great interest in the images taken from the bell.

"See," he said, pointing to the charcoal impressions on the paper. "This says 'Nothing is sacred.' It doesn't mean that there is no sacred thing. It means that the element of nothingness is sacred: all things are sacred including nothing. It gives us a good idea of the studies of the monks at Five Mountain Temple. They meditated on nothingness and found it to be sacred. They thought God was so completely apart from corporeal existence that he himself is not invisible or visible, he is beyond nothingness and he is not created. So if nothingness is sacred, how sacred must God be?"

With that the story was ended. I reminded the professor that I'd made an oath of secrecy to my friend Thomas. I asked him to respect that.

Gessho said, "I will."

I still keep in touch with Dr. Suzuki, who is a prolific letter writer.

I told Thomas about the interpretation of the carvings, and he was impressed. He asked me, "Can Gessho keep a secret?"

I told him, "Yes." He seemed satisfied with that.

A couple of months after we went to the raft, I was at the local grocery store picking up a few items when I bumped into Copper in the produce section.

"How you doing there, Joshua? How are the vegetables this week? Are they fresh?" he asked me. "How was the Alsek River? Did it treat you well?"

"Yes, it did," I said, "but it was scary at times."

"The elders knew what they were talking about, didn't they?" he said.

I nodded yes.

Then, turning his head, he looked me straight in the eye with the steeliest stare you ever did see, and as clear as the sound in the mountains that night, he said, "Bong!"

Kennedy's Weather Vane

One Friday night I was in the workshop, my feet up, with a hot cup of coffee and two Hungry-Man TV dinners. When I was too tired to cook, they hit the spot, and I expertly garnished them with my own herbs and spices to bring them close to gourmet status. CBC was showing a rerun of *The Man from U.N.C.L.E.* Napoleon Solo and Illya Kuryakin were saving the world from evil THRUSH agents, but all I cared about was trying to get my hair to look like Illya's.

There was a knock at the door.

"Hello, anyone in here?" Thomas called.

"Come on in," I said.

Thomas poked his head around the corner and walked in.

"How you doing?" I asked.

"Fine, fine. Every time I come here, it's looking more like a clubhouse than a workplace."

"Yeah, I know. It takes more and more work to clear things out so I can work."

"Just like my garage."

"Can I pop a Hungry-Man or two in the oven for you? I add my own secret spice recipe, and they come out real tasty."

"No, I'm fine. Rose has dinner ready at home. I dropped by to see you about this crashed DC-3 you mentioned. I can't get it out of my mind, especially the gold and wads of money."

"I don't forget about it either," I said.

"Well, I want to go back there with you," Thomas said.

"And why would you want to do that?" I asked, taking a bite of Salisbury steak soaked in what the packaging called gravy.

"I'm not greedy. I just want to grubstake the future for my wife and kids. You said you saw gold and cash money in the plane. You can't leave all that just sitting there going to waste. I could retire with security. I don't think my pension is going to be able to support my big family. If it weren't for my son, Elias, bringing home two or three moose every year, I would be hard-pressed to pay the grocery bill. I want to do this for my family."

"Well, maybe someday we could go back."

"Listen to me, please. You're not understanding what I'm saying. A family is a big responsibility. Wait until you have one. Then everything changes, believe me. Let's go get the gold, Joshua. I'm not kidding. I need this."

"Thomas, you're a good guy, and you and Rose have been the best of friends to me. If I can help you in any way, I'll do it."

Thomas looked pleased with that and shook my hand vigorously.

"Let's go and get that gold, Joshua."

"Right, we will," I said.

"Thank you," he said, and headed home for dinner.

I knew Thomas was trying to support his family—his generosity was well known—so I didn't mind taking him to the gold.

Thomas wanted to start straight away. He had holidays coming and he booked off for four weeks.

"The time is right, Joshua. Let's get going. Rose is talking about taking the kids to Disneyland in California. I want to go, but I can't afford it."

Two weeks later we were headed for Atlin with Elias and Arnold in tow and a ton of supplies.

Thomas worried that I might not remember how to get to the place. "How will you know where it is? You told us yourself you travelled with a map and compass."

"I have a photographic memory when it comes to places, faces, pi and constellations. Going back along my hiking route and finding that plane will be easy."

Thomas gave me a knowing look and said, "Some old-time Indians had the same skill. Some could even find gold by its smell."

"Another adventure, eh?" Arnold said. "I hope we don't get the hell scared out of us again like we did on the last two. I nearly jumped out of my skin when I heard the Japanese monks' bell."

"No one was scared but you," Thomas said.

"Did you ever get that kitchen renovation finished for your wife?" I asked.

"Naw." Arnold laughed, and his cheeks went red. He had reached the point of feeling guilty about his home renovation.

Atlin was a sleepy little town. We waited there for three days for the Beaver float plane to return.

"It got hired away by some prospectors," Hugh, the store owner, informed us.

In the meantime we visited with Rose's family, the Jacks. They greeted Thomas warmly, and we had a pleasant time.

The plane came back at midday, and the pilot buzzed Atlin to let people know he'd arrived. We walked down to the dock to watch it come in. The pilot swung out across the lake, turned around and headed toward the dock. The floats touched the water in perfect synchronization, the pilot cut the engine and the plane glided up to where we stood. When the cabin door opened, a young woman stepped out onto the pontoon and threw a rope to Elias, who secured the plane to a metal tie-down.

The scene was classic. I almost expected a brass band to play "O Canada" when the pilot climbed out and put his arm around the woman. Together they stepped onto the dock. If ever a bush pilot looked the part, it was Timmy Benghazi Lake. He was tall and handsome and wore red woollen shirts and brown breeches tucked into high-laced boots. He had a brilliant smile, smoked a pipe and exuded confidence. His pretty blonde wife, Wendy, was his co-pilot and the model of a northern bride. I was sure they'd walked among the pines and she'd sung "Indian Love Call" to him. She would be Jeanette MacDonald, he would be Nelson Eddy and they would profess their love for each other.

Timmy was a first-rate pilot, and people staked their safety and lives on him. He was born in Libya to a Canadian diplomat and his archeologist wife, hence his middle name of Benghazi.

"You must be the Shackelton party." They greeted us on the dock, and we shook hands all around.

I had my original maps, the ones I'd used a few years back, and showed Timmy our destination.

"I know the area. Why are you headed up that way?"

"We're prospecting for gold."

"Well, let's pack up and head out within the next hour. You guys are ready, right?"

We were ready after sitting around for three days. It took thirty minutes to pack our gear in the plane.

Wendy stayed at home in Atlin, so Thomas sat in the co-pilot's seat while the three of us reclined on the pile of baggage stored in the cargo area. The plane taxied across Atlin Lake and, with a deafening roar, lifted off the water. Timmy circled the town once, and then like a majestic bird soared down the valley and over the white sleeping giant glaciers to our destination. We'd arranged to be dropped off on the Stikine Plateau between Teslin and Telegraph Creek. Timmy swung the great yellow bird through the valleys and landed perfectly, hardly causing a ripple, on a small, unnamed lake west of the Tuya Mountains.

After giving clear, explicit instructions about where and when we were to be picked up, we pushed the plane out from the shore. It drifted away, and Timmy started the engine with a huge cloud of white exhaust, taxied down the lake and, with another great roar, raced across the water and flew into the sky. He circled once, tipped his wings in goodbye, climbed and disappeared over the mountains.

Elias, Arnold and Thomas got their packs ready, but I pretended to watch the plane. I was deep in thought about the time when I travelled here alone and how strong and independent I was.

Thomas must have been reading my mind. He looked around and said, "You were out here all by yourself, Joshua?"

"No," I said. "Angst and I were out here together. He doesn't like flying, so I didn't bring him this time. He had a bad experience flying into Telegraph Creek. The pilot buzzed the lodge too low, and the angry owner upset Angst."

We shouldered our heavy packs and set off to the northwest. Hiking, twelve hours a day, we crossed some of the roughest terrain I'd ever experienced. At the end of each day we threw ourselves down, bone-tired and barely able to eat or make camp before we climbed into our sleeping bags.

"I'm totally out of shape," Thomas groaned. "I can't believe how hard this is. I have to remember I'm doing this for my family."

I showed him no mercy. "If you left a few doughnuts for others and didn't sit on your butt all day doing that cushy job of yours, you might be in better shape."

Thomas tried to laugh, but his sore back wouldn't let him, so he just groaned.

Elias and Arnold, being in better shape, carried some of Thomas's load. The dry weather held, but we suffered from soaked boots and wet clothes when we waded streams and marshes. Our feet became sodden and looked like white brain coral. We used a needle and a bottle of peroxide to break our ballooning blisters and liberally applied salve and bandages. The bandages slipped off when our boots got soaked and didn't last the day.

Thomas and Elias politely questioned me about my directions. I had no trouble answering them. "Do you remember that tall pine tree we ate lunch under a few miles back?'

"Yes."

"I ate dinner under it when I was here before. And do you see that valley in the mountains over there? When we camp, I'll show you two trees growing close together that are perfect for hanging a hammock. Just ask, and I'll tell you things every step of the way."

"Just checking, just checking," Thomas said, waving his hand to dismiss his inquiry.

The valley widened, and we entered an area where sparse vegetation covered the rock mantle. The going got easier, and I remembered more specific rock formations, lakes and clumps of forest.

That night after dinner I told the three of them, "We're on the right trail."

Thomas looked over his cup of tea at me, nodded in appreciation and took a long sip. "Good tea," he said.

I led the way directly to the plane, but when we came upon its crash site, we saw nothing but rocks and trees. I stopped dead in my tracks, and Thomas came up and bumped into me. Elias bumped into him, and finally Arnold bumped into Elias. If anyone had been watching, I'm sure they would have thought someone was making a Keystone Cops film.

"That's what you get for walking with your heads down," Arnold said.

"Pack's heavy," Thomas said.

They had no idea what I was staring at. Where the fuselage of the DC-3 had been jammed between the rocks, nothing remained. Not one sign of the plane was evident.

This is not good, I thought. My mind raced a million miles a minute. What was I going to do? I could keep on hiking and say I lost my way and couldn't remember. Or I could run off into the woods and hide, then move to South America, but I didn't want to leave Angst behind. Or we could hike farther and make camp, and I'd go for water. When I came back, I'd tell them, "I slipped and hit my head. Who are you guys, anyway?" Acting out amnesia is complicated, though, and it would be a lie to my friends. As the plane had been, I was stuck between a rock and a hard place.

In my heart I knew truth was the best. I smacked my forehead with my open palm. The sound got their attention.

"What's up, Joshua?"

"I don't know."

I dropped my pack and reached for the black grease-baked cast-iron frying pan tied to it.

"What are you going to do with that?" Elias asked.

"I'm going to hit myself really hard over the head with it. I don't believe what I'm seeing."

Thomas looked down and noticed faint scratch marks on the ground. "Is this the place?"

"Yes," I said hopelessly.

"So where is the plane?" Elias asked quietly.

"It's gone," I said weakly, pulling my hat over my eyes and stretching my arms out in front of me, reverting to the childish notion that if I couldn't see them, they couldn't see me.

"It's what?"

I spoke up louder. "It's gone, damn it! Listen to what I'm saying."

Thomas slung his pack off his shoulders and threw it to the ground. "What do you mean it's gone?"

"How the hell does a plane disappear? Where's the plane?" Elias said. He not only dropped his pack, he threw it about ten feet. Then he ran over and kicked it like a football.

"Don't look at me! I didn't take it! It was right there, jammed between the rocks, damn it," I said, gesturing wildly at the crash site.

"We showed you the raft," Elias shouted. "It's not fair if you don't show us the DC-3!"

"I knew it! I knew this was going to happen, I felt it in my bones. It was too good to be true, and if something's too good to be true, then it isn't. I knew it, I knew it, I knew it," Thomas said. "I should have gone to Disneyland like Rose wanted."

He walked away, sat down and put his head in his hands.

No one spoke, but we all rubbernecked at the scene around us.

"Maybe we're in the wrong place," Arnold said with a weary sigh.

"Yeah, maybe we're off by a few miles," Elias said hopefully. Then he lit a new cigarette from the one in his mouth, chain-smoking faster than ever.

"No, we're exactly where we should be. Everything is exactly the same except that the plane is missing. I spent a few days here. I know this place."

Thomas rubbed his face vigorously with both hands. "Damn," he said.

"I never believed it in the first place," Arnold said.

Still confused and wondering what had happened, we made camp, gathered firewood, cooked supper and turned in for the night. We barely spoke to each other. None of us could sleep.

In the morning I skipped breakfast and went out to look for clues. From a distance everything seemed perfectly normal, but I took a closer look and saw paint on the rocks where the plane had scraped on impact. Thomas and Elias were working around camp, so I called them over and pointed out what I'd found. The restoration was perfect; where the plane had damaged rocks, paint and grout had been expertly applied to match them. From five feet away we couldn't tell the difference. We had to get down on our hands and knees to see it.

"Holy cow! Now I believe you. They really did a job to hide their tracks, but how in the hell did they get that plane out of here?" Thomas said.

"With a Sikorsky S-64 helicopter. It could pick up a barn if it had too," Elias said. "I read about them in *National Geographic* magazine."

We stood around for a few moments and then split up to take a better look. It became clear that there had been a wide-scale, thorough cover-up. Every single scrap of the plane had been taken, leaving absolutely no evidence of it. Even the oil and lubricant stains had been covered over.

"Slick job. These guys were real experts," I said.

The others nodded in agreement.

"It looks like government work," Arnold said. "The FBI and CIA for sure, and maybe even the President of the United States of America, came out here to help with this. He probably took some of the cash for his wife to redecorate the White House."

"Yeah, he probably has the kitchen half torn apart like you," I said.

We made a wider search farther from the crash site. About a mile away we came upon the remains of a camp. For all their care in covering up the plane, they left plenty of evidence where they'd lived. We found a firepit, K-ration tins, boards made into benches and spent rifle cartridges.

After further examination Thomas blurted out, "Damn, they had target practice with the Mannlicher-Carcanos! What a bunch of crazies."

"Probably sighting them in for another Kennedy assassination," I said.

I gathered up about thirty of the spent cartridges, and when I returned home, I pounded them into the butt end of one of my cabin's logs facing the street. I have a house number, fifty-nine, made of the same bullets that killed a president.

We hung around for another day, but it was evident what had happened.

Thomas said, "Joshua, if you had just taken the time and stashed some of that gold, we would all be rich today."

I asked, "How do you know that I didn't and I'm just too lazy to go get it? Gold is heavy, you know."

Thomas looked serious for a moment, then he laughed. Elias and Arnold joined in, and soon our laughter carried out across the landscape and disappeared into the hills. It felt good.

Our packs were lighter, but the hike back was just as tiring. We had only a few hours to wait before Timmy swung his Beaver over the lake right on schedule and touched down as gracefully as anything I'd ever seen. We packed our gear and flew back exhausted, not cherishing the long ride home on the dusty gravel highway. We stopped in Whitehorse for the day and then headed west to Haines Junction. It took me about a week for my bones and muscles to recover from the hike.

"I'm sorry about your pension plan, Thomas," I said. "I really wanted to help out you and Rose."

"Don't worry about it, buddy, things always work out for us anyway."

None of the events in my life just end—they seem to go on and on until there's a solution or conclusion—so I wasn't surprised by what happened next.

A year after our hike into the bush, one sweltering Yukon July day when the thermometer registered an eye-popping 84°F, I met the conclusion of our gold-seeking story. He was standing beside a broken-down truck on the Alaska Highway about five miles north of Haines Junction. The hood was up, and steam boiled over from the radiator. I stopped to help the man and ended up offering a tow to the repair garage and a meal at my place. His name was Pat Marshall and he turned out to be a retired army sergeant who'd worked at the military air base in Fairbanks, Alaska, for almost thirty years.

"I was an aircraft mechanic and worked on all types of fixed-wing airplanes, mostly piston pounders," he said. "There wasn't anything I couldn't fix. I worked on them all."

Pat bragged on about the capabilities and might of the American army.

"We could blow those Russkies to hell in the blink of an eye if they came over the North Pole," he said. "We have atomic weapons."

Right, I thought. And Canada, my adopted country, is the perfect place to explode them—we wouldn't want to get Alaska contaminated.

Just when I had convinced him that we should go check if his truck was ready, he started on another story altogether. It seemed he wanted to tell a stranger in a small, remote town something he could never tell anyone else.

"A number of years ago we had a real top secret thing happen. We got this plane delivered—well, parts of a plane—and it was a crashed DC-3. I don't know where it came from. They set it up in a hangar guarded by more security than I'd ever seen before. There was a tank at the front entrance, for God's sake. All these secret service types were poring over it and picking it clean. You know, the real intense type, working in a white shirt and thin black tie with a crewcut and a gun holster. Real pencil-necks, all of them, if you ask me. I was allowed in on a few occasions to consult on the plane's manuals, but otherwise we were kept out. This went on for about a month. Then one morning they were all gone, finished, but the plane wreck was still sitting there.

"I asked my colonel, 'What should we do with this plane?'

"'See if anyone wants it for scrap. We could make a buck from it,' he said.

"And we did sell it as scrap. Someone bought all the parts, and by jeez, they shipped it somewhere and formed a club and restored it."

I sat there, not believing what I was hearing, and said nothing.

Pat took no notice of my expression. "Well, time's up. Got to get moving. Wife's expecting me in Seattle in five days. Let's go get that truck," he said.

I dropped Pat off and never saw him again.

It's a funny thing when two separate and seemingly unrelated thoughts enter your mind at the same time and complete a picture. About two weeks after I met Pat Marshall, I was lying on the couch after eating a late dinner. I was thinking about driving into Whitehorse the next day to pick up Thomas and his family, returning from Disneyland, when I remembered the DC-3 airplane on display at the entrance to the Whitehorse airport.

A light went on in my head. Could that be the Kennedy DC-3? I'd heard the Yukon Transportation Museum had restored different planes over the years.

In my travels I'd kept a diary crammed with poetry, observations, recipes and other notes. The only thing I took from the DC-3 was information I'd copied from a small plate attached to the left of the rear door. My curiosity overwhelmed me. I grabbed my coat, diary and Angst and headed into town with an aluminum extension ladder strapped to the top of Thomas's Chevrolet van. I'd be one day early to pick them up, but that was okay.

It was almost midnight when I arrived at the airport, but the sun shone as bright as high noon. The restored DC-3, the world's largest weather vane, according to the *Guinness Book of World Records*, pivoted on a steel column. It was there in recognition of its role as a workhorse of Yukon aviation.

The wind was dead calm.

"You don't need a weatherman to know which way the wind blows," I said to Angst as I carried the ladder the hundred yards from the road to the plane.

I extended the ladder and leaned it against the fuselage. Angst climbed up twenty feet immediately and positioned himself on the top rung. I climbed up after him and, with diary in hand, read the numbers and letters off the plate. They were identical. I slapped the fuselage and laughed. "Good to see you again, old girl."

As Angst and I stood on the ladder confirming the numbers, an angry voice commanded gruffly, "Get down now! And stop slapping that plane."

Looking over my shoulder I saw two burly airport security guards scowling up at me. They had completely ruined my moment of discovery. As they repeated their command, they grabbed the ladder and shook it.

"Hey, take it easy there," I called.

I patted the plane's fuselage, held Angst tightly and climbed down. Angst growled.

"Control that dog," the tall one said, and Angst whimpered at his tone.

"Dog can go up but he can't come down, eh?" the short one said.

I wished people would stop saying that.

The tall one snatched my notebook from my hand and asked, "What in the hell are you doing up here?"

"Just checking," I said. "My dog wanted to take a look."

"Checking what? And what was your dog wanting to look at?" Shorty demanded. "A place to party when we're not around?"

"He likes planes," I said.

"You and your dog are both under arrest, smartass," Shorty said.

Feeling like criminals, we were bundled into the back of their dusty, aging, windowless van and driven off to the airport security office.

It was almost 4:00 a.m. by the time I finished explaining why I was up on the plane. The two guards, Bob and Ben, were mesmerized and had long since stopped taking notes. They listened in silence, feeding me cups of warm coffee and stale doughnuts, which Angst wouldn't eat.

"He likes them fresh and with jelly inside."

Even the young RCMP officer they called in sat listening, looking at his watch as if he had to be elsewhere, but wanting to hear how the story ended.

At the end I said, "And that's why I was on a ladder looking at the DC-3 manufacturer's plate."

Bob tossed my notebook across the table. "You can go, but only because that's a great story and one hell of an excuse for climbing up on the plane."

"Yeah, you should write it someday, but no one will believe a word of it," Ben said.

The police officer nodded in agreement and left.

I got up to leave. "You're right, I'll never write this story. No one will ever believe me."

Angst barked in agreement.

The next day Thomas and his family piled into the van, and we drove past the DC-3 out of the airport.

"See that?" I said and pointed to the plane.

Thomas was very quick. His eyes went wide as he looked at me, back at the plane and back at me again. I thought his head was going to swivel off. "No," he said.

"Yes."

And that was all we said as we drove back to Haines Junction. Thomas would go into deep thought for about five miles and then exclaim out loud, "No!" I would immediately respond with, "Yes!" We were annoying the hell out of Rose, sitting in the back seat, who eventually told us to shut up and cuffed Thomas on the back of the head.

After that day we never mentioned the plane again. I think it was best; we would have made powerful enemies and placed ourselves in the path of danger if people knew what we knew about President Kennedy.

Crepitus Creek

Billy de Beers sailed from South Africa to Vancouver on a passenger ship after reading Jack London's *Call of the Wild.* He memorized word for word almost all of Robert Service's poetry. Standing on the bow of the SS *Ivernia* he quoted to the porpoises and any fellow passengers within earshot "The Cremation of Sam McGee." When the boat docked, he caught a bus to Whitehorse, took the "de" off his name and called himself Beers.

"Beers suits the Yukon, and I like the sound of it better," he said, although no one ever saw him take a drink.

Billy Beers toured the land from top to bottom. He visited Dawson City, then caught a ride to Mile 71, the end of the Dempster Highway, with a wood-cutter. Then he followed the outline of the winter road over the tundra into Old Crow. It took him three weeks, and he was chased by bears twice before he strode down the village streets at four o'clock in the morning under a bright, warm midnight sun. The children of the town were out playing; the adults slept at night, and the children during the day. They could play alone above the Arctic Circle, since there was nothing that would get them into trouble.

"Where did you come from?" the surprised youngsters asked him. "We never saw anyone walk that way in many years."

He hitched a ride on the *Brainstorm* barge that delivered supplies to Old Crow and Fort Yukon and travelled back to Dawson City via the Porcupine and Yukon rivers.

He thumbed a ride to Stewart Crossing on a transport carrying bundles of asbestos out of Clinton Creek. He went east to Mayo, Elsa and Keno City, then south to Pelly Crossing and Carmacks, over to Ross River and south again to Watson Lake. He inspected every community and spoke to many inhabitants.

"What's work like here?"

"Not so good."

"Do you have a Kiwanis Club?"

"Nope."

"What's the apple pie like in the restaurant?"

"What restaurant?"

And so it went until he visited Haines Junction and, like me, found the perfect place and settled down. He bought a small property across the street from mine.

"I'm glad to have you for a new neighbour," I said as we shook hands.

"Dawson City's too rowdy for me, Joshua, and Ross River needs to pull itself into the 1960s. You can't live in the 1920s forever, I really must say. I like Keno City, but you can hardly call it a city with so few citizens."

From the start he went out of his way to show affection and hospitality to all peoples.

"They practise apartheid in South Africa, you know. They put signs up saying that only certain people can swim here or eat there. They made it the law. Disgusting thing, hate. When I denounced it, my neighbours shunned me. You have no idea of the freedom you have here. I read about Canada, and when I saw pictures of the mountains and rivers, I fell in love with it."

"You must be happy here, being away from all that trouble," I said to him once.

"I am, but I think of home and my friends every day. For all its trouble South Africa is a beautiful place, something like the Yukon but with lots of unrest. It's all political, and I hate politics and corrupt politicians. The honest ones are okay. If I had the money, I would go back to South Africa and support a democratic party to make changes. I know democracy is the worst form of government—except for all the others—but what can be done about that? People are dying. You have to forge ahead."

At Mac's Books in Whitehorse he bought a package of postcards that pictured the gold rush miners working by their sluice boxes. He showed them to me, then copied their clothing and appearance. Every day he wore a John B. Stetson ten-gallon hat—it really held three quarts—a red bandana around his neck, woollen bush pants tucked into knee-high cowboy boots or rubber boots, suspenders and expensive heavy plaid shirts. He trimmed his sandy blonde moustache and beard so that he looked like a character out of Buffalo Bill's Wild West Show.

Walking around town with a shovel and a gold pan, Billy convinced the tourists he was a true sourdough. "Just off the creeks and taking my gold poke into town to be weighed," he would tell them. "I think I've found the motherlode this time."

"Oooh," the tourists would say, greatly impressed. They would pose for pictures with an arm around his waist before they got back on the bus.

Billy carried a bulging moosehide poke decorated with beads, but what was in it was anyone's guess.

"Marbles," Copper Johnson said and laughed at his own joke.

"Burned flapjacks," said the cook at the restaurant.

"Eye of newt and toe of frog, wool of bat and tongue of dog," said Rebecca the piano teacher, who read Shakespeare.

Billy worked in the local grocery store and wore his getup under a clerk's stained white apron. Billy had a boyish enthusiasm about him, laughing easily and joking with the customers.

"That friendly clerk is going to boost your business," Thomas told the store owner.

"He's a lot better than the crabby ones you've had in here over the years," said Rose, pushing her cart toward the till.

Billy loved to act. He tried to get me to go in with him on a play.

"Come on, Joshua, it will be fun."

"Absolutely no way am I going to act in front of anyone," I said.

He asked Arnold, Elias and Thomas. They all laughed.

"Arnold, you look like Richard Burton. You should be in acting."

"I've got a kitchen to renovate," Arnold said.

One summer Billy wrote and produced a one-man show and called it *A Man and His Yukon*.

"I would have called it *Five Men and Their Yukon* if you guys had helped me out. I can write anything—one- or two-man shows, even fifteen-man shows."

He put up posters and invited the tourists and townsfolk to see the act for a modest sum. Held in the community hall, it consisted entirely of Billy lip-synching to scratchy LP records of Johnny Horton singing "North to Alaska" and other songs on a green and white portable record player. He even threw in a Mel Tormé tune called "Get Me to the Church on Time" from *My Fair Lady*, which brought quizzical looks to faces in the small audience.

"Shouldn't have included the Velvet Fog," Billy told me later. "He wasn't appreciated."

Next he gave a lengthy recital of Robert Service's poetry. People slunk away after an hour. Only when I was the last person in the hall did Billy end the show with a stirring rendition of "O Canada." I stood and enthusiastically joined in.

"Thank you for your support, Joshua. This concludes the evening's entertainment."

The show closed after opening night. Word got out quickly, and no one attended after that.

"Worst damn stage presentation I've ever seen for my fifty cents," Arnold said, "and I took the wife for a night out. Now she is really going to want that kitchen renovation finished."

Billy went around town to give the money back. He was honest like that. A few accepted it, but the crowd in the coffee shop told him, "Just keep it. The show wasn't that bad."

This encouraged him to recruit Rebecca and her piano for a show called *A Woman, a Man and Their Yukon*. It consisted entirely of Rebecca playing the piano dramatically like a musician in an orchestra pit at a silent movie while Billy sang Robert Service poetry out of tune.

They lowered the admission to ten cents but closed the show after two nights.

"I've never been so embarrassed in all my life," Rebecca said.

Billy gave her the entire box office take, $1.75 plus a five-cent Vancouver bus token.

Ever since Billy arrived in Haines Junction, Albert's wife, Rose, had had her eye on him as a husband for her sister Marsha and a father for Marsha's five grown boys.

Rose and Marsha had attended all the shows. "He isn't any Jack London or Robert Service, but I think he will do, Marsha. Pickings are slim around this town anyway."

Marsha was hesitant. "Isn't he a little weird?"

"Yeah, but he has a job and he doesn't drink or gamble. That's half the battle right there."

"It's a stretch to think any man would take on that many kids," Thomas said.

About the time Rose and Marsha were planning a dinner for Billy, he caught gold fever. Gold fever has no physical symptoms like spots or rashes. It shows itself in people's actions. There is no known cure. Gold fever is mental blindness. When the blinds are drawn, people lose sight of reality. Billy wanted gold so badly to help his country that he was unable to resist the fever's influence.

"I can't stop thinking about it, Joshua. All these stories about the motherlode are firing my brain up. That gold has to be around here somewhere."

I don't get gold fever. I hardly get excited about anything. Too much material wealth can distract one from life. Besides that, I was never a good business man, so the making of money eluded me.

When the story came out in its entirety, people said Billy was prospecting up northeast of Beaver Creek on a small creek that he followed through Willow Marsh and down into a small valley. The creek, which he named Crepitus Creek after some moose bones he found, was where he made the discovery. Apparently at that point he went stark raving mad with happiness.

His work became zealously intense. He quit his job and toiled alone for long periods of time at a pace that would have killed other men. Billy spent months staking everything everywhere and keeping things very hush-hush. He staked discovery claims, leased claims, mineral claims and placer claims all over a wide area of impenetrable forest.

Twice he hired a helicopter at $350 an hour to bring supplies into his camp, promising to pay in gold when the mining started. He had spent all his savings. Business was slow, so the owner of the helicopter took Billy's word that he was good for it.

"I'll pay you, and you've got a bonus coming for trusting me," he said.

The pilot gave the thumbs-up and flew away.

With white knuckles gripping the steering wheel, Billy bounced over the gravel washboard highway at breakneck speed with Herb Albert and the Tijuana Brass blaring from the battered '59 Ford's eight-track stereo. Dashing into the Whitehorse mining recorder's office, he threw paperwork and cash down on the counter and secured his claims.

The prospectors who were picking up their mail met in the lobby of the post office. There was a buzz among them that some activity was happening— all the signs were there—but Billy had done all his staking long before anyone else had a chance to move in. All they could do was scratch their heads and wonder what he was up to. A few prospectors staked the peripheries of his claims and tried to pry information out of the helicopter pilot, but true to the code of the North, he said nothing.

"What's going on up there, anyway?" one miner asked, having flagged down the helicopter pilot on the road.

"Can't say a word," the pilot said, placing an index finger over his lips, and drove off in his pickup.

I met Billy coming out of the post office and queried him on the rumours of a big strike. He was dishevelled, his clothes and hat were tattered and dirty and his eyes shone like a madman's.

"I got it this time, Joshua! I've struck the big one, and I'm rich!" he laughed.

He looked exhausted. I was puzzled by his demeanour. I had known gold miners who struck it rich, but Billy was acting different and strange. Usually they were sedate about their finds, much like card players holding four aces and keeping a poker face.

"Good," I said and shook his hand. "If you need any help, just give me a call."

"Everything is fine, but thanks for the offer."

Then Billy jumped in his truck and sped off. I was worried for him.

Soon the talk in the post office, coffee shop and grocery store was that Billy had flipped out; there was no strike, and there was no gold. The day after I spoke with him he drove into Whitehorse for a 10:00 a.m. appointment with his banker at the Royal Bank downtown on Fourth Avenue.

Once in the manager's office, Billy gleefully dumped out a canvas bag of small rocks and pebbles on the polished mahogany desk. Then he sat back in his chair with a wide grin and declared loudly so all in the bank could hear, "Yahoo! See, I've struck it rich! What do you think of those apples?" He then wiped the tears of joy from his face with a dirty handkerchief.

The manager didn't think too much of those apples.

"Well, I don't know. Let's see here. Billy, this is just a pile of rocks," he said.

Fortunately the manager was a compassionate and understanding family man who, instead of booting Billy out on his ass, called for help.

"Would one of you tellers come in here, please, and help me out with this?" he called from his door.

A tall young teller in a white shirt and tie swept the "nuggets" back into the sack, telling Billy with less sympathy in his voice than there had been in the manager's, "There will be no deposit here today."

None of us had had any idea of how far the fever had burned into Billy's brain, but some of the old-timers in the Mountain Sunrise Senior Citizens' Home said it was the worst they had ever seen.

"I'm surprised he still has a brain in his head," Copper told the elders at Burwash.

"We will say prayers for him," they said.

Billy spent months in the hospital under the care of the doctors, nurses and shrinks. They gave him lots of attention.

I visited a few times, taking a bucket of Kentucky Fried Chicken, but Billy was in no mood for his favourite food. Mostly he lay in a fetal position, sleeping under the influence of drugs. Slowly he came around but insisted on not leaving the hospital. The shrinks worked on this refusal and got to the root of the problem. Billy was embarrassed. He realized how foolish he had been; he knew he'd gone all cock-eyed.

"I want to go back home where no one knows of this."

"You're better off facing the music here than going back to apartheid. You have to leave the hospital sometime, Billy, or we'll start charging you rent for your room," the shrink said.

Sheepishly he returned home, hoping to be left alone. He didn't have to worry. People were understanding. They knew Robert Service had said it all when he wrote, "There are strange things done in the midnight sun / By the men who moil for gold."

"Don't worry about this, Billy. This is the stuff legends are made of. You'll go down in history. People will be talking about this for years to come," I said.

Billy spent two years working to pay off the bills from his staking venture. The helicopter rental alone came to over five thousand dollars, never mind all the camp equipment and supplies that still sit out there rotting and rusting away.

"I wished so much for gold I thought that rocks were gold," he said.

"We know," I said.

I resisted adding "All that glitters is not gold." I thought he had figured that out.

The next summer Billy went into a big production and presented the melodrama *Gold Stole My Heart on Crepitus Creek*.

Billy directed it. I played the part of Billy with a fake beard and all. Rebecca pounded the ivories like she was backing up the Rolling Stones in concert. Thomas played the part of the hospital shrink—exceptionally well, I might add—and Arnold finally finished the kitchen renovation and was able to play the part of the helicopter pilot. The musical was enthusiastically received by all who attended.

A year after Billy's fever, I went over and joined him in his backyard. He was standing on the back deck, coffee cup in hand, looking wistfully northward.

"Still thinking of the gold?" I asked.

"Ah, the gold, the gold. Joshua, my friend, what I was going to do to apartheid with that gold. I was going to change the government and change the world. In reality money won't change apartheid."

I nodded in agreement.

He raised his cup in a toast. "Here's to dreams and South Africa, Joshua. May they both shine on."

No Good Deed

Living in Haines Junction improved for Billy Beers once he settled down and enjoyed life without a cause. He lived alone, went to work at the local grocery store and came and went as he pleased. Hiking the mountains around the town and reading were his hobbies, and if it weren't for a slight loneliness and his own bad cooking, he might have remained a bachelor.

Billy took time to relax after his gold fever breakdown on Crepitus Creek. Once he left the hospital, he followed his doctor's advice to get out more and socialize with people. He graciously accepted an invitation for dinner at Thomas's. Rose barbecued steaks, and her sister Marsha roasted potatoes and mushrooms. I was invited to join them.

It pleased Billy to be among friends. He sat beside Marsha the whole evening, and at one point Marsha—giggling all the time—cut a piece of Billy's steak and fed it to him. Billy blushed but he liked the attention.

"Do you like that song 'Get me to the Church on Time?'" Marsha asked Billy between mouthfuls.

Unwittingly Billy smiled and said, "I like the way Mel Tormé and Johnny Mathis sing it. It's my favourite." Maybe he'd forgotten the song was about a wedding or didn't realize they were giving him a hint.

"I love your name, Billy," Marsha said, pinching his cheek so that he blushed again.

"That man has the reddest cheeks," Thomas said later.

Marsha wanted to get married again. She liked Billy, and they were friends. At her age she knew the importance of companionship, and her five boys needed a father. She'd had a good relationship with her previous husband, a federal government employee who'd travelled from Ontario to work at the experimental farm just north of Haines Junction. He'd drowned in a boating accident on Kluane Lake years ago, when her youngest son, Adam, was six months old.

"No person can survive more than five minutes in that icy water," said the RCMP sergeant who'd pulled the body out.

Three months after the dinner Billy and Marsha surprised everyone with a marriage announcement. Two weeks later they were hitched in a private ceremony by a Justice of the Peace in Whitehorse. They honeymooned in Hawaii.

"Billy tried to surf but almost drowned. He was the only guy out there with a life jacket on," Marsha told us over dinner one evening.

"I never was much of a swimmer," Billy said. "It's hard to learn back home in South Africa when the sharks are all about."

They returned to Haines Junction tanned and happy and settled into marital bliss. Marsha's five teenaged boys—Adam, DanDan, Tyler, Carl and Harrison—moved in and brought their motorbikes, sports equipment, games, snow machines, boats, ping-pong table and box after box of personal belongings.

Billy was a good father to his new sons, and they got along well with him. They called him Pops.

"Hey Pops, you want to play ping-pong?"

"Only if you let me win."

"Sure we will."

But they never did.

Billy always made time for the boys. He also framed and finished two new rooms over the garage to give each his own bedroom. He said, "It's important for kids to have their own space."

The boys had a 1953 two-door Chevrolet Bel Air with side windows that rolled down to create one opening. They'd been working on it for two years, but progress had been slow.

"My dad gave my sons that car before he passed away. He told them they could have it if they got it running again," Marsha told Billy.

"I can't wait," Harrison said. "I love Grandpa's car."

Billy helped tow it over and set it up on blocks in the garage. He and the boys hoisted its engine with a block and tackle, backed the car out and dropped the engine on a supporting rack, which they rolled out of the way to move the car back in. The boys let Adam "drive" while they pushed the car out and back. He clutched the wheel as though he were going a hundred miles an hour. With Billy's help and money, the repairs sped up. The Chev was a good, safe vehicle for the boys to ride around in.

"That car will give them confidence," Billy said, "and I won't have to drive them to school."

Billy's tools were scattered from one end of the garage to the other; things would never be kept neat again. He figured as long as the tools came back to their boxes at the end of the day and the kids had fun, it was okay with him.

Inside the home Marsha lived and worked in the spacious kitchen, turning out pots of soup, stews, roasts, fresh bread and buns, pies and cookies. Billy and the boys heartily devoured everything as soon as it came off the stove or out of the oven. They dipped slabs of hot buttered bread in man-sized bowls of the *soupe du jour.* There were roasts on Sunday with vegetables from the garden, and on special occasions up to forty relatives and friends sat down together. It was a lot of work, but Marsha and Billy didn't mind. They were in love, and the boys were happy and healthy.

"Joshua, I love my life. I never thought I could be so happy," Billy told me as we worked on the Chev one day.

The boys were big people. Adam, the youngest and the baby, outweighed Billy by fifty pounds and lived in the cocoon of being everyone's favourite.

The first-born and the smartest, Harrison, towered above everyone by a foot and a half and outweighed them by a hundred pounds. Harrison was level-headed and took his role of eldest brother seriously.

"Without Dad around I had to step up and look after things."

"Harrison never had a childhood," Marsha said.

Carl, the second oldest, was mechanically inclined and did most of the work on the car. He told me, "I can fix anything—cars, snow machines, boat motors, you name it, I'll fix it—except Husqvarna chainsaws. I hate them and won't touch them. I had one that never worked."

The second youngest, DanDan, was attached to his mother and spent time with her cooking in the kitchen and working in the garden. He said, "I want learn to cook so I can work in the fanciest restaurant in Paris."

Tyler was the middle child, handsome, academically inclined and quick-witted.

"You don't want to get into a war of words with Tyler," Billy warned me. "He's too smart and he'll beat you every time."

Marsha appreciated Billy's help with the boys, but when it came to discipline, she had them in line, and they rarely gave her trouble.

"If you boys want to fight and argue, then I'm going to fight and argue with you," she said, shaking a finger covered in doughnut dough in their direction, "and if that doesn't work I'm sending you over to your Uncle Thomas so he can have a word with you."

More than anything the boys dreaded the embarrassment of being talked to by Uncle Thomas. That threat usually straightened them out. If it didn't, Marsha wrote a note, sealed it in an envelope and instructed, "Take this over to your uncle and let him read what you've done."

Thomas disliked the notes as much as the boys did, but as the closest thing they had to a father before Billy came along, he would address the issue.

"So you refused to tidy your room?"

"That's what Ma says."

"Well, don't do it again."

"Okay."

That was the end of the lecture.

Now that Billy and Marsha lived across the street, I became a friend of the boys. They cut my sparse lawn in the summer and made quick work of the snow in my driveway in winter. In payment they sat in the workshop while I was out working, watching TV and helping themselves to the pop in the fridge. I think they used it as a hideout and skipped school a few times. On occasion they ate my Swanson Hungry-Man frozen dinners. Over the years I figured it cost me twenty-five dollars every time they shovelled the snow or mowed the lawn. I didn't mind. They were good kids, and Angst became their friend and followed them everywhere. He learned to sit up on the handlebars of Adam's bike and, keeping an eye peeled for potholes, rode around town this way.

It was mid-April when Billy and the boys dropped the Chevy's engine back into place and drove the car for the first time in two years. Hundreds of hours and dollars had gone into it, and they were right proud that the engine ran perfectly. For now the brown primer paint coat would have to do; later they could paint it a metallic blue.

Pine Lake lay just east of Haines Junction. It was a common practice for people to drive across the winter ice, taking a shortcut to the Alaska Highway.

Now that they'd fixed the car, Harrison and his brothers planned to head into Whitehorse on a Saturday morning for a day of shopping and visiting friends.

"The Bay store should have some new spring clothes in."

I wanted to buy some new camera equipment at Hougen's Department Store so I asked if I could ride along.

"We'd be very pleased if you went with the boys," Billy said. "It would make me feel a whole lot better knowing someone was keeping an eye on them."

I almost said that I didn't want to babysit but I let it go. I knew I'd end up watching them anyway.

The brothers dressed in their best jeans and shirts, slicked their hair and fought over who would ride in the front. Both Billy and Marsha had to come out and decide who went where.

"Harrison, you drive. Carl, you sit in the front with Joshua. Angst, you stay home with us. Tyler, DanDan and Adam, you three get in the back and stay there. And no fighting," Marsha ordered, "or I'm sending a note!"

Harrison gunned the engine and raced down to the end of Pine Lake. The sky was clear, and we anticipated a pleasant drive and a day in town. A slick of water lay on top of the ice. Harrison pulled the wheel to avoid it and skidded into a pool of slush. He quickly put the car into reverse and started to back up, but before he could, the front end dipped and sank halfway up the hubcaps.

We jumped out to inspect the damage.

"You've done it now, birdbrain," Carl said.

"Shut your face, idiot stick," Harrison said.

"This is not good," DanDan said.

"It's dangerous," Adam said.

"It's only stuck a little ways. Pops will be able to pull us out easy," Harrison said.

"One of us will have to go for help," Carl said.

"You're a real scientist," Tyler said.

"Yeah, well, Adam and DanDan can make the hike back while we wait here," Harrison said.

"Why us?"

"Because you're the youngest and you're both lard butts. You need the exercise."

Adam and DanDan looked to me for support, but I raised my hands and said nothing. The babysitting had begun.

Adam and DanDan wondered if they should continue this conversation or just go for help. They decided on the latter.

The two hikers shrank to dots at the end of the lake while we sat on the hood of the car soaking up the sun. We didn't sit inside because every once in a while the car would jerk and slide a little lower. The boys dug into the basket of sandwiches and baking their mother had packed. Between mouthfuls of egg salad sandwiches and swigs of cold pop, they discussed a plan to get the car out.

"Piece of cake. When Pops gets here, we'll be out in a shake and on our way again," Harrison said.

"You'd better hope that happens," Tyler said.

About two hours later we heard Billy grinding the gears of his four-wheel-drive flatbed truck; recently he'd been fixing up the weather-worn one-ton army surplus vehicle. They heard the jingling as its chained wheels hit the ice, grabbed firmly and sped toward the car.

"Why does everyone have to drive like a madman on this lake?" Harrison asked.

"You're such a hypocrite," Carl said.

Billy pulled up a hundred feet from the car and jumped out with Adam and DanDan in tow.

I walked out to greet him.

"This doesn't look too bad, Joshua. We should have you out and on your way in a jiff," Billy said.

"See? I told you," Harrison said.

Both Adam and DanDan, hungry from their hike, headed straight for the food basket.

"Where the hell has all that food gone?"

"You shouldn't have taken so long. We would have saved you a few crumbs."

Billy inspected the car, walked back to the truck and kicked the lever to release the winch's steel cable. He and I pulled it across the ice and hooked it to the rear frame. The boys watched us do it.

"Stand clear," he said.

Billy locked the truck's brakes. Harrison jumped back into the car and put it in reverse. The winch started to pull, but the Chevy's wheels only spun a rooster tail, showering everyone with slush. The car didn't budge but slid deeper. The truck's tires didn't grip, and the truck slid forward.

No one noticed the rear end of the truck dipping into the slush until I looked back and shouted, "You're sinking, Billy! Your truck is sinking!"

But it was too late. The truck had sunk over the rear wheels so that the front end tilted upward. Billy slackened the winch cable and turned the engine off.

"Oh no, what happened there?" Harrison said, grabbing his head. "We'll never get to town now."

"We could have taken the highway and been in Whitehorse already," Carl said, "but now look where we are."

"Well, this changes everything. It's turned out to be more serious than I expected," Billy said. "I'm going for help before both vehicles drop through the ice." Then he set off at a jog.

"Watch the boys, Joshua!" he yelled back.

"Sure thing."

DanDan and Adam, still complaining about the sandwiches, shared the last can of pop.

"If Grandpa's car goes to the bottom of this lake, Ma is going to be writing notes for a week," Adam said.

"Nobody's car or truck is going to sink. We'll get them out. Wait and see," Harrison said.

Back in town Billy came across Arnold from Burwash parked outside the grocery store, drinking coffee. He was on his way back from Edmonton where he'd bought a new four-wheel-drive three-quarter-ton Ford pickup. He was driving around town with a couple of his cousins, showing it off.

"That's a beautiful new truck," Billy said and explained the situation.

"Sure I'll come and help," Arnold said, happy to show people what his truck could do.

Arnold drove across the ice, parked a hundred feet behind Billy's truck and jumped out to inspect the conditions. The boys gathered around him.

"Hey Joshua," he said.

"Can you get us out?" DanDan asked.

"No problem, DanDan. It seems solid," Arnold said, jumping up and down on the ice. "You guys must have driven into a soft spot."

Arnold pulled his own winch cable to the one-ton with Billy's help and hooked it to the truck's rear frame. They told the boys to stand clear, and Billy told Harrison to gun the Chev when they start moving. With thumbs up each of them jumped back into his vehicle.

Revving the engine, Arnold slowly pulled both the vehicles out of their holes. More rooster tails of slush rocketed skyward. Grey exhaust floated in clouds along the ice, and for a moment, all three inched back. The boys cheered, and the drivers had big smiles, but their triumph was short-lived. Harrison felt the car drop and wisely scampered out as it sank up to its hood. Since the windows were open, water poured in and the added weight forced the car further down. Billy watched his cable go taut and knew what was happening. He jumped out and yelled for everyone to get clear. Then he shouted to Arnold to drive forward and slack off his line so he could unhook it.

"Otherwise your truck's going to get sucked in like mine!" he yelled.

It was too late. The car plummeted completely through the ice and out of sight. The cable zipped back, cutting the ice as a wire cutter slices cheese. Billy jumped back in behind the wheel of his truck and floored the engine. But it was to no avail. The tire chains only ripped into the ice. He was held fast by the dead weight of the suspended car.

"Get out, Pops, get out!" the boys screamed.

Billy did just that, throwing himself onto the ice.

The car now hung sixty feet directly below where they stood. For a moment it seemed nothing was happening. Then the truck gave a jerk and dove below the surface with a crash of ice and a splash of water. The cable connected to Arnold's truck now sang like a violin string.

Arnold's eyes grew as big as saucers. "Grab the chainsaw! Get the damn chainsaw out of the back!" he yelled.

Billy jumped into the box, grabbed the saw and threw it to Arnold. Arnold caught it, and in one smooth motion, fired it up—thanks to expert saw maintenance—and in desperation tried to cut the cable.

Chainsaws are made for wood, not steel. The only result was high-flying lines of yellow and red sparks before the chain ripped off the bar.

There was nothing anyone could do but watch as Arnold's new truck slid forward, wheels locked, engine running, signal light flashing and tape deck blaring "Stand by Me" by Ben E. King. It slipped into the water to join its companions. The lights would stay on in the depths until the battery ran out.

Arnold sat down on the ice beside the still-running chainsaw and watched the air bubbles return to the surface.

I walked over and switched off the saw. The silence was deafening. The seven of them stood around, not knowing what to do. The loss was so complete that only an empty feeling remained.

"At least none of us were hurt," Billy said, "but damn, I just got a new rear end put in that truck, and those tires were only two months old. And I left my glasses on the dash."

"I feel for your loss," Arnold said with a touch of anger in his voice. "I've only got payments of $135 a month for the next thirty-six months for a truck I don't even own. My wife isn't going to be happy with this."

In single file we headed back to town. Arnold phoned for his cousins to come and get him. The rest of us sat glumly in the living room, waiting until Marsha came home from shopping with an armload of groceries.

"What happened?" she asked. "I thought you were going to town."

"We lost Grandpa's car," Harrison said.

"You what!" Marsha screamed.

"And Billy's truck."

"And Arnold's brand-new Ford."

Marsha was silent and sat down. "What happened?"

As Billy explained, Adam cried and DanDan almost cried.

Arnold sat quietly staring at the floor, probably trying to figure out what to tell his wife.

Harrison tried to blame Carl, and Carl tried to blame Tyler, but no one took this seriously. Others had crossed the lake earlier that morning with no problem.

"You might have all drowned," Marsha said, wringing her hands. "We can always get another car. I'm grateful you're not hurt or worse."

"That was Grandpa's car. Now it's gone. I was hoping to give it to my kids," Adam said.

There was a honk in the yard, and Arnold left.

Weeks later a rumour ran around town that Arnold would have to sue Billy for the loss of his truck, but nothing came of that. In the end he said, "I've got to take responsibility. I went out there to help. No one thought this would happen."

"Thanks," Billy said.

The insurance company refused payment on all three vehicles because they'd been operated "in an unsafe and careless manner."

No one argued. Arnold fired up his old truck and drove that for the next three years until he'd paid for the lost one. Then he drove to Edmonton and bought the exact same model with the same paint job and all the same accessories. He even bought a new Ben E. King tape.

In late July, Marsha, Billy and the boys launched a freighter canoe with a 40 hp Mercury motor and crossed the lake to where the vehicles had sunk. The lake was like a mirror, and using a marker on the shore, they were able to find the spot of the sinking.

DanDan peered over the side, looking down into the crystal clear water and shielding his eyes with his hands. He was humming "Octopus's Garden" from the *Sergeant Pepper* album.

"I think I see them," he would yell enthusiastically every few minutes.

They sat for half an hour, keeping the canoe in place with occasional sweeps of a paddle. Then a small blob of oil drifted from 150 feet below and dispersed on the surface in a sheen of blue, yellow green and red.

"Probably axle grease," Harrison said.

"Probably the tube of Brylcreem you're always lathering on your head," DanDan said.

Later that summer the Yukon Scuba Club dove Pine Lake because it was deep and the visibility was 100 percent. Before and after the dive they stopped by Billy's house because they'd heard about the trucks and car.

"They're there, all right. We saw them. In the deepest part of the lake too."

"Did you find my glasses?'

"No, they must have fallen out on the way down. The car and the flatbed are vertical and the new Ford landed on top of them sort of like Stonehenge. The winch cables are draped over them like spaghetti."

"Did you bring anything back?"

"We brought back the license plates."

Billy nailed the licence plates to the side of the garage and above them posted a neatly hand-painted sign that Tyler made. It said, "No good deed goes unpunished." Below it one of the boys had scrawled in pencil, "Just ask Arnold and Pops."

Beano's Angel

My life in Haines Junction was enjoyable. I had good friends, work I enjoyed and a comfortable home. I never thought of leaving. A knock on the door changed all that.

The prettiest woman I had ever seen stood on my doorstep. Her blonde hair was in a braid, and she wore a beaded blouse and faded bell-bottomed jeans with sandals. Over her shoulder was a canvas satchel crammed with books and a tripod.

Nice, I thought. I was momentarily tongue-tied and must have blushed.

"Hi. I'm Angel Featherstone and I'm looking for Joshua Shackelton," she said with a confident smile.

"That's me." I felt happy—almost giddy—that she'd found me.

Giving me a look as though she'd seen that response before, she rolled her eyes and ignored my enthusiasm. I held the door open. She took that as an invitation and walked past me into the house. I could smell the perfume of her hair.

She turned and faced me, looking prettier than she had a moment before. "I'm writing an article for *National Geographic* magazine on Kluane Park, and your name keeps coming up when I ask who knows what around here. Are you that man?"

I didn't really hear what she was saying and didn't know the answer. I covered my confusion by asking, "Would you like tea?"

Angst stared at her and wagged his tail slowly, assuring her that I was all right.

"Tea is okay," she said, and sat on the couch.

I took out the cups and put the water on the stove, trying to appear as domestic as possible and hoping she wouldn't look at all the clutter.

"What's your dog's name?" she asked, looking around the room.

"Angst."

"Interesting," she said with a laugh.

I was pleased that it amused her.

Angst didn't improve my domestic hopes when he offered her a length of caribou leg bone he'd happily gnawed on for days.

That was the beginning of our friendship. For the next week I drove Angel around the town and Kluane Park. She took pictures and notes, and I introduced her to everyone I knew. She went over to Thomas and Rose's at night and slept on their couch. The boys and Angst took a liking to her. She was kind and gave them attention. Angst stayed over with her, abandoning me.

Rose, seeing a potential bride, praised me to the roof to Angel. "Joshua is a good man. He looks out for my boys and works hard."

I didn't care that Rose was matchmaking. In a distant part of my mind, a voice was saying, "Marriage is okay."

"What a nice dog," Angel said, sitting on the couch and rubbing Angst's ears and head. The dog closed his eyes and smiled a dog's smile. I thought he was going to fall over.

"A friend of the sasquatch," I said.

"Angst is a friend of the sasquatch?"

I entertained Angel with the stories of my life on Vancouver Island, finding a crashed DC-3 airplane in northern BC and discovering a Japanese raft left high and dry above the Alsek River.

"You should write a book."

"Maybe I will someday."

"You have the most amazing life here, Joshua, with all these friends and your cabin. I've lived with a friend in Dawson City for the past six months but I haven't fit in as well as you have."

"Every town is different. I don't think I could live in Dawson unless I had a special reason." I thought, you would be my special reason, Angel.

Angel gave me a warm hug and a kiss on the cheek when she boarded the silver Greyhound bus back to Dawson City. I couldn't keep that hug and kiss out of my mind. I pondered it deeply for the next few days. It was real, I told myself, and the only sign I needed to move to Dawson City. I was sure Angel had feelings for me, and over time a romance would develop.

Angst looked at me and whined.

I checked the *Whitehorse Star* classifieds for employment in the Dawson area. Two jobs were listed. One job for a dog catcher included a note that it came with a generous insurance package because the work was highly hazardous. Apparently the good folks of Dawson City didn't want anyone bothering their pets. The other read, "Wanted, gas jockey for Hughie Ford's Chevrolet Automotive Garage in downtown beautiful historic Dawson City. Slackers need not apply. Wages are $1.75 per hour. Accommodation is available."

I dialled the phone number in the ad.

"Hello."

"I'm calling from Haines Junction about your advertisement in the help wanted section."

"Advertisement? What advertisement? And speak up. I can hardly hear you."

"The one in the paper for the gas jockey," I yelled.

"You don't have to yell my head off!"

"Okay," I yelled more quietly.

"Can you stand the smell of gas? Because the last one couldn't, and we had to take him to the hospital. He threw up for two days."

"Gas doesn't bother me."

There was silence on the line for a few moments, and I heard a muffled conversation.

"Are the wages okay? We don't want any quibbling once you get over here."

"The wages are fine." I would have worked for nothing to get to Dawson and Angel.

"Okay. I'm Hughie. My brother Mordechai and I own this joint, but we're hardly ever here. You're hired. When can you start?"

"In about a week. I'll need the accommodations. What are they?"

"A cozy furnished sitting room above the garage so you won't be late for work in the morning."

"Fine. I'll see you in a week."

"Okay." After we hung up, I realized I hadn't given him my name.

It took me a week to board up the house, pack my truck and let everyone know where I was going. I had dinner one last time at the home of Rose and Thomas before heading out.

"Chasing some skirt, eh?" asked Thomas.

"Must have been a full moon when you met her," said Billy Beers.

"I just love it when people are in love," said Rose.

"Crazy as a loon," said their son Elias.

"Woof!" Angst agreed with everyone.

I arrived in Dawson on a cold, grey, drizzly Sunday evening. Hungry and tired after driving over the Top of the World Highway, I parked the truck in a field of grass next to the garage. In the morning I was roused by a rap on the window.

"You have to move your truck. This isn't no RV park, you know," the gruff voice said.

The windows were fogged, and we couldn't see each other, but I recognized the voice of Hughie from my phone call.

"I'm your new employee, Joshua."

"I don't give a damn who you are. Get off my lot right now." He tried to open the locked door.

A voice behind him said, "Yeah, get the hell off our property."

I knew that was Mordechai.

This wasn't working so well. I rolled down the window, and Angst stood on my chest, dug in his claws and leaped out. I shrieked in pain. Hughie thought he was being attacked. He yelled, covered his head and stepped back.

"Crap, that scared me!" Hughie clutched his chest and repositioned his green faux tortoiseshell glasses. He was fat and bald and could barely see over the bottom of the truck's window. His brother stood behind him, and from where I lay, I could see only the top of his head.

"It's me, your new employee from the Junction, the one you talked to on the phone, the one you hired to pump your gas."

"Oh. Why didn't you say so?" Hughie demanded. "Come inside and have a coffee. Leave your truck where it is."

That was the start of my tenure at Ford's Chevrolet Automotive Garage. I pushed back my hair, grabbed my coat as I jumped out of the truck and followed them into the garage. Both men looked as wide as they were tall, and their jeans were belted so high they almost touched the bottom of their plaid shirt pockets, which were stuffed full of papers, pens and notebooks. Hughie and Mordechai Ford turned out to be good guys. They were Jews born in Poland who fled to Palestine after the war.

"Yeah, we did a little work in the resistance," Hughie said once, leaning against the office desk. He had a steely resolved look when he said it.

"We made those Nazis pay," Mordechai said.

My cozy sitting room over the garage turned out to be a one-room apartment in need of a paint job. It had a broken chair and matching table, a creaking bed with a thin mattress and old Christmas decorations around the window. The dishes consisted of a fork, spoon, plate and bowl, all stamped CPR.

The brothers led interesting lives. They had business investments from Haifa to San Francisco and an arm's-length method of management that they reinforced by hiring the right people. They were shrewd judges of character. Mordechai told me, "That's why our business is so successful. We know who to hire." They treated me well and appreciated my work, and we became lifelong friends.

Besides the garage and placer mines in the Yukon they had sheep farms in Australia and a tin mine in Bolivia. In 1967, while they were prospecting, they ran into Che Guevara hiding in the hills.

"Che and his men were worn out and sick. We helped them as best we could with what little we had. We had to be careful not to be seen. Soldiers were all over the place. Che's men were in bad shape but committed. I had never seen such commitment to a cause. The whole country was buzzing with news about them. We encouraged Che to get out by boat and go back to Cuba," Hughie said.

"We said, 'Look, Che, we know something about what you're doing. We were in the resistance against the damn Nazis. We learned when to run and fight another day,'" Mordechai said.

I had always been interested in Che and the Cuban Revolution. I had a T-shirt with the dramatic picture of his handsome face on it. It was worn out. Mordechai had given me a wink the first time he saw it.

"Why didn't he leave?" I asked.

"He was in too deep. He wouldn't give up—he believed so much in the revolution. The success in Cuba might have gone to his head, and he thought he could instigate a worldwide revolution."

"Bit off more than he could chew," I said.

"We offered him money, but he showed us bags of it. He was well funded. I think Fidel took care of that. His main problem was that the peasants weren't supporting him, and his men were split up and out of communication. He didn't want to leave them behind. Plus he had asthma. He was wheezing all the time and needed medication.

"Shortly after that the soldiers cornered him in a narrow canyon where they wounded and captured him. We were still in the vicinity and heard the shots. We cleared out of Bolivia until things cooled down," Mordechai said, "but we went back later."

"Were you armed? Did you participate?" I asked.

Hughie gave me the same steely look as when he talked about the Nazis. *"No comprendo,"* he said.

"C'est la guerre, but it was sad," Mordechai said. "Che was a likable fellow and a good leader."

"I would have hired him," Hughie said.

Brian was their trusted garage manager and mechanic. He was a good guy except for one quirk: he thought space aliens were living among us. He checked everyone out, convinced that he had the ability and the knowledge to spot aliens. He was slim, not very tall, and his thin black hair was parted neatly above a handsome round face.

"Don't mind Brian and his space saucers. It's only his hobby," Hughie said.

It wasn't a hobby, I found out. He was dead serious.

"Do you know anything about aliens?" he asked.

"I lived near Roswell, the alien capital of America, in a little town called Artesia."

"Did you see the place where the UFO crashed and the aliens fell out?"

I thought I might as well play along. "We had a field behind our house, and I think that's where they crashed. If you stood quietly and listened closely you could hear the play-by-play broadcast of the Los Angeles Dodgers in the Coliseum hundreds of miles away. I think it was because some of that spaceship's metal was scattered about."

"That is so weird."

From that day on Brian questioned me every chance he could about my life in New Mexico. He would ask, "Did you ever notice anything strange?"

"What kind of question is that? There are strange people everywhere."

"No, no. Did any of your friends at school have pointy ears or two different-coloured eyes?"

"We had a teacher, Mr. Barry Baines, who had a glass eye that didn't quite match the real one. He bought it on the GI Bill after the war. He'd lost an eye fighting on some island in the South Pacific."

After I settled in, Mordechai had John the Painter paint the apartment. It took two days to spruce it up. "We should have done that before you moved in, Joshua, but no one has lived up there in years." They also supplied furniture and a new bed. It actually turned out quite nicely.

One day on the job I asked Brian about Angel.

"Yes, I know Angel Featherstone the writer," he told me. "She lives up at the north end of town with her boyfriend, Beano."

I spat coffee all over the table and coughed and choked for another five minutes. "What the hell do you mean, her boyfriend? She told me she lived with a friend. I thought it was a girlfriend. And why does a girl like that go with a guy named Beano?" I yelled, wiping coffee from the front of my overalls.

Brian looked surprised. Then the light went on in his head, and he said, "You're that friendly guy she talks about who helped her in Haines Junction."

"Yes, I am that friendly guy. Or I should say I was that friendly guy until now!"

"Maybe she thought you wouldn't be so helpful if you knew she had a boyfriend."

"No, she's not that kind of girl. I should have thought it through. It's just my wishful thinking that brought me over here."

Brian crossed his arms on his chest and stroked his chin. "So you came over here to see her and you didn't know about Beano."

"I had no idea about Beano."

"Beano isn't a bad guy."

I threw a rag onto the workbench. "I don't want to hear it."

Over the next few days I came to grips with my dilemma and asked Brian to keep our conversation under his hat.

"I'll tell you the strangest stories you've ever heard about living near Roswell if you help me out here," I said, knowing how one little rumour of personal business can fly around a town like Dawson City.

"Okay, you got it, but the stories have to be good," Brian said. He had no idea of the tales I was going to spin to keep him quiet.

Brian sealed our agreement with a six-movement handshake he swore was taught to him by someone who learned it from an alien encounter. After we'd practised it, we could do it at blinding speed. The kids in town picked up on it, and the handshake became a regular greeting.

"See how things go, Brian? It starts out as a simple handshake and ends up as an everyday thing," I said.

I met Beano when he came to the garage. He was short and pale with a head of curly, jet-black hair. I couldn't help not liking him. Angel was glad to see me and gave me a hug. Angst was over the moon to see Angel and danced around until I told him to stop. I knew how he felt, though.

"I never thought I would see you in Dawson City. I've been trying to convince Beano to move to Haines Junction. Maybe if you're here we could rent your cabin."

Great, I thought, they're going to live in my place, make it their very own love nest and I'm going to be stuck here. Maybe I should send Angst with them to complete the deal.

Then Angel introduced Beano. "Beano, darling, this is that nice man I told you about who was helpful when I was in Haines Junction doing the *Geographic* article."

I hated that she called him darling.

"Pleased to meet you, Joshua," he said, flashing a toothless smile. He didn't offer his hand to shake.

He knows, I thought.

"Likewise," I said and went back to work.

Later I was sweeping the garage floor, wondering how a grown man got a name like Beano. It seemed that Brian was reading my mind. He poked his head around the corner of the overhead door and said, "Beano got his name from reading the English comic strip *Dennis the Menace*. You know, that tough little guy in the red and black striped jumper, the one with the dog named Gnasher? It came out five days after the American comic of the same name, but plagiarism wasn't suspected on either side. It was just a coincidence."

That afternoon I started paying my debt to Brian with stories from Roswell. He sat on the workbench, and I pulled up a chair.

"There was this radio station in Roswell that reserved two hours from 8:00 to 10:00 p.m. every Saturday night for requests. You could call in and dedicate a song of your choice to your friend or whoever. Well, the station kept on getting this request for 'Purple People Eater' by Sheb Wooley over and over again. And you know what they figured out, Brian?"

"What?"

"They figured it was the aliens calling in for their favourite song."

"Oh." Brian sat in silence for a while looking at the floor. "You know what, Joshua?"

"What?"

"The next dog I get, I'm going to call him Sheb." He got up and headed for the door, yelling, "Lock up behind you."

I met Tobias, the writer, reporter, historian and all-around good guy. I spent time with his parents, Rebecca and Hudson, who took the place of my friends Thomas and Rose in Haines Junction. Through Tobias I got to know the Halloos, a large extended family living at Rock Creek. The three brothers who headed the family were known as the Rock Creek boys. They didn't really head the family—their wives did—but we let their husbands dream on. At first I didn't get along with the Halloos, but we patched things up, and they introduced me to their favourite niece, Missy.

Soon I found a way to spend one evening a week with Angel. When I heard that she'd signed up for lessons at Mr. Waldo's Dancing School, taught in the cavernous Diamond Tooth Gertie's Community Hall, I signed up too.

Mr. Waldo was from Hungary. He had the most painstakingly trimmed pencil moustache you ever saw and a physique without an ounce of fat. Since he was barely five feet tall and weighed a hundred pounds, some of his students dwarfed him. He knew all the moves, though, and was a graceful dancer. In his heavy accent he boasted, "I danced for royalty at the Astoria in London and the Ritz in Paris."

No matter how cool it was in the hall, he danced in sleeveless undershirts. He didn't shave his underarms and smoked like a chimney. It amazed me that people could work puffing on a cigarette. Mrs. Boss went into a coughing fit while practising the foxtrot when Waldo exhaled and she inhaled.

Victor the gypsy came in but left.

"He's okay dancer but he's no Freddy Astaire," Waldo said. "I'm glad to see him leave. I do not like gypsy."

More buxom women than men were taking lessons. Chief Daniel was eager but old as the hills, Skinny Craven was a beanpole who danced rigid like a beanpole and Walter Rather, the store owner, was a naturally lousy dancer. All three of them stumbled about, forgetting every single instruction that Waldo gave them. In the end all they did was a one-two-three waltz around the floor, looking at their feet to get it right.

Every chance I got, I danced with Angel. We foxtrotted, tangoed and mamboed. At one practice Beano arrived to take her home and leaned against the wall, arms folded, glaring as hard as he could as he watched us.

I was the one everyone chose to dance with because I could at least keep time and didn't forget the steps. By the end of each class I was so exhausted I was tripping over my own feet, but Mr. Waldo looked like he was just getting warmed up. Thankfully some of the women danced together, taking the load off me.

I enjoyed my days at the garage, changing tires, pumping gas, chatting with the customers and doing mechanical work. I also took over some of the management since Brian had met an African American woman from Miami named Maude and was distracted from his duties.

"Don't tell anyone, Joshua, but I think I've found the real deal. This woman all but admitted to me that she is an alien."

"Well, you'd better go get her. You don't want her to fly away in a spaceship, do you?"

"Nope," he said, and went off to pursue Maude.

I bumped into Angel and Beano from time to time in the grocery store or the laundromat. I could see their closeness by the way they laughed and talked together.

One day a poster was thumbtacked in the garage office announcing a community potluck and dance. The New Tones orchestra from Whitehorse was playing, and it promised to be a great evening of dining and dancing.

I showed up early in my tweed jacket and tie to get a good seat, but the darkened hall was already packed and noisy. The New Tones, decked out in their red glittering pants and jackets, were tuning up to play dinner music. Angel sat with other students from the dance class and Mr. Waldo. Beano wasn't with her. She waved me over to the empty spot beside her. I squeezed between rows of folding chairs, excusing myself all the way, and sat down.

"Where's Beano?"

"Beano is in Whitehorse finishing up some paperwork. We're moving. That *Geographic* article I did landed me a job in Vancouver, and I have you to thank for helping me."

My head spun, but I kept my feelings inside.

The plates of hot food were served by an army of white-smocked volunteers who deftly manoeuvred over people's heads. I worried they would drip gravy down someone's neck or ruin a Clairol home perm.

Angel was excited about her new job. "We'll find an apartment, and all of you are invited to come and visit. Beano is going back to university to study math."

Funny, but a guy named Beano who couldn't replace his missing front teeth didn't strike me as a mathematician.

Angel took a drink of her soda and looked at me over the glass. As though she'd read my mind, she said, "He's studying for his master's degree. He is brilliant. NASA material."

I didn't really want to know, but I was starting to understand what she saw in him.

Everyone at our table ate every last morsel on their plates. The volunteers wheeled carts around to collect the dishes and hauled them off to the kitchen, where a din was getting louder by the minute as they washed up.

The band started to play dance music. Angel grabbed my hand. "Come on, Joshua, let's show them what we learned from Mr. Waldo."

Waldo clapped his hands. "Yes, you two were my best students. Go show them, please."

We walked out onto the dance floor, and a waltz began. I couldn't resist saying, "I'm going to miss you."

She smiled. "You're a sweet man, Joshua. I'll miss you too."

We danced all evening, and our skill must have shown. When we sat down people applauded. The Halloos from Rock Creek seemed to have bees in their bonnets about something and shot me glances all night.

Skinny Craven came over, slapped me on the back and did a quick foot shuffle. "That's pretty good footwork you're doing there, boy. If I was thirty years younger, I'd be doing the same thing."

"I have a talented partner," I said.

The band played its last dance, the jaunty but haunting "Midnight in Moscow," at 1:00 a.m., and we all went our separate ways. I sat in my room under a bare bulb, trying to write my feelings for Angel in poetry. I couldn't find anything that made sense and rhymed with Beano. My best line was, "You have to leave Beano so we can be togethero."

Tired, I put my head on my pillow for only a moment but woke the next morning with paper and pencil in my hands and a kink in my neck. The poetry didn't look any better in the light of day so I scrapped it.

On Monday morning Brian grabbed me before I even had my coveralls on.

"Joshua, that last story about Roswell was fascinating," he said, pushing me toward the coffee room. "Tell me more."

"Do you want to hear about the strange craft that flew over the farmer's yard? After that the chickens only laid eggs with three yolks and the farmer's wife gave birth to triplets."

"Yes, tell me," he said eagerly.

"Well, this spaceship flew over this house, and the chickens had three-yolk eggs and the farmer's wife had triplets."

"What else?"

"There is nothing else. But oh, I just remembered, the farmer grew three more toes on each foot."

"Okay."

Two weeks later Beano and Angel drove into the garage. Their roof rack was piled high with strapped-down boxes and suitcases, and the back seat was packed full of blankets and books. Through the back window I could see that Isaac Newton's *Principia Mathematica* sat on top.

I checked the oil and filled the gas tank. Beano was wearing a red and black striped jumper. What else would he wear? I thought. After all, he's a comic book hero.

He went inside to pay, and I crouched down beside Angel's side of the car.

"Goodbye," I said, and held out my hand for her to shake.

She shook my hand and held onto it longer than necessary.

"Goodbye, Joshua. Thanks for being my dance partner."

"My pleasure."

Angst came over and put his paws up on the door. Angel patted his head.

"Goodbye, Angst."

"Goodbye," I said, playing at being Angst. I grasped his paw and waved it.

Angel laughed.

Beano came out of the garage, putting papers in his wallet and stuffing it into his back pocket. Brian tagged along behind him. Beano didn't stop but walked around to the driver's side, saying, "Goodbye, Joshua," over the roof of the car.

"Goodbye," I said. Then I added, "Hey Beano, if you ever get a dog, call him Gnasher."

That made him laugh. He reached across the roof and shook my hand. "You're all right, Joshua."

I still disliked Beano but I respected him for that.

Angst and I stood and watched until they drove out of sight. After a few minutes Brian stuck his head out of the office and called, "Hey Joshua! Let's go have coffee and talk more about Roswell."

"Okay. Have I told you the one about the aliens marching in the UFO Parade in Roswell? Everyone thought they were ordinary people dressed in costumes."

"No, wow, I can hardly wait."

The Wedding

A year after Angel moved to Vancouver with Beano, I received a postcard from her. It showed a picture of a totem pole in Stanley Park. The brief message said she and Beano were settled and I should let everyone in Dawson City know so they could come and visit. I told no one and didn't keep the card. Angst growled when I threw it in the garbage.

The Klondike had caught my interest, and I was beginning to like living in Dawson City. I hiked the creeks on weekends, climbing over the mothballed gold dredges and digging around the massive bucket draglines to look for nuggets that might have slipped through. I revelled in the history of the gold miners and I volunteered at the museum where I read from books bearing Robert Service's signature.

In the winter I helped organize the 210-mile Percy de Wolfe Memorial Dog Sled Race from Dawson City to Eagle, Alaska. Someday I wanted to compete in it myself, but for now dogs, dog food and sleds were expensive.

I was still working at Ford's Chevrolet Auto Garage. My boss Brian had married the love of his life, Maude, and he wasn't so interested in my Roswell alien stories anymore now that he was convinced his wife was an alien. This was fine with me. My stories were becoming more far-fetched, and I thought for sure he was going to start questioning them.

A few months later I received another postcard from Angel. This one was different. It had a long, crammed note telling me how much she missed Dawson City and seeing her friends, especially me. She signed it "Love, Angel" and put three Xs at the end.

Something was up, I thought. Things couldn't be right with her and Beano, but how could anything be right with a guy named Beano? And things weren't right. She phoned me the next day at work.

"Hello, Joshua, how are you?"

"Fine, Angel. It's nice to hear from you."

"I want to come back. Things haven't worked out so well. I'm lonely. I want to see you."

"Oh?" I looked out the garage office window. Three cars were lined up at the gas pumps, and the drivers looked impatient.

"Beano hasn't been nice," she sniffled.

"I can't get involved," I said.

It was true. I couldn't get involved in another couple's breakup or troubles. If Angel was going to bounce around between men, I wanted no part of it.

"Oh."

"I can't get involved," I said again.

The line clicked and went dead. She'd hung up.

I looked at the phone and thought maybe I'd been too hard. I didn't feel good about what I'd done, but I thought I'd done the right thing for myself.

Missy, the Halloos' niece, walked into the office as I hung up. A few times during the year I'd visited Rock Creek to see her, and I was always happy when she came to the garage.

Today she was a sight for sore eyes, dressed in bright cotton pastels with her blonde hair in braids. Lately we were seeing each other more often, and she always seemed to be bringing the Halloos' vehicles into the garage.

"Hi, Joshua, I think my truck needs an oil change," she said.

"Clutch brought it in last week."

"Oh. One of the windows is stuck."

I checked them. "The windows seem okay."

"What about the carburetor?"

"What about it?'

"It might be stuck."

At that moment I came to my senses. Something else was going on here. Then I realized she was here for me. I felt flattered and pleased. I hadn't had a woman's attention for the longest time.

"Okay, Missy," I said. "I'll fix anything on your truck, but let's go for lunch at the Flora Dora to discuss this further."

As we walked along the boardwalk, I could feel that she wanted to walk close to me. We smiled at each other, and I felt light-headed. I put my hands in my pockets, and she held my arm. I liked her touch, and I thought we looked like the album cover of *The Freewheelin' Bob Dylan*. I felt as though we were strolling in Greenwich Village.

Missy drove in every day from Rock Creek to have lunch. Sometimes we went to the Flora Dora and sat with our friends, and other times she brought a basket from home. I could tell her aunts were involved because she would say, "Stella baked this especially for you, Joshua, and Lulu wants you to try these bread-and-butter pickles."

I tried them all.

Her uncles were different. After all, I was courting their favourite niece. When they drove up to the pumps, they weren't so friendly. They gave me that narrow-eyed stare and spoke sharply but politely. "Morning, Joshua, how ya doing? Are you behaving yourself?"

"Good morning, gentlemen. Yeah, sure I am. Why wouldn't I be?" I said as I pumped their gas.

"That's real nice you called us gentlemen, because that is what we are. Right, brothers?"

OP and Clutch, sitting in the cab and staring out the window at me, nodded in agreement with Winch.

"And we appreciate gentlemanly behaviour in others, don't we, boys?"

OP and Clutch nodded again.

"We wouldn't want to hear of any ungentlemanly behaviour in this town, now would we, brothers?"

OP and Winch shook their heads.

I was getting the point. "Okay, okay, I hear you. Only gentlemanly behaviour."

The brothers liked that and broke into grins. Winch, who'd gotten out of the truck to pay the bill, slapped me on the back with his big meaty hand. I was beginning to dislike those signs of affection.

"Okay, Joshua, but we're just the messengers. Uncle Zak wanted to make sure everything was crystal clear."

They laughed some more and drove away. When they stopped at the first stop sign half a block away, I could hear them still laughing.

Missy took a job with Parks Canada and moved into town. "My uncles didn't like me moving in on my own. They said if you visit me in the evening, you have to be out by eight o'clock."

I was out by 7:30 just to make sure.

"That Joshua is a very respectful gentleman," the brothers told people.

Missy and I met in the library, read the magazines and discussed literature. We shared the same interests in writing. One Saturday afternoon we talked at length about marriage. I wasn't too surprised when she took my hand and in a library-soft voice asked, "Will you marry me, Joshua?"

I liked it that she asked me. I liked independent women. "Yes, of course I will."

"First you'll have to ask my uncles for my hand."

"Okay."

Two weeks later there was an engagement ring on Missy's finger, and I was happily but nervously sitting in the dim, seldom-used living room of the Halloo home.

The Halloo men gave every indication that they ran the family, but the power behind the tree stump was the elder Halloo women, Stella, Lulu and Olive. They were the real authority and made all the decisions. I was pretty sure that they'd already made up their minds about Missy and me marrying— they liked me—and this meeting was just a show for the men.

Winch, Clutch and OP sat on an ancient couch that was struggling not to sag under their combined weight of almost twelve hundred pounds. The two-by-four blocking that I saw sticking out from the bottom offered the support they needed. OP, in the middle, stretched out his arms and drew his shoulders together to make more room. Their beards flowed down their chests, and their hair was parted in the middle and tied back with leather laces.

Earlier, in the kitchen, Olive had tied a bow in OP's beard with a red ribbon. Lulu then tied an array of small colourful rag bows throughout Winch's beard—he liked it and had Lulu do it when the occasion called for him to dress up—and Clutch had a big gold-flaked brown barrette in his. Sometimes the Halloo women made their men their playthings. The men didn't complain. They enjoyed the attention and thought it was funny. So did the children. "Uncle OP looks like a birthday present."

The brothers had taken off their boots, and they all wore clean red and white striped socks that matched their T-shirts under their bib overalls. The Halloo women also dressed their men.

The Halloos ignored their cramped discomfort and eyed me intently.

Uncle Zak sat on a kitchen chair with his legs crossed, looking as though the proceedings were going to amuse him.

Winch's famous Hunker Creek axe, the one he used to remove his own gangrenous toes, hung on the wall above our heads. I didn't know if meeting under it had any significance, but I couldn't help but notice it.

Outside in the hall other family members had their ears glued to the door. I could hear them rustling around, giggling and whispering.

"So our Missy asked you to marry her, did she?" Winch started.

"Yes sirs."

"And what do you think of that?"

"I liked it. Missy has an independent spirit. It shows who she is."

"And you accepted her proposal?"

"Yes, I did. I was happy to."

"You got a steady means of employment?" Zak asked.

"I work at Ford's Chevrolet Garage."

"Are you going to keep our niece living in the style she is used to?"

Seeing as Missy lived a pretty simple life, I said, "Not only will I do that but I will strive to improve both our lots."

"Good," Zak said.

"Ever been married?" OP asked.

"No."

"Ever been incarcerated?" Clutch said.

"No."

"Ever voted Conservative?" Winch said.

"No."

"Ever beat your dog?" Zak asked.

"No, never beat anyone. I don't intend to either."

"Ever take the last slice of pie?" Winch asked.

"No."

"Yes you have, we seen you do it, but that's okay because we take it all the time," Winch said.

"Trick question, that pie thing," OP said.

"Do you love our niece Missy?" Clutch asked anxiously.

I let the question hang in the air for a moment before I answered, "With all my heart. I love Missy with all my heart. We'll be good together."

With loud whoops the brothers leaped out of the couch—with some difficulty because they used each other to push off from—and rushed toward me. I instinctively put my arms up to protect my head, but they picked me up and crushed me with hugs and slaps on the back. I felt as though I was being beaten up. I understood this to mean that they'd given consent.

"Yahoo! Hullabaloo! Joshua, welcome to the family, son!" And I was beaten up some more.

Zak smiled. When things settled down, he got up and shook my hand and gave me a gentle hug. "Welcome to the family, son," he said, and left to go about his business.

"Joshua is family now," the brothers shouted for the hallway crowd to hear. At that prearranged signal their wives and a dozen other people swept into the room, yelling, "We're going to have a wedding! We're going to have a party!"

Winch pointed his big meaty finger in my face. "You're family now, Joshua. Nobody but nobody messes with you or your dog."

Nobody had ever messed with me, but I somehow felt more secure knowing the Halloos had Angst's and my back.

Missy was waiting out by the river. When she heard the ruckus, she knew the brothers and Zak had consented and came in to hug me.

"I'm so happy," she said. Then she went to thank the men. She didn't need to thank the women since they'd made their minds up weeks ago and wouldn't let the men say no anyway.

Missy and I wanted the wedding to be a private affair, but the Halloos insisted on a grand celebration.

"That's our favourite niece you're marrying there, man. We have to do this right."

We relented to make everyone happy. After all, they wanted to show their love. They also wanted us to move out to Rock Creek and live with them.

"You can't stay in Dawson by yourselves. You have to be with your family," Lulu said.

They gave us one of the larger rooms on the third floor. It had its own bathroom and a magnificent bay window seat overlooking the Klondike River. Missy moved back out to Rock Creek, and I would move in after the wedding. We were happy to do that.

"We're here all the time anyway, Joshua. We might as well move in," Missy said.

Missy was related to the Halloos through her grandfather, Bertrand, who was related to Alice Halloo, the mother of Winch, Clutch and OP. After a year of university, Missy had come to the Yukon for a visit and stayed.

The protests from her parents did not budge her. "You must come home, Missy, and finish your schooling. The Yukon is no place for a lady like you."

Missy responded by sending pictures of herself chopping firewood and packing the hindquarter of a moose out of the bush. She wrote, "Mom, Dad, I'm okay. I love it here."

She told me later that since she'd met me, she wasn't leaving for anything.

When her parents, George and Swan Nottage, arrived, they could see what a good life their daughter had and they were more than pleased with her choice of husband.

"It's lovely here, the air is so fresh and Joshua is a prince."

I didn't try to change their opinion.

Among Missy's many relatives were four distant cousins who'd lived all of their lives in Kemptville, a small town outside Ottawa. Two brothers—Buster and Jack McKan—attended the wedding and enjoyed a holiday by visiting Dawson City and meeting people.

"Friendly town, that Dawson. I met a sourdough who knew Skookum Jim, the gold discoverer, and another old man who told me he had a seven-shot Smith & Wesson revolver but forgot where he put it. I believed the sourdough but not the other fellow."

On our wedding day, Stella, her sisters and their best friend, Maude, hugged Missy and me a hundred times.

"We are just so happy for you two," Lulu said, drying her eyes with her hanky.

Thomas, Rose, Billy, Marsha and the boys came over from Haines Junction loaded with presents and good wishes from everyone in the town. Their five boys were glad to see me, and I made a point of talking to all of them.

"Copper Johnson couldn't make it on account of his age but he sent this package," Thomas said.

While Missy undid the twine and wrapping, I explained to her that Copper was my elder friend from Burwash. Inside the package were two pairs of children's moccasins, brightly beaded with flowers, one in blue and the other in pink.

"Copper said this is the children you will have—his wife had a dream—and you are to put Copper and Pearl in their names," Rose said.

Missy kissed Rose on both cheeks and asked her to thank Copper and his wife for us.

I was delighted and looked forward to the day we had Copper and Pearl.

Missy looked radiant in her dress with flowers in her hair. We were friends and lovers, and I knew we would be happy.

"You're so handsome in your suit, Joshua," Missy said.

The suit actually belonged to Tobias, my friend; his mom even tied my tie for me.

Tobias and Lulu acted as our witnesses, and we recited our vows for everyone to hear.

"The first day I saw Joshua at the garage, I knew he had to be mine," Missy announced to the guests after the ceremony.

"And when she asked me to marry her, I thought I was the luckiest guy in the world," I said.

The crowd gave a roar of approval, "Way to go, Joshua!"

Then the dancing and the feasting began. The wedding was exactly what the Halloos wanted: good food and hundreds of family and friends gathered together on the lawn alongside the Klondike River. By late afternoon all that was left of the barbecued side of beef were bones turning on the spit. We'd eaten sixty pounds of coleslaw, three hundred baked potatoes, hundreds of pounds of fresh vegetables and two hundred ears of roasted corn.

As dessert was being served, people got up and made toasts to Missy and me.

Zak and his wife, Frieda, stood up and raised their glasses of punch. "The Missus and I have been married longer than any of you, so the best advice I can give is never to get angry at the same time."

Billy and Marsha stood up. Marsha said, "I know you two lovebirds will always be together, so the best advice Billy and I can give is to respect your vows. In the bumpy times the keeping of your love and loyalty will get you through." Billy nodded in agreement, and they both sat down. Their five boys sitting in a row clapped enthusiastically.

Brian and Maude came forward next. "Never ever think your wife is an alien," Brian said. "And if you do," Maude continued, "treat her like the Queen of the Klondike, and everything will be all right."

Winch, OP and Clutch got up next. "If three brothers marry three sisters, then head for the hills, because you're never going to win. Just kidding, just kidding," they said and sat back down to the crowd's laughter and cold stares from their wives.

"Maybe we shouldn't have done that," OP said. Winch and Clutch nodded.

Jack from Kemptville stood up next. "My wife Ruby asked me to marry her when I was fifteen and she was sixteen. Two things influenced my decision, the first being I was failing grade nine for the second year and couldn't stand school; the other was that I figured that a good-looking woman like that would only come along once in a lifetime and ask you to marry her."

There were titters of nervous laughter from the guests.

"We eloped, and when I turned sixteen, the Department of Social Services quit chasing us and we were able to return home. I went to work in my father's hardware store. We have had our ups and downs. We both took anger management and stopped throwing the dishes at each other. Besides, it was getting expensive even buying those cheap sets from Simpsons-Sears. She has a few beers and likes to dance with the guys at the Legion Hall, but it's all in good fun, right?"

There was more nervous laughter, and a few people clapped their hands as Jack took his seat.

"I didn't need to hear that," Lulu said to Maude in a whisper with her hand over her mouth.

After the toasts the music started, and the brothers turned up their amps. "We want to be heard all the way into town and let everyone know what they are missing," Clutch said.

"Great wedding, but I blew an amp on 'Purple Haze,' trying to keep up with Buster on his bagpipes," Winch said days later.

Buster had brought his bagpipes along to pipe the bride and groom in, and after that he joined in with the band to play a few tunes. No one had ever heard of such music before.

"You must be a born-in-the-Yukon man at heart. Only a person born on the creeks would play Hendrix on the bagpipes," Clutch told him.

Buster loved the compliment. "I feel like I've lived here all my life."

The dancing went on until the midnight sun dipped along the horizon and rose again.

After the wedding Clutch and Buster packed up a truck with supplies and drove all over the Klondike, visiting placer mines and old dredges and panning every creek they came to. By pure luck Buster panned out a nugget the size of his small fingernail with the very first pan he ever dipped into a Yukon creek.

Clutch was amazed. "Wow, that's something! You must have the spirit of the Yukon running through your veins, Buster. The only thing like that I've ever seen was when I was standing on a road talking with a guy and he looked down and picked up a nugget right off the ground."

"Now I know what those gold discoverers felt like on Bonanza Creek that day," Buster said, admiring his find.

Camped out under the stars, Buster told Clutch, "This is a wonderful country you live in. The spirit is so great and real here."

Clutch noticed Buster had a special glint of light in his eye that he'd seen before, but he couldn't put his finger on it. "You should move up here."

Buster tossed a stick into the fire. "I don't know if I could. I've got two more brothers back home and a family hardware store that has probably fallen apart because I'm not there."

When the men returned to Rock Creek, Buster invited Missy and me to come and visit them in Ontario. I said, "That sounds like a good idea. I've always wanted to see Eastern Canada."

Olive thought it was so nice of them to invite us that she invited the McKans to come and stay at Rock Creek. "Bring your family. We have lots of room and would love to have you any time."

Olive hadn't noticed Lulu's attempt to kick her under the table.

Buster grinned and thanked her. "That's wonderful, Olive, but I'm tied to that store. I could never get away."

Lulu looked relieved. She'd seen the glint in Buster's eye and knew it was gold fever.

The Unexpected Pilgrims

A few days after our Klondike wedding, Missy and I flew back to Ontario with her relatives Buster and Jack.

Ruby, Jack's wife, met us at the airport. She was as pretty as he'd mentioned at the wedding and, as he'd also described, gave Jack trouble as soon as his feet touched the ground. "You were to be here five days ago. Where the hell have you been?"

"At the wedding."

"Likely story."

Buster grabbed his bags and headed for the car, and Jack got around to introducing us. "Ruby, I'd like you to meet the bride and groom, our relatives Joshua and Missy, who've come to visit."

Ruby changed from a dark storm cloud to a bright sunny day. "How very nice to meet you. What a lovely couple you are."

Then she turned back to Jack and actually raised the corner of her lip to show her teeth.

We stayed a week with Missy's parents in their white bevel-siding home surrounded by fruit trees and flower beds. From the start they treated me kindly and like a son.

Then we stayed with Buster, his wife, Tammy, and their five kids. "You're welcome to stay as long as you want. We just love having relatives visit."

Their big rambling home on Harvey Street in downtown Kemptville was beautifully furnished, and a collection of boats and cars filled a large garage. On the lawn were a badminton net, trampoline and other toys and games.

There were kids everywhere.

Buster and Jack were back at work behind the counter in the hardware store they owned with their other two brothers, Moe and Chipper. Buster said, "This store has been in the family for over eighty years, and the McKans will probably be here for another eighty."

Missy and I drove into Ottawa to visit the Parliament Buildings and the National Art Gallery. It wasn't actually a national art gallery because there were no paintings from the Yukon displayed there. Then we drove to Quebec City and enjoyed the restaurants, poutine and Plains of Abraham for a couple of days. When we got back, I took a tour of the brothers' store and was impressed by the amount of stock they had.

"If we don't have it, no one else on the planet does," Chipper said proudly. The aisles, walls and floor areas were covered from top to bottom with every tool, nut and bolt that I could imagine. The brothers scoured the world for items as though they were Marco Polo trekking to the Far East and bringing back spices. Many items were forged tools from China and India packed in grease and wrapped in heavy brown waxed paper.

"Half the damn job is getting stuff out of its packing and cleaned," Chipper said, unwrapping a large crescent wrench. "Our older kids come in on weekends and after school to help out. They have to learn the hardware business. Someday they'll be the ones behind the counter."

All four brothers were about the same height and weight. They had comb-overs and wore the same style of glasses and the same khaki work pants. The only difference was their shirts. Each had his own favourite colour and style. Moe wore green, red and blue plaid. Buster preferred a white shirt and a bow tie of a different colour every day. Jack wore brown or beige corduroy. Chipper chose blue denim and a tie showing a mackerel or some other fish with a hook in its mouth attached to an infinite fishing line.

"He has over fifty of those fish ties but he doesn't fish and won't eat fish either," Buster said.

"Each one is a piece of art," Chipper said. "The one I'm wearing I bought for fifty cents at a sidewalk yard sale in New York. By its width it must be fifty years old. I think it's a trout on the line."

"Today a trout, tomorrow a marlin," Jack said.

Then the three brothers Buster, Moe and Jack broke into song. "Today a trout, tomorrow a marlin, today a trout, tomorrow a marlin," they sang, dancing in a circle, following one another. Then, just as quickly as they'd started, each brother shuffled down a separate aisle and went back to work. Chipper laughed merrily as he opened the cash register, which gave its never-ending ding, and dropped in the float of coins and bills.

We had coffee together every morning, and I found the brothers pleasant to be with. We were talking about the North when Buster said, "After visiting the Yukon I feel strangely out of place here. It's as if I'm in a different world or something." His eyes glinted.

Missy said later, "I think Buster enjoyed his visit to the Klondike and he's fallen under the spell of the Yukon. I think he's becoming aware that Kemptville has some limitations."

Also, Buster had found a gold nugget on Too Much Gold Creek and wore it around his neck. He played with it constantly. Gold fever infected the spell of the Yukon and sent him into a tizzy.

"This is Billy Beers all over again, Missy," I said.

"Who is Billy Beers?"

"Do you remember the South African guy who came to our wedding? A few years back he went bonkers with gold fever up by Beaver Creek and just about ruined himself. If it wasn't for his friends, he might have never recovered."

Moe and Chipper were influenced by Jack and Buster, who talked constantly about the Klondike. The store was a place of coffee pot conversation, so the customers joined in.

"I know what you're talking about. I worked for a highway construction crew on the Alaska Highway up around Destruction Bay for a few years in the fifties," rasped Peewee Smitherman, the oldest and skinniest living resident for many miles around. "It was the most beautiful place I ever saw, and the people were friendly as hell, especially the Natives."

"The sunny days were nice, and the midnight sun was unbelievable. I panned out gold on a creek at two o'clock in the morning. It was like two o'clock in the afternoon," Buster said.

Jack bought every book on the Yukon he could get his hands on. He found two copies of Pierre Berton's *Klondike* in the second-hand book store across the street and placed them on the counter to be thumbed through by the brothers and customers alike.

Robby, Buster's oldest boy, asked me in the store one day, "Joshua, have you seen that picture of the people hiking over the Chilkoot Pass? I wonder if a person could still climb it."

"Yes, hikers do it all the time," I said, "and if you come to the Yukon, we can climb it together."

"Real cool," said Harley, Chipper's son.

Kemptville had been the centre of the McKans' universe for generations. Now it no longer interested them. They started to consider their lives dull. Church attendance, which had been compulsory ever since their father helped build the church in 1930, seemed intolerable. The hardware store, which was their reason for getting up every morning, was now a burden, a mausoleum whose back rooms and aisles the brothers trod like ghosts. Their hearts had been stolen and now lay in the Klondike.

"Joshua, say something to help them. They're confused. I don't think they know what is happening," Missy pleaded.

"No, I'm going to let this unfold on its own. One should not interfere in another person's spell of the Yukon."

The McKan wives—Tammy, Molly, Ruby and Holly—grew tired of hearing the stories, and at the supper table the kids groaned, "You're not going to talk about the Klondike again, are you, Dad?"

This preoccupation drew their attention away from the store. Crates of tools remained unpacked in the overflowing aisles. Customers' orders went unfilled, and phone calls went unreturned. Paperwork crowded the front counter so that the cat didn't like the disarray and found himself another place to sleep.

"Maybe we shouldn't have invited those two to the wedding, Joshua," Missy said.

"It's way too late now, sweetie."

The wives were doing the men's work.

"What would your father say if he was here to see the mess this place is in?" Tammy asked as she picked up a heavy crate. "And your children are taking time off school to help!"

"If only your mother could see this now," Ruby added, sweeping piles of sawdust and other packing material into a dustpan.

The men knew the store was getting out of hand.

Late Wednesday morning Buster called a meeting of his brothers. "You can stay, Joshua. This will interest you."

They turned around the OPEN sign to read CLOSED and locked the door. They'd never done that before; rain, shine, snow or hail, the store was always open to the public from eight to five, Monday through Saturday, except for holidays and funerals.

Customers rattled the handle and squished their faces up against the glass, leaving smudge marks. The brother could hear them talking and stood at the counter watching the faces come and go like a slide show.

"Those faces look weird," Moe laughed.

"Do you think they're being robbed? Maybe we should call the police," one round red face said.

Jack sighed, unlocked the door and went out to assure them that everything was okay. "We'll be open shortly. There's some family business we need to attend to."

The small crowd dispersed from the sidewalk and came back later.

"My lord, if we ever left this town, I think the whole place would fall apart," Chipper said.

The brothers gathered around the counter and the ancient cash register that had seen innumerable dollars pass through it. Each of them wondered what Buster was up to.

He got right to the point. "Tammy and I are leaving Kemptville."

I was surprised, but not as surprised as the brothers. They stood in stunned silence. Moe got teary-eyed. Buster was his big brother, and they were inseparable.

Chipper slid off the counter, put his arm around Moe's shoulder to console him and asked, "What do you mean you're leaving, Buster? You can't just get up and walk out of here."

"We're leaving. We've made up our minds. Tammy, the kids and I are moving to the Yukon. Dawson City, to be exact." He had that glint in his eye when he said it.

Chipper, Jack and Moe swivelled their heads back and forth to look at each other and said in unison, "We're going too!"

And that was that. After eighty-seven years of owning a family business— a tourist attraction because of its ability to find and sell almost any tool or piece of hardware that mankind had ever made from Detroit to China—the McKans were moving on.

Buster said later, "I was pleased with the way things worked out, Joshua. I knew if I asked my brothers to come along, there'd be endless days of arguments about giving up a family business. When I told them I was leaving, they joined in."

The process of extracting themselves from the deep roots attached to their friends, homes and business was excruciating. It took two months of hard work, giving up countless pieces of their lives—furniture, dishes, books and other household effects—in a dozen yard sales before the belongings going to the Yukon shrank to a manageable number.

The townsfolk didn't believe the McKans were leaving. The uproar was led by Peewee, who said, "They've been here for almost a century. Where are they going? They can't leave. They belong here. There're ours. Those McKan boys belong to us and they can't leave."

Peewee's lament garnered wide support even in the town's outlying areas. "My family bought chicken feed off their great-grandpappy. Peewee is right, they can't leave," a farmer called Jones said.

"They made this town. There have been more McKan mayors than anyone else. Hell, half the cemetery is filled with McKans, and I'm headed there pretty soon myself to lie alongside them, which will be an honour," Peewee said.

The store was listed for sale, and interested buyers came out to kick the tires, but none of them really appreciated the history and value of the business. The brothers were pleased when the agent called with an offer from a young man, Dicky Sheepshanks, who happened to be a distant cousin of the McKans. He knew a good deal when he saw it and bought the place with the help of his brother and two sisters. They ran it successfully for another fifty years.

"You wouldn't believe the antiques we found cleaning out the warehouse," Dicky said.

A large farewell party packed the school gymnasium. Some of the speeches were tearful, and others praised the brothers and reminisced about their father, mother and family history. A few speakers shook their heads while they spoke and said, "We can't believe you are going."

Peewee had prepared a speech but couldn't read it. Saddened by the night's event, he sat on a set of stairs at the back of the stage.

The evening concluded after midnight with the crowd standing, hands over hearts, to sing a rousing and emotional "O Canada." It was hours before the room emptied. No one wanted to say goodbye.

There were some benefits to leaving, though. The McKans were also discarding a lifetime of gossip, innuendo and lies.

"Life in Kemptville has not been easy," Moe said, "Dad was a philanderer and our mother an alcoholic because of it. There were hurtful things said. Small towns have no mercy."

"We are leaving a lot behind," Molly said, "some good things, some bad."

On a bright August morning, when the maple leaves were turning to their glorious golden plumage, a long caravan of new trucks pulled out of Kemptville loaded with furniture and household goods and interspersed with cars driven by the wives and packed with kids, dogs and cats. Missy and I were last in line, driving a one-ton flatbed piled high with boxes and crates.

Half the town lined the streets as though it were Canada Day and waved flags in one final goodbye. Peewee stood with tears running down his cheeks and staining his GWG work shirt. He had known the brothers' great-grandparents, grandparents and parents. For Peewee it was the end of an era.

"We're off to Shangri-La," Molly said with a laugh and a last wave of her hand.

The brothers had been astute and careful businessmen, and unlike others who went north seeking their fortune, the brothers were taking one with them.

Ten days later, at four in the morning on a late August day, the convoy pulled into the Halloos' front yard. After running the last 333 miles from Whitehorse, we turned off the vehicles and sat in silence as the lights in the house started to come on. Olive opened the front door dressed in her nightgown with a sweater draped over her shoulders and holding a cat that was trying to jump out of her arms. Behind her tiptoed Stella, trying to see who was there. Missy jumped out and ran ahead to hug her aunts.

Buster stepped out of the truck, placed his hands on his hips, arched his back and walked stiffly past the vehicles full of sleeping kids and tired drivers, right up to the porch.

"Well, Olive, we took you up on your invite. Here we are, the McKans with your Missy and Joshua."

Olive was surprised and dropped the cat but managed a smile. She told Stella to get Lulu. "The McKans are here, all of them, and Missy and Joshua are with them."

Stella hurried off while Olive held the door open and invited Buster inside.

"You all come in now, and I'll get the coffee on," she shouted, waving a welcome.

One thing about the Halloos: they were like the nomads of the Arabian Desert. It was their honour and pride to extend generous hospitality.

Lulu came down with Winch and asked nervously, "It's nice to have you as our guests. How long should we prepare your rooms for you?"

"Well it might be a while, maybe until spring. We plan on getting a property and building our own homes, so that will take a while," Buster said. "And if we go gold prospecting in between, well, we might be here longer."

Lulu's face went stiff, but she managed to smile and say, "Well, we'll see how things work out." She forced another smile.

Missy and I grabbed our few suitcases, went upstairs and gratefully collapsed exhausted in our own bed.

The next morning activity overwhelmed the house. Bedrooms that had been hastily assigned the night before were now being sorted out. There was enough room for everyone; someone just had to organize the space. Lulu was at her best in these situations. "Tammy and Buster, you and your kids can go in the two bedrooms at the back. Molly and Moe, you can go next door in those two rooms with your kids."

There was also a dorm bedroom for the older boys and another one for the older girls.

Over the next few days we unpacked the furniture, boxes and luggage and carried them into the house and barn. A stream of helpers lined up near the trucks to pass things from hand to hand.

"Only eight adults and eighteen kids! Couldn't you have squeezed a few more into the vehicles, eh? Are you sure you didn't leave anyone behind? I'm not moving out of my room. Someone will get a sharp stick in the eye if you try to move me," Zak said. "And I don't want those damn cats and dogs in there either."

"No one is moving anyone anywhere. We have room as it is," Stella assured him.

"We don't want to be any trouble. It's just that we don't know anyone else here," Tammy said.

"We'll get you sorted out," Olive said, and she went to get more linen out of the closet.

Zak was right. All these people were too much. If the others shared his view, they didn't say anything, but there was some grumbling. The McKans were generous in their financial support of the household, and this smoothed things over. The Halloos appreciated it, since there had been times when guests took advantage of their hospitality.

The McKan children adjusted surprisingly well. They made friends with the Halloos, and the bunch of them had adventures in the barn, by the river and in the surrounding forest. Having the Halloos for relatives made life easier in their new school. No one messed with them.

The men found work in town. Jack worked at Hughie Ford's Chevrolet Automotive Garage with me and Brian. The first time they sat down for coffee, Brian gave Jack the alien quiz.

"How did your parents shake hands?"

"Like normal people."

"Do you have relations living around Roswell?"

"Never heard of the place."

"If you had the choice of pointy or round ears, which would you choose?"

"The ones I have."

"Nope, he isn't an alien, Joshua. He failed the test. Besides, no alien with any sense of style would have a comb-over."

I introduced Moe and Chipper to people in town, and they found work on the creeks with the placer miners.

Buster went to work for the Downtown Hotel as a desk clerk. At the hardware store he'd been the workhorse, and he welcomed the respite from physical labour.

The women helped out with the daycare, in the gardens and around the house. Like the Halloos they liked things clean and fresh. "The kitchen floor has been scrubbed so many times I think that linoleum is going to wear out," Stella said.

The McKans worked hard and made an effort to fit in, unlike the Halloos when they first arrived. This was their home now, and they wanted to live under the midnight sun and the aurora borealis, snug in the family ties of the Halloos' friendship and the goodwill of the people of Dawson.

"Respect for each other is so important. Here's hoping we gain the respect of the townsfolk," Buster said.

"Show your respect for others, and everything should be okay," Lulu said.

Although the house was crowded, everyone seemed to be getting along. In the evening the young adults reclined on blankets beside the Klondike River. The children played croquet on the level spot down by the barn, and the parents with infants sat on the porch drinking tea and watching the children. Classical music played on CBC radio, and Glenn Gould's renditions of Bach cast a rich, pleasant air over everything. Across the fenced vegetable gardens toward the hill a baseball game was in full swing. The shouts of "Batter,

batter, batter!" and the crack of the bat drifted across the valley to embrace Bach. From the shop came hammering and a splash of red sparks from the grinding of metal as the men worked late repairing equipment and vehicles.

Missy and I spent hours with Tobias when he came out to visit. He was a good friend who was researching the Halloos when he was home from journalism school.

I got along well with both sets of brothers and told the McKans how I'd discovered a Japanese raft beached high above the Alsek River and a crashed DC-3.

"Either you're a hell of a good storyteller or you've led one hell of an interesting life," Chipper said.

"Just go look at the DC-3 weathervane," I said. "That's proof enough."

"Sure, sure. Someday," Chipper laughed.

I didn't appreciate him not believing me.

One month later the first snow arrived. This winter was one of the earliest and coldest in memory. The temperature plunged to forty and fifty below and stuck there. Nothing moved. Trucks froze, schools closed, transportation of fresh food on the highway dwindled to a crawl and only the bravest ventured out. The airlines quit flying, and woodpiles disappeared into stoves more quickly than expected. The moose migrated higher on the mountains, searching for warmer temperatures. Tires froze flat on the bottom, and it took a mile before the passengers stopped bouncing up and down and the tires rounded out.

The days and nights were clear. Without a blanket of clouds the warmth flew to the stratosphere like a helium balloon. The pale sun rose around 10:00 a.m. and disappeared by 4:00 p.m. The air bit into our lungs, and metal became brittle. Other than the occasional raven there was no sign of outdoor life. The dogs buried themselves deep into the straw inside their log houses, and we added an extra chunk of tallow to their food to burn against the cold. Winch wired a 100-watt bulb into each doghouse to keep the dogs comfortable. At night we could see the light through chinks in the logs, and that reassured us that the dogs were warm.

Our social centre was in the oversized kitchen around the stove, where we drank coffee and ate the baking as soon as it came out of the oven. No one wanted to go outside unless it was absolutely necessary. Wood detail was quick and efficient, with everyone pitching in to load firewood into the basement.

The Halloos took the weather in stride, but the McKans were beside themselves. The cold took the shine off their image of the Yukon.

"Do you really live like this?" Tammy asked.

"Sure we do. What choice do we have?" Lulu said, sounding sensitive to a criticism she could do nothing about.

The McKans started to show signs of strain. An argument broke out between husbands and wives and moved on between the brothers and their sisters-in-law. When it started to pull in Zak, his wife, Frieda, Lulu, Olive and Stella intervened. "This is going no further. We're not getting involved. This is about a few people not handling a Yukon winter."

"I was just getting started on those cheechakos," Zak said.

"We know. That's why we're calling a halt to this."

One Saturday evening the living room was packed with hockey fans in their team jerseys desperately trying to bring in CBC's *Hockey Night in Canada* on a snowy TV screen. Molly sat on the arm of the sofa and bent over to hug Moe, disturbing everyone in the room during the week's most uninterruptable program.

"I just want to go home! I just want to go home! I miss my home! We have to go and buy it back! We never should have sold it! This is like living in Siberia," she sobbed. Tears streamed down her cheeks, and her nose ran. "No, I take that back, this is like living in hell," she said, and sobbed even louder.

"This is Siberia," Zak said. "It sure as hell isn't Miami Beach, not with all that snow out there, or haven't you noticed?"

Holly told Zak to hush. He didn't like it a bit and left the room in a huff just as Danny Gallivan started announcing the game play-by-play.

"I think we have the sound but no picture," Winch said, and got up off the floor. He'd been crammed in behind the TV, turning dials.

Molly's sisters-in-law tried to comfort her, but she rushed off to her room, slamming the door so hard it reverberated through the building.

"There go the hinges," OP said.

"Shouldn't do that in another person's home," Olive said.

Moe hurried after her but came back. "She locked the door."

There was nothing anyone could do. The cold was a reality, and the conditions it imposed were real. It was a trial of faith that spring would return, life would come back to the land and people would rediscover their freedom and happiness.

The McKans started looking for property. They ventured out in the cold to trudge through the snow with a real estate salesperson, inspecting property lines. I went out and helped them, making sure they didn't freeze anything. "Damn it, leave the truck running! Don't turn it off to save gas at forty below!"

They bought acreage next door to the Halloos and set about making plans and ordering material for construction in the coming spring.

"We are going to be neighbours," Jack said.

"About time," Zak said.

By mid-January some of the McKans were barely surviving the cold, darkness and cramped quarters. Molly was faring the worst.

"Get me out of here! Take me home, Moe!" she often shrieked, lacing her demands with profanities.

Moe was shocked into silence. He and his brothers never swore but instead expressed themselves with terms like shoebox, dagnab it and binder-grinder.

Molly was the love of Moe's life, and he bought her everything she wanted. They had left a beautiful home surrounded by acres of gardens for the cold of the Klondike. He felt responsible for her anguish.

A few days later, before anyone had gotten out of bed, Molly packed a dusty paisley carpet bag with nonsensical things such as a checkerboard, canned food and all her makeup. She started walking down the middle of the road to the airport about a mile east of Rock Creek.

As her breath flowed in a cloud behind her, she pouted and complained, "I'm not spending another minute in that place. I'm flying out of here and going home. Those people who took my house had better be gone by the time I get back."

It was Sunday, and there wouldn't be a plane until Tuesday, if one could fly at all in the cold weather.

A Yukon territorial grader operator named Moose Rednapp, heading out to clear the Dempster Highway, drove up behind her. Moose knew something was amiss because Molly wore a pink printed summer dress, a straw hat with yellow and white silk daisies, sandals and no coat, gloves or boots. Tears had frozen to her cheeks, and her exposed skin was turning bright red. Her nose had run and frozen to her top lip, and frost was caught in her hair from her breath. He stopped and climbed down out of the cab. Moose had on quilted overalls, but the cold made him shiver as he put his gloves and hat on.

He ran to catch up with Molly. "Hey there, miss, don't you think you should be dressed a little warmer?"

Molly stopped and faced Moose. "I'm going home, damn it." Then she let loose a cloud of obscenities that seemed to hang and freeze solid in the arctic air.

Moose was an old soldier and had seen this type of breakdown before, although the swearing was something new to him. "Wow, that's a few new ones."

It took some convincing, and he had to half-carry Molly into the warmth and safety of the cab. Shutting the door behind her, Moose jumped in, radioed ahead to the government garage and drove into town as fast as the lumbering grader would go.

The families got an early morning phone call, and almost every last one rushed into Dawson City and filled the nursing station. The doctor had a difficult time getting through the packed crowd in the reception area. He announced, "Only Lulu and Moe will be allowed to see her today."

There was a loud collective groan, and people started filing out.

"She's not up to visitors, I'm afraid. She's had a bit of an ordeal and has suffered from frostbite. This is not an uncommon occurrence at this time of year, but rest should help," the doctor said.

"How could she go out barely dressed?" Moe wanted to know.

"You're just lucky that Moose found her," the doctor said.

Molly kept all her fingers and toes despite the swelling and pain. Her hospital stay and the kind words of her visitors helped her come around. Moe sat by her bedside all day.

"Catching that plane seemed like the thing to do," she said.

"Was she trying to harm herself?" Moe asked the doctor.

"No, Molly was escaping being housebound. Running out is a northern anomaly. There is no way to prevent it."

I had a chance to visit Molly and Moe on the last day she was in the hospital.

"I'm not going back to that house, Joshua, never again," she told me.

Moe rented a spacious suite on the top floor of the Occidental Hotel and moved their kids and belongings in. Apart from the late-night drone from the bar and the smell of beer, it was pleasant enough, and they had more room. Molly, Moe and the kids ate French toast in the restaurant for breakfast, the special for lunch and à la carte for dinner. But the change didn't work.

Molly demanded that Moe return her to Ontario, the land she loved.

"Take me home, Moe, or I'm taking the kids and going myself."

Moe believed her; she had already proven her intentions to leave. He drove out to Rock Creek and packed up one of the pickups with their belongings. "I'm sorry, guys, but she won't stay. We're moving back."

No one questioned him. They let him go.

It was a cold, dark morning when Moe and Molly drove out. She insisted that they not stop, and they passed by the Halloos without saying goodbye. "I don't want another look at that damn house and all those people in it as long as I live."

She changed her mind by the time they got to Whitehorse and made a long teary pay-phone call to say goodbye. "I was afraid if I stopped, you would talk me out of leaving. I have to go," she sobbed.

"You do what you think is best, dear," Lulu said, "and if you ever need help, we'll be here for you."

"Thanks," Molly said.

Moe told me later, "We drove all the way to Ontario. When we arrived in Kemptville, people were surprised but didn't give us much attention. They had gotten over us leaving and had moved on with their lives."

"This is terrible," Molly had said. "I feel like a stranger in my own town, and those people living in my house are just horrid, I know it."

As they drove down the streets, Molly waved frantically at everyone, but few waved back. Maybe people didn't realize it was her. They weren't expecting her and Moe back so soon.

The people they did talk to wanted to know how Peewee Smitherman was doing. Apparently, he had left for the Klondike to visit the McKans.

"After two weeks of staying in a hotel, we couldn't stand the change in attitude toward us," Moe told me. "Our business was gone, our house and garden were gone, our status in the community had been given to others. Kemptville had become a lonely place. In fact it wasn't our place any more.

"Molly insisted on parking outside our old house, and before I could stop her, she jumped out of the truck and ran up to pound on the door. It was heartbreaking to see we no longer belonged there. When the owner answered, Molly was speechless. She turned around and walked away. We were lucky the police weren't called."

"Take me back to the Yukon," Molly now demanded. "Take me back, Moe. I cannot live here another second. We have to go back. I made a mistake."

Moe was happy. If he'd fought with her, she would never have returned to Dawson on her own.

It was a road-weary family that drove into the Halloos' yard exactly thirty days after driving past without saying goodbye. The Halloos and the McKans all came out to greet and hug them.

"Look at the early birds that spring has brought back to us," Stella said.

"More like two cuckoos," Zak muttered.

"We're here to stay," Moe said. "You'll all be happy to know we are moving back in."

Oh God, thought Lulu.

Oh no, thought Stella.

Yikes! thought Olive.

"Damn," said Zak for everyone to hear.

But they all smiled and offered their hospitality once again.

Peewee Smitherman

Late in the evening two days after Molly's rescue by the grader operator, the noisy crowd playing cards in the kitchen heard a loud banging at the kitchen porch door. Everyone went silent, eyes riveted on the door as though a creature from a horror movie lurked outside.

"What the hell is that?" Clutch jumped up from the table, spilling his coffee.

The pounding resumed, louder this time, accompanied by the sound of a muffled voice.

"What's that, Joshua?" Missy asked.

I had no answer for her.

"Damn, it's the police!" OP said, and ran out of the room.

"Open the door," Zak said.

"You open it," Clutch said.

"What the heck, you bunch of chickens!" Missy got up and pushed the door open, letting in a cloud of cold fog.

A tall figure stood on the porch, head and shoulders wrapped in heavy woollen scarves that had frozen in place. Shivering uncontrollably, it was encrusted with frost from head to foot, and its breath came out in spurts through the scarves like exhaust from a truck in need of a tune-up. It clamped a suitcase in each mittened hand.

An angry male voice demanded from deep inside the scarves, "Let me in! Can't you see I'm freezing to death? Dagnab it."

The man dropped his suitcases and staggered forward, holding out both arms like Boris Karloff in *The Mummy*. I guided him to a chair, where he

151

collapsed with a groan. Lulu and Stella stepped forward and helped remove his layers of coverings.

OP got over his fright and came back into the kitchen. "No cops?"

No one answered him. Everyone was too interested in this new arrival.

"Who on earth is under all this?" Stella asked, unwrapping another layer.

A pile of scarves and coats dropped to the floor and built up around the chair, forming puddles as the snow thawed. An ancient red face appeared, bespectacled with gold glasses, and shouted, "Are the McKans here, dang it?"

"Yes, the McKans are here," Lulu said, standing back to see this new visitor.

"All of them?" the old man asked.

"Yes, all of them, damn it," said Zak.

"Good. I've come to the right place. Get one of them for me. No, wait, get the oldest. Buster's the only one with brains," he said as he rubbed the tops of his legs with his red hands.

Zak laughed and whispered to me, "The only one with brains? This is my kind of guy, whoever he is."

"Joshua, go get Buster," Olive said.

The unexpected guest sat pulling off his rubber boots, muttering all the time, "Binder-grinder."

Lulu and Olive looked at each other and mouthed the word. "Binder-grinder?"

OP helped pull off the boots, which were tight because of the three pairs of grey woollen socks the old man wore.

"Just about damn well froze to death walking from the airport. I couldn't see a damn-blasted thing and I fell into the ditch a couple of times. Snow must be ten feet deep in there."

Buster came in, and his jaw dropped. "Peewee Smitherman, what in hell are you doing here?"

Peewee stood up and hugged Buster. "I've come to see you guys. How could you leave without me? I wanted to go with you so badly, but no one asked me. You know how long I've known your family? Shoebox, I missed you guys. Kemptville was never the same after you left. And I just about died getting here, and it cost me three months' pension." He covered his eyes with his hand, and I saw a few tears slide down his red cheeks.

Zak patted him on the shoulder and said, "There, there, old-timer. You're safe and warm with us. We'll take care of you now."

I set a mug of coffee in front of Peewee, and he cupped his hands around it and took a sip.

"Ahhh," he said, and managed a smile.

Clutch just rolled his eyes and asked under his breath, "When will this ever end?"

Zak said, "Don't ask me. I only live here."

Buster shrugged his shoulders. "I had no idea about this."

The Halloos couldn't send Peewee back to Ontario, so he moved in along with the others. I carried his suitcases up to his room like a hotel porter and helped him unpack his belongings. His small room had a metal-spring bed with a striped mattress and a stack of army blankets. He hung his clothes in the closet and arranged his toiletries on the chest of drawers. His needs were simple; he reminded me of soldiers I'd seen in barracks in my brief army career before they discharged me for colour blindness.

Zak and Peewee hit it off right away and sat up drinking coffee and swapping stories.

"He's a vet! He blew up those Nazi Huns like I did!" Zak said.

"We were both at the Battle of the Ardennes in January 1945. By the sounds of it, we might have been shooting at the same guys," Peewee said.

"It's funny how killing bonds people," Tobias said, taking notes of the entire goings-on. He was out spending the night, as he often did when he was interviewing the Halloos.

Peewee was happy to be with the McKans and got along with the Halloos just as well. He took a shine to Lulu and followed her around the house, sitting for hours drinking coffee and watching her work in the kitchen.

"What the hell is with this guy?" Winch wanted to know. "Is he making a play for my wife or what?"

This only produced laughs and warnings from the other men. "Better watch that old geezer. He looks like a Valentino."

"Can't you see? He's been a bachelor all his life, and Lulu is like his sister," Missy said.

It was about this time that Stella Halloo and Ruby McKan, who had bossed her way into the kitchen, much to the chagrin of the Halloo women, took a dislike to each other. Harsh words may have been said about the discipline of the children, or maybe there was a comment about how a certain food was cooked, or maybe the cold winter was finally getting to everybody. In any case, rumours spread like wildfire through the house.

Ruby complained to Jack, "Stella has been talking behind my back."

Stella complained to Clutch, "That woman is nothing but trouble. She talks far too much."

Clutch found Jack reading Milton's *Paradise Lost* in a quiet corner of the living room and asked, "Why is Ruby so hard on Stella?"

"Don't ask me," Jack said.

Things soon went from bad to worse. More people were drawn in, and more facts were left out, and there had been few to begin with.

Jack spoke sharply to Zak, who was just waking up from a nap and had no idea what was going on, about his unkindness to Ruby.

Zak greatly resented Jack's tone. "You got the story wrong, Jack. I never complained about Ruby's cooking. Hell, I eat just about anything set in front of me except sushi. I can't stand raw fish."

Stella cried to Lulu, and Lulu went to Winch. Winch also wanted nothing to do with this squabble and misunderstood Lulu. He went and gave Zak hell again.

"Zak, why in hell are you causing all this trouble?" he demanded.

"What trouble? What the hell." Upset, Zak threatened to drive into town and stay at the Occidental Hotel for as long as it took for things to settle down. Lulu talked him out of it.

Peewee got involved, although he had only been there a short while, and cried, "Peace has to be restored in this house. I didn't come all this way to hear quarrelling."

"Who the hell does he think he is?" Clutch wanted to know.

The families were now in a complete uproar. Cold shoulders inside the house mirrored the cold weather outside. The days seemed darker, and people reached for their vitamins to perk themselves up.

"I knew this was going to happen the day they arrived," Zak said. "You can't have this many people living under one roof without trouble. Especially if they're strangers as we are."

"We're all adults," said Missy, throwing up her hands. "Why can't we get along?"

Lulu finally had enough and decided not to let this whirlwind go any further. She instructed the older children to go around the house, shop and barn and tell the adults to meet at three o'clock in the kitchen. Lulu knew the warmth and coziness of the Halloo kitchen had a positive influence on most moods. She baked a large plate of coconut cookies and put the coffee on. Everyone turned up promptly and crowded in—brothers, sisters, aunts, uncles, nieces and nephews—with only the children excused.

Missy and I sat in the back.

"Don't get involved in any of this, Joshua, just let it be," Missy said.

"I hear you, sugar."

When three o'clock came, Jack and Chipper were still in the shop.

"We don't have to go to any meeting. We've got better things to do," they told the teenaged girl that Lulu sent to request their attendance.

While the families waited, Lulu hastily wrote a note, folded it and sent one of the older boys running to deliver it. Almost immediately the two men appeared. They left the shop so fast that neither of them had put on hat or gloves. Jack handed the note back to Lulu with a chastened look on his face and took his seat.

"Sorry, Lulu," he said.

To this day very few people know what Lulu wrote on that piece of paper. There are rumours that she threatened in graphic detail what would happen if they didn't show up immediately. Zak always said it had something to do with Chinese water torture and bamboo slivers. In truth all the note said was "Binder-grinder."

"Must have meant something to them, because it worked," Lulu told me later.

Lulu waited for the room to go quiet before she spoke as the Halloo matriarch. She was intuitive and needed only to shake a person's hand to have their life—good or bad—flash before her eyes.

"Sometimes I hate what I know," she said to Stella.

Her radar was accurate enough that she was careful not to discuss her understanding of one person to another. She couldn't wear a watch because it would stop, speed up or slow down, never telling the correct time. Her jewellery would change colour, and her diamond wedding ring would sparkle as if it had a light inside it.

Winch never really understood Lulu. I heard him tell Tobias, "Either it's her love for me in that wedding ring or the power of her brain flashing in those diamonds."

Lulu had seen this conflict looming long before it happened. Experience had taught her that few people accept advice, especially advice based on intuition. Knowing the arguments were not life-threatening, she'd let them unfold on their own.

Now the kitchen was silent. When a child cried down the hall, Lulu recognized its voice and signalled with a nod for its mother to go and attend it.

"This cold weather is difficult, but it's no reason for this kind of behaviour. I'll get right to the point. One thing I cannot tolerate is harsh words and criticism. Words behind people's backs are destructive and ruin relationships. The weather is a factor but weather comes and goes. Families remain."

Heads nodded in agreement, but a few people kept their eyes averted and gave no indication of agreement or disagreement. They knew she was right but felt certain that they'd done nothing wrong; others were to blame.

There wasn't much else Lulu could say, but she did speak privately and separately with Ruby and Stella. She took Missy along and told her, "You might as well see how to handle these things while you're young."

"Please be civil for the sake of the household, especially for the children. Fighting affects them badly," Lulu told them. She also advised Ruby, "Maybe it would be best if you spent less time in the kitchen."

The men shook hands and forgot about it, but Ruby and Stella were a different story. Their deep dislike wasn't going away.

Peewee had been napping and missed the meeting; as an elder he would have been excused anyway. When he awoke, he thought the battle still raged and said to no one in particular, "This place is just too crazy. I'm going into Dawson for some peace and quiet."

By then it was late evening, and the kitchen was empty. Without asking permission Peewee took the keys off the rack and went out to fire up the old International Harvester. When it was warm, he jumped in—dressed in his slippers, pants and plaid shirt—and drove toward town to find a hotel room. It was common Yukon practice to make a dash from a warm vehicle to a warm building, forgoing the parkas and boots.

He thought, first thing I'll do is have the cook fry me a New York steak with all the trimmings.

Peewee wasn't a good driver. His shaky hands jerked the steering wheel, and the truck drove back and forth across the road. The dashboard fans didn't work, and only an eight-inch-high half moon thawed on the windscreen. As he hunched over, Peewee's neck developed the worst of kinks. Soon he was driving almost blind, snatching quick looks down the road every hundred feet.

Five miles out of Dawson City, Peewee missed a corner and drove over the bank and down into an ice-covered dredge pond. The truck plowed into the deep snow, and despite Peewee's attempts, the powerful four-wheel drive couldn't pull the truck out. It was almost midnight and fifty-four degrees below zero.

Back at the house Clutch and I stoked the wood stoves for the night, and everyone went to bed. We all assumed Peewee was fast asleep and the truck was still in the yard.

Stuck in deep snow on the icy dredge pond, Peewee pounded the steering wheel and cursed under his breath. "Shoebox, dagnab it."

He opened the door, forcing back the snow that was packed to the windows, and stuck out his head to check that the exhaust was flowing clear. He closed the door and wrapped the heavy oil-stained seat blanket around his shoulders. For the next two hours the motor warmed the cab and cleared the windows.

Peewee nodded off to sleep and woke only when the engine gave a cough. It sped up for a minute, coughed again, shuddered and stopped. Peewee tried to restart it until the battery went dead. The fuel gauge registered empty.

The cold crept in immediately; the laws of physics dictated it. The temperature in the cab plummeted. Peewee folded his legs up on the seat and wrapped the dusty blanket tighter around his head and shoulders. Thinking there might be a jerry can of gas in the back, he climbed out, pushed through the deep snow and opened the tailgate. His bare hands stuck to the metal. He climbed up in the box and kicked around in the snow but found nothing. When he stubbed his toe on a spare tire, it hurt all the more because his foot was cold.

"Shoebox!" he yelped.

Back in the cab, his hands and feet ached from the outdoor excursion. He waited another hour and began to tremble violently. It was three o'clock in the morning, and the dredging field was as still and quiet as a moonscape. The cold clouded his mind. Instead of climbing up to the road, he decided to walk through the bush along the edge of the cliffs, thinking it was a shortcut into town. It was a mistake.

I've seen those Ski-Doos and dog teams run over there, he thought. The path should be packed.

Without a hat Peewee had no way to stop the heat loss from his head. His body started to feel excruciating pain. He stopped to rest, but the cold brought on amnesia, and he forgot how long he'd sat. Getting up almost immediately, he began to plow through the snow again. The cold also induced apathy, and Peewee abandoned the urge to warm himself. His blood thickened, his oxygen consumption dropped and he started to hallucinate.

"Moe, Chipper, how did you get out here? Give me a hand, will you?"

As his constricted blood vessels dilated, Peewee felt extremely hot. He tore off his shirt and pants and kicked off his slippers. In his shorts he crawled another hundred yards before lying face down. He just wanted to rest for a while. He didn't get up. Peewee thought of a girl he'd known a long time ago. The moon shone off his bare white shoulders like light reflected off a porcelain doll.

At the house all was quiet. Everyone slept peacefully in their warm beds, unaware of the tragedy unfolding down the road.

OP stood in the kitchen drinking his morning coffee and looking out the window at the vehicles parked in a row in the front yard. Where the International Harvester had sat since late fall he saw only a bare rectangle of ground covered in leaves and last year's grass, surrounded by snow.

Taking a sip, he shouted over his shoulder to anyone within earshot, "Who took the International?"

Clutch came over to the window and nudged OP out of the way to take a look. "I don't know. It was there last night. I remember parking next to it. Maybe someone stole it."

"I wouldn't think so. Someone would have to be crazy to steal that old clunker. They'd have taken Zak's or my truck instead, the keys are even in it," OP said.

It was mid-morning before anyone put together the missing truck and Peewee. It was early afternoon by the time Missy made a few phone calls into town and the Halloos raised the alarm on his behalf.

Moose, the grader operator, phoned around three o'clock. "I see your corn-binder is stuck in a ditch a few miles out of town. I checked, but there's no one in it. I saw tracks heading over to the cliffs."

Four trucks piled with men and snow machines left immediately. The families stood in the kitchen watching them pull out.

"I sure hope Peewee is okay," Ruby said, and started to cry. Stella went over and put her arm around her shoulder.

The truck was easy to find. With sinking hearts the men looked at the trail leading away through the snow.

"Why in hell did he walk off in that direction?" I asked.

No one answered.

While the McKans winched the International back onto the road, Winch, OP and Clutch unloaded the snow machines and roared off, following Peewee's path.

"Hop on with me, Joshua," Clutch yelled over the roar.

We didn't have far to go. In minutes we found Peewee stretched out, face down, with a dusting of fresh snow on his back. His head rested on one arm, and the other arm stretched out in front of him.

We got off as the others drove up and lit up the area with their headlights. Clutch knew Peewee was gone but removed his glove and felt his shoulder anyway.

"It was like touching cold stone," he said later.

Clutch rolled him over. Frost covered his open eyes and eyelashes. His mouth was set in a frozen grimace.

As I walked back to pick up Peewee's clothes, two RCMP officers drove up on their snow machines and took charge.

"Don't touch those clothes or anything else. Thanks for your help, guys, but please back off and let us do our job."

After a quick look about and a conversation with Zak and Clutch, the officers understood what had happened.

"He lived with us for a short while," Clutch told them. "He took a truck into town last night and never made it."

"Inexperience," Zak said.

One officer wrote in a small notebook until his pen froze, then asked if anyone had a pencil. Another took pictures and measurements. Fifty below facilitates quick decision making. The corporal said, "That's all we need. You can move the body now. It's pretty clear what took place here."

We wrapped Peewee in a tarp and loaded him on a sleigh, then towed him back to the highway. A large crowd of curious onlookers and helpers waited on the road. They'd left their trucks running, and the headlights pointed in all directions across the valley, illuminating the hills. Great clouds of exhaust floated above the scene.

Clutch and I drove up the bank and stopped among them. Despite the cold, the onlookers removed their hats while we placed Peewee on a gurney and loaded it into the ambulance. The doors slammed shut. With sirens wailing in a frozen lament, he was sped off to the hospital.

"No need to speed. Nothing's going to help that fellow now," Moose said. "He was stiff as a board."

The next day we hauled cordwood up to the grove of trees above the baseball field and lit a fire to thaw the frozen earth. The melting snow turned to water, and fingers of soot radiated out and flowed down the hill. It took two men two days of digging and two cords of wood before Lulu inspected and gave a nod of approval. The grave was deep enough.

Zak and I set about making the coffin.

"Thanks for your help, Joshua," Zak said.

In the workshop OP showed me where he'd stored a stack of oak planks above the radial arm saw. We inspected every board and checked it for flaws and grain. Working late into the night and the next day, we hand-planed each piece so it looked as though it were machine milled.

"We have to do Peewee justice, Joshua. He was a vet who fought so that every one of us could be free. He deserves a nice final resting place," Zak said.

At the head of the coffin we cut the pins first and then the tails for the dovetail joints. At the foot we cut the tails first and then the pins. This was something Zak's grandfather had taught him to do.

"It dates back to the old country, where it signified change. You come into this world of change and when you leave it's still changing. It will always be changing. No one has any control over it," Zak said. As an afterthought he added, "I wish that damn fascist Hitler had realized that. It would have saved everyone a lot of trouble."

We dadoed in the bottom and dropped the top lid into a rabbet. The fits were so precise that the box would hold water. Zak heated a can of beeswax with a plumber's torch and rubbed it into the wood to bring out a rich reddish brown. The children and women hand-polished the wood for hours. The men couldn't; they choked up.

The McKans carried the coffin into the living room and laid it on two chairs. Lulu brought in a brightly woven Hopi blanket she'd bought in Arizona and laid it on the bottom. Over that she tucked in a pillow in a case embroidered with colourful birds and flowers. We placed Peewee's glasses and personal effects on the side.

The ambulance brought his body at mid-afternoon. He had been washed and wrapped in clean linen. When the attendants carried the stretcher into the kitchen, a path opened through the human bodies packed throughout the house. Winch and Clutch placed Peewee in the coffin and covered him snugly with the blanket so that his head rested on the pillow.

"That will keep him warm now," Missy said.

Lulu wouldn't let the men use power tools to fasten the coffin lid. "Have some respect. How would you like someone drilling over you when you're dead?"

Clutch was partial to power tools, but the men did as told and used a #8 Robertson screwdriver.

The McKan brothers carried Peewee up the hill and cried every step of the way. The Halloo men followed, ready to help if anyone should slip.

The weather had been warming since dawn, and it was now a balmy ten degrees below zero. The sky was cloudy and overcast, and the snow became slush where people walked. A gentle wind swayed the tops of the trees.

Missy read prayers. The McKan men chanted "Requiem Aeternam Dona Eis, Domine." Then they lowered Peewee into the ground and, after everyone had paid their respects, shovelled the earth over him. Tobias had painted a flywheel headstone from a D8 Cat in sunburst yellow, and Clutch had used welding rod bead to write on it in script, "Harold (Peewee) John Smitherman. Soldier, Friend. b. 1885 d. 1970. Came from Ontario and froze in the Klondike."

After we filled the grave, Winch, Clutch and OP stood on one side with shovels in hand. The McKans—Buster, Moe, Jack and Chipper—stood on the other side with picks in hand.

"It's too bad that old fellow came all this way just to freeze and die," Winch said.

"Peewee didn't have an ounce of fat on him," Chipper said. "He could have frozen on a cold night in Jamaica."

"It's not so bad," Jack said. "Peewee was with the people he grew up with and loved."

The women had prepared a meal, and it was past midnight when the last guest left for home.

"It was a nice funeral. His friends were here, and you can't hope for anything better than that except to die in your sleep," Missy said as we washed the dishes.

"I liked Peewee," Lulu said. "From the moment I shook his hand, I liked him. He was a gentleman."

"Binder-grinder," Zak said.

Saved by the Tuba

Forgiveness is not a well-developed virtue, as yet, among the good citizens of the Yukon. People think that in order to survive in the Klondike they shouldn't forget, and that to forgive is to forget. But even forgettable matters never really go away and instead get woven into the warp and woof of families and communities.

In the spring, after a difficult winter living together under one sprawling roof with their Halloo hosts, the McKans started to build new homes on the property they'd bought next door. First they hauled in four trailers to set up temporary residences. Then they excavated and poured four concrete footings. Next they built the foundations and started framing the houses.

I watched this process with interest and offered my advice when I thought it might be helpful. The four McKan brothers knew a good deal about plumbing, heating and electrical work but they didn't know much about carpentry. They hired the twins Orville and Peter Buttery-Byrds, who quickly sized up the McKans' inexperience and took over the job, working at their own discretion and leisure.

"We always start work at ten and take a two-hour lunch break. We need that extra hour for a snooze. We work hard, you know," Orville said. Peter stood behind him and nodded in agreement. Peter was the silent one, almost like Harpo Marx without the horn. Orville was talkative, too talkative according to Buster McKan, who told me, "If he would just keep quiet and work, that's all I'd ask."

Orville and Peter snoozed on the grass when it was sunny and under a finished roof when it rained.

They were okay carpenters who swore they didn't need measuring tools. Each wore his cap twisted to one side, Orville to the left and Peter to the right.

Orville told me, "We can do all that measurement stuff by eyeball like our father taught us."

"We don't need no stinking lines, levels or squares," added Peter, a man of few words who got right to the point.

Nothing was square or plumb on the buildings.

Both Peter and Orville were a few inches over five feet, and their wives were even shorter. Their children were taller. "Must be all those chemicals in their breakfast cereal that's making them grow like that," Orville said.

Every day Orville's wife, Matilda, and Peter's wife, Jean, a midwife who was never out of work in the Klondike, drove out together from Dawson with picnic baskets full of lunch. Plates of pickles, cheese and cold cuts were laid out on a checkered cloth along with bowls of potato salad and jelly for dessert. Their large assortment of children ran back and forth from play to the food, breathlessly grabbing mouthfuls and running off again. They climbed over the construction site like goats in a tree, and one scrambled to the peak of a roof. Lunch was interrupted to chase her down.

"You're going to fall and break your silly neck," Matilda yelled. As a former gymnast she'd encouraged her children in the sport but didn't like them climbing over buildings.

Orville had to get up and order the kid down himself. He shouted, pointing a piece of celery, "Workman's compensation will never cover your fall from there."

After the men ate and snoozed, Matilda and Jean would visit with the McKans and the Halloos until quitting time.

"I don't mind them visiting once in a while, but every day of the week those kids are just too much," Lulu told Winch on a Friday night after work when everyone had gone home.

It took the better part of a month and a bit more money than they wanted to spend before the McKan brothers' business sense kicked in and they supervised Orville and Peter better.

"We have to get going, guys. Winter's coming on, and we can't laze around."

"You can't shorten our lunch break. We're going to the union," Orville cried.

"This isn't a union job. One hour is enough," Buster said, frustrated. "And please get here on time."

The Buttery-Byrds brothers complained and twisted their hats to more of an angle but began turning up on time and taking shorter lunch breaks.

"They hardly have time to finish dessert," Matilda complained.

Jack asked me, "Would you help us and take over the job, Joshua? We can't supervise what we don't know, but you're a carpenter."

I wanted to get back into construction. I'd had enough of garage work, and the smell of gasoline was getting to me. Brian, the garage manager, offered to raise my wages if I stayed. "I'll give you fifty cents an hour more. That should be enough to keep you here."

"Thanks, Brian, but I'm going."

I told the McKans, "I'll build for you on one condition. I want to bring my pal Arnold over from Burwash to help. With the four of us banging nails, we'll be sure to get most of the work done before freeze-up."

Arnold was glad to come over as things were slow in Burwash. He brought his wife and kids and moved into the Halloo house down the hall from Missy and me.

It turned out all the Buttery-Byrds brothers needed was a lead hand to get them going. They were never late and always the first to start after lunch. They even let themselves be talked into using a line and level to plumb and square things up.

We were able to frame and clad all four houses to the weather by the first of October.

It was about that time that Clutch and Ruby ran off to live in Mayo. The first Missy and I heard of the disaster was Stella, clutching a note to her chest, screaming and wailing in the kitchen like a wounded grizzly. She ran out of the house and collapsed on the front lawn. Her children gathered around and tried to help, but she buried her head in her arms and sobbed all the more. Lulu and Olive came out, helped Stella to her feet and carried her back into the house with her legs collapsing every few steps. Her face was streaked with tears, and she sobbed incoherently. Her children sobbed along with her, and Olive and Lulu wiped away their own tears.

Jack McKan was shingling the roof of his house when his unsuspecting brother Moe handed him a note that he'd found propped against the Tabasco sauce bottle on the kitchen table. Jack put down his tools, tucked a leg under him to sit on the slope and glanced over the way to the scene on the Halloos' lawn as he tore open the envelope. He read the contents and understood what the ruckus was about. He let the wind take the note from his hand and without a word walked up to the roof's peak. Without hesitation he threw himself off onto the farm equipment parked below.

Moe screamed in disbelief and grabbed his head. He ran to the ladder, slid down and ran around to the side of the house.

"Oh my God! Oh my God!" he yelled.

Jack lay face up on the tractor, his body suspended awkwardly on the steering wheel and the metal seat. Blood dripped from his mouth, his eyes were glazed and he breathed rapidly. He waved his arms aimlessly in the air as if trying to get up.

By the time the ambulance arrived, half the neighbourhood had gathered around to help. Carefully they braced Jack, lifted him off the machinery and laid him on the ground.

"Careful, his back might be broken," I said.

The paramedics arrived and moved him to a stretcher and into the ambulance. Halfway to Dawson City, a Trans North helicopter circled once, landed on the highway and whisked Jack off to Whitehorse. There he was stabilized, then flown to Edmonton and placed in intensive care. His condition was listed as critical.

One of the children picked up the note that had blown off the roof and gave it to Lulu. She read it and put it in her apron pocket.

Everyone was spitting mad. Winch said, "When we get our hands on those two, there'll be hell to pay."

It was as though a bomb had gone off. No one had suspected any such relationship existed between Ruby and Clutch. Stella's intuition had told her something was up, but she would never have guessed this. Even Lulu had missed it.

"It's so farfetched I couldn't imagine it," she told Missy and me as people gathered in the kitchen.

"We're going to Mayo now!" Winch yelled, "Get in the truck, OP."

Lulu grabbed me by the arm. "Go with them, Joshua. I'm afraid there's going to be violence."

I jumped into the truck before Winch and OP got in.

"Where the hell do you think you're going?" Winch growled. "Get out!"

"Lulu told me to get in," I said.

Winch growled again and slid behind the wheel. OP got in on the passenger side. There was barely enough room, never mind me sandwiched between them with my shoulders compressed together. I couldn't move my arms. I had to sit sideways, with my back to OP and facing Winch, which wasn't pleasant as he kept muttering to himself.

Winch sped down the highway, throwing up gravel on sharp curves. I could see the speedometer going over eighty miles an hour. We roared into Mayo in record time. Clutch and Ruby had rented one half of a Yukon Housing Corporation duplex. A few questions at the store, and we had directions. When we knocked, Clutch opened the door. OP grabbed him in a headlock, and both men fell into the kitchen. OP was on top, squeezing the life out of Clutch's head.

"Why did you do that to Stella?" OP asked, strengthening his grip.

"Murmmmpfh," said Clutch.

Winch and I took hold of OP and pulled him back. I was grateful for Winch's help. I'd have been unable to handle OP alone.

Clutch was still on all fours. Without looking up he raised one arm and said, "Okay, okay. Let's talk." His voice was nasal, and blood ran from his nose down his beard and onto the floor. He picked himself up, covering his nose with his hand, and said, "No fighting, okay?"

Ruby sat at the kitchen table and didn't move. Winch ignored her and pushed Clutch into the living room, grabbing a towel off the sink and handing it to him as they went by. He directed Clutch toward the couch and pulled up a kitchen chair to sit in front of him. He waved OP off to the other side of the room, and with his knees touching Clutch's so they looked like two walruses standing belly to belly, he said, "We have to talk, little brother. You have totally ruined everything—your marriage, kids, home and family. What the hell were you thinking? And how long has this been going on? You've embarrassed the whole family. Halloos don't do this kind of thing. We're family people!" By the time he finished, Winch was yelling and sweating.

Clutch started to cry. Between wipes at his nose and tears, he said, "I just love Ruby so much. I've never been so much in love with anyone in all my life."

"What about Stella and the kids? You love them, don't you?" Winch said.

Clutch didn't answer. Sobbing, he looked down at the floor as though he hoped the answers to all his problems would appear written in the linoleum pattern.

"Let me tell you something about love, Clutch. If it hurts this many people, it isn't love. You're a fool. You screwed up badly. I never thought my brother would be so stupid. If you had problems, you should have come to us," Winch said, pointing to himself and OP.

"You could at least have talked to Lulu. She would have helped out," OP said.

The mood was starting to soften. Winch was beginning to feel sorry for Clutch and Ruby.

"It wasn't anything I could talk about. It just happened," Clutch said.

Ruby said, "I'm sorry for this trouble, but Jack and I had been on the skids for the longest time. I don't know what happened, but Clutch and I just hit it off at a time when we both needed somebody," Ruby said.

Winch pointed his meaty index finger at her. "Shut up! You sound like a lovesick schoolgirl. There's no good reason for what happened. Too many people have been hurt! Your family can deal with you. We'll deal with our own."

Then Winch realized Ruby didn't know about Jack's injuries. He got up and sat down at the table across from her and said, "Jack took a fall off the roof and is in hospital in Edmonton. They flew him out."

Ruby's eyes widened. A stricken look filled her face. "Oh my God," she said, "Jack has been injured? What about the children? Who's looking after the children?"

"He jumped off the roof when he read your letter," OP said. He had no sympathy for Ruby, and if it wasn't for Winch, he would have said more.

"You two pack up and come with us. We won't solve anything here, and Jack and the kids need Ruby," Winch said.

Clutch nodded in agreement, and he and Ruby went and got their stuff.

Ruby sat between Winch and Clutch and cried all the way home. OP and I drove Clutch's truck behind them, and I was grateful to have more room in the cab.

"The McKans will blame us for this," OP said, "and sure as hell the Halloos will blame the McKans."

"Maybe it will just blow over."

"Like hell it will," OP said, and we drove the rest of the way in silence.

Winch dropped Ruby off at her trailer. She looked lonely standing there, suitcase in hand. The curtains on the window moved, and before he drove away, the children ran out and hugged their mom.

Clutch walked into the cold kitchen, empty except for Stella. Everyone had cleared out and distanced themselves. I followed him in and went upstairs. Stella sat at the table and didn't look up. Her face was red and swollen from crying. The wood stove was unlit; Stella had on a heavy sweater with a well-used hanky tucked up her sleeve. Clutch took off his hat but didn't remove his coat. He sat down.

"How could you do this to the children and me?" she asked in an exasperated tone. Her face was full of hurt as she looked him in the eye.

"I don't know. It just happened," Clutch said.

They sat in silence for a few minutes. Then Stella got up and went to her room.

Stella took Clutch back for the sake of the children, though she never fully trusted him again for the rest of their life together. She told Missy, "My kids need a dad. I can't throw him out."

Ruby went to Edmonton to see Jack. He eventually recovered but walked with a limp and had backaches when the weather was damp. He also bore a crescent scar on the back of his head from hitting the tractor's stick shift. Jack forgave Ruby; he was too much in love with her to do otherwise.

"Be a man. Kick her out," OP advised.

"I can't. The children would be heartbroken," Jack said.

Between Stella and Ruby there was serious tension. The families tried to keep them at a distance.

Ruby and Jack, like Stella and Clutch, went on with their lives as best they could. But in cases like this, parts of marriages are lost, some for a time and others forever.

"You cannot unring a bell," Zak told me sadly, "so make sure as hell you don't mess up in the first place. There has to be a law of the Yukon in there somewhere."

Music was the one thing that refreshed and calmed our souls. The Halloos kept on with their regular jam sessions in the barn, and the McKans were also a family of musicians. In the early evenings they would gather in a trailer or, if the weather was warm, inside one of the framed houses. Missy and I would sit in and listen, clapping in time.

The McKan women played autoharps, violins and cellos. The men played brass instruments and guitars. The kids clogged while the parents played. The family sang songs their relatives had sung back in the Appalachian Mountains generations ago before they moved north and settled in Ontario.

"It's old-timey music, the sound of the North American settlers and one ancestor of today's rock 'n' roll," Tammy said, drawing a bow across her violin.

They also had an old, discoloured, dented tuba that they hauled out on occasion.

"Great-great-grandpappy Captain Isaiah McKan was a bandmaster in the Confederate Army," Buster said, and proudly showed a soldered metal patch on the tuba's horn that had repaired a Yankee bullet hole.

"Grandpappy never did play the tuba after being shot at. Our relatives say he took up the Bible and church organ. He felt safer there, since no one ever shot up a church," Buster said.

"Well, not back then, they didn't," Chipper said.

"Grandpappy thought the tuba saved him once and he didn't want to tempt fate again. We have a studio picture of him in his uniform with his finger stuck through the bullet hole. It was right by where his head went. He still looked concerned."

The McKans decided that they had to excise the affair, as they collectively referred to it from that time on, by continuing their association with the Halloos.

"Music is a good place to start. No need to talk, just play," Moe said.

"I'm staying home," Ruby said.

"I'm staying too," Jack said.

One evening a while later, as I listened in to the Halloos practising down in the barn, there was a knock at the door.

"Someone must be awful polite to knock before entering a barn. Will you get that, Joshua?" Winch asked.

I did. In walked three of the McKan brothers and their wives, holding their instruments.

There was an awkward silence. A few people looked down to avoid eye contact.

Ruby and Jack, like overdue library books, were conspicuous by their absence.

Buster spoke first. "We've been listening and wondering if we might join you."

"We played a little back home with the local musicians," Holly said with a hopeful smile.

After another moment of silence, Winch cleared his throat. "Do you know any Blood, Sweat & Tears?"

Smiles broke out, and a sense of relief filled the room.

"Play them all the time," Moe said.

"Fleetwood Mac?"

"Our favourite."

"What's Bo Diddley's real name?"

"Ellas Otha Bates."

"That was a tough one," OP muttered to me.

"Jethro Tull?" Clutch asked.

"Never," Tammy said.

"Neither do we," Winch said. "I don't play the flute and can't stand on one leg too long on account of my weight."

"Picture a three-hundred-pound stork in bib jeans," OP said.

"Who wrote Manfred Mann's 'Blinded by the Light'?" Clutch asked.

"Springsteen," said Chipper.

"Which one?" OP asked.

"The Boss," said Moe.

"What are the lyrics to the Kingsmen's 'Louie Louie'?" Winch asked.

"No one knows, not even J. Edgar Hoover, the head of the FBI," Molly said.

"We agree. It's a secret of the universe," Winch said. "We glued our ears to that record for hours. It's unintelligible at any speed."

"Even backward," Clutch added.

"Okay, let's have a vote. Are the McKans in or out? Joshua, you count the yeas and nays," Clutch said.

Everyone in the barn put their hands up. The McKans voted for themselves. Clutch went through the trouble of counting them.

"It's unanimous. You're in," he said.

From the start there was goodwill and co-operation as they made music. A new bond developed, and the band sounded pretty good. The two sets of brothers and the McKan wives could read and write music. It was impressive to listen to them discuss chord arrangements.

Molly, Holly, and Tammy added strings to Electric Light Orchestra and Rolling Stones classics. The men added horns to Chicago tunes.

Stella was happy that Ruby stayed home. It would have been too much if she'd shown up. Stella might have asked her to leave.

In May the Yukon territorial government sent an official letter requesting a quote from the Halloos to provide entertainment at the Commissioner's Ball that was held every year in Dawson.

"That's the social event of the year. We would play that for free," Winch said.

"I'd play it just for the steak dinner," Zak said.

"You're not even in the band," OP said.

"Yeah, but I'm your best roadie, and anything you're eating I'm eating as well," Zak said.

Winch had me mail off a quote of fifteen hundred dollars. Days later I got a phone call from someone official-sounding in the Department of Tourism.

"A contract is being mailed. Please sign and return it," he said. "You should also know that this year the GG of Canada is making a special appearance, so we're requesting that band members dress appropriately in suits and ties."

"GG? What the hell is a GG, some kind of horse? Joshua, what is a GG?" OP asked.

"Governor General. GG means the Governor General of Canada, the Queen's representative in this great land of ours. He is going to be there, and they want you to look sharp," I said.

"Great, we're playing for the big shot. I'll put on a tie but no suit," Winch said.

The Mckans were beside themselves. They'd never thought they would perform for such important dignitaries as the Governor General of Canada, the Commissioner of the Yukon and a Member of Parliament.

"It's nothing. The Yukon is full of opportunities like this," Missy said. "Everyone rubs shoulders here. Heck, if the Commissioner was your neighbour, he'd probably come over and borrow your lawn mower."

After a late-night practice just days before the ball, Chipper said, "We have to get a new name. We're a new band and we need a new name."

No one had thought about changing the name, but he was right. It was a new band and it needed a new name.

"Crazy War," Clutch said quickly. "I want to call it Crazy War."

There was an awkward silence. No one agreed with Crazy War.

Then a long night of wearisome argument began.

"Nothing," Chipper said.

"Why would you want to call a musical group Nothing?" Clutch argued, feeling miffed that Crazy War had drawn such a blank.

"Because that is what I believe we are before being created. Nothing, zero, zilch, non-existence," Chipper said.

"Then why don't you call yourself the Nothing Choir if you're going to bring religion into it?" Clutch said, not even trying to hide his annoyance.

"Sounds good to me," I said, being facetious.

Tammy wanted the name Influenced by Lucy. She'd seen every Lucille Ball TV show that had been produced, and Lucy was a great influence in her life. She'd dyed her hair red and curled it like Lucy's. No one paid attention to her suggestion either.

I spoke up and suggested the band's name should be My Dog Angst. We could draw Angst's picture on the front of the bass drum.

"I like The Myooz. It's a play on the word 'muse,' meaning 'to think thoughtfully," Moe said.

"It's going to be a long night," I said.

And it was. We sat up until three in the morning. Some left after signing a sheet of paper allowing others to vote for them by proxy. Finally they agreed on Saved by the Tuba either because they were too tired to continue or the name really sounded good to them.

"I like being called a tuba," OP said.

"I hate it," Clutch said. "No energy to that at all. How can I play music and be named after an instrument that has so little to do with rock 'n' roll? It's ridiculous."

Under the moonlight they marched in a tired row up to the house to get whatever sleep they could before morning.

The Commissioner's Ball was held in the historic Palace Grand Theatre in downtown Dawson City. As chairman of the Klondike Visitors Association, Maude introduced the Right Honourable Governor General of Canada, Lyon Beaverstock, the Commissioner of the Yukon, Robert Service Jack, Member of Parliament Robb Henderson, Members of the Yukon Legislative Assembly Ted Planner and Imogene Hogg and the Commissioner of the RCMP, Sterling R. Uptown. Everyone had gone to great expense to dress in the finest 1898 period costumes.

I helped carry the equipment in, being careful not to mess my tails and top hat. As I was setting up the stage, the McKans arrived, though Ruby and Jack had stayed home. They took the event seriously. The men wore tuxedos, ties and crisply starched paisley print shirts with matching cummerbunds. The Halloos wore their new Round House–brand overalls with bright red bow ties on robin's egg blue shirts.

The groups looked each other up and down.

Moe said what everyone was thinking. "Who dressed you?"

"Our thoughts exactly," said Clutch. "I never thought we'd be playing with a bunch of penguins."

"And we never thought we'd be playing with the cast from *Hee Haw*," Tammy said.

"But by the by, your women look stunning," OP said.

The McKan gals had been decked out by the Halloo women and Maude in their finest designs.

"You'd have to go to Paris to find the equal of these creations," Maude said.

They all wore identical full-length empire line dresses with puffy sleeves made of the same material as their husband's shirts. The only difference was that the Halloo women wore white runners with knee-high woollen stockings, and the McKan women wore sensible black low-heeled pumps with no socks.

Saved by the Tuba set up on the stage where The Frantic Follies played for the summer tourists. During the meal the band played light background music, but as soon as the speeches concluded and the tables were cleared away, Winch grabbed the microphone and asked in his booming voice, "Are you ready to rock 'n' roll in the land of the midnight sun?"

A resounding "Yeah!" came back from the two hundred guests cramming the dance floor. Then another single "Yeah!" followed.

Someone was out of sync.

"I can't hear you!" Winch yelled.

There was another loud "Yeah!" followed by another solitary "Yeah!"

"Who the hell is that?" Winch wanted to know and shielded his eyes so he could look out into the audience.

Zak stood up and waved from the back of the room. He had gotten his steak, and yelled across the floor, "I'm eating."

"Then eat, don't yell," Winch said. He roared again to the crowd, "I still can't hear you!"

This time the "Yeah!" almost took the roof off the building and could be heard all the way down the street in the Flora Dora Café. Then The Tubas launched into "Born to be Wild" by Steppenwolf. No one could resist, not even the kitchen help, who abandoned their work and jumped onto the dance floor.

The wife of the Governor General never suspected in all their years of marriage that her spouse could dance. He performed the Swim, the Monkey and the Twist with reckless abandon. Nothing was outside his repertoire; he commanded the dance floor, whirling and twirling as if a dervish spirit had been born into him. He jumped higher in the air than ever before and made moves that only an upper-middle-class white man from Forest Hill in Toronto could perform. His wife laughed and took pictures.

"I'll blackmail him," she shouted over the music.

On stage, watching the Governor General dance, Moe shouted to Clutch, "I'm convinced that the air in this part of the world makes people become their true inner selves."

Clutch thought the Governor General was just another party animal.

While the band took a break, Chipper sent me out to the truck to fetch the tuba. He pulled up a chair front and centre onstage, adjusted the mike and played the most soulful rendition of "Stairway to Heaven." Some say there were tears mixed with the thunderous applause that greeted the last note. Chipper politely bowed and left the stage.

"Civil war meets Led Zep," Moe said. "Odd combination."

From that time on, the band was never allowed to end an evening without a rendition of that song on the tuba.

The evening was a success. The Governor General thanked each and every one of the Tubas personally. "You guys are great. If you lived in Ottawa, I'd have you at all my affairs."

Zak asked him, "Does this mean we're getting the Order of Canada? I sure hope so. I should have got one for what I did at Dieppe."

The Governor General smiled at Zak as though he'd heard a thousand similar requests before.

It was a happy evening for the Halloos and the McKans. There were hugs and handshakes all around. Hugs for the men at least. The Halloo brothers didn't hug women, but shook their hands.

"Grandpappy McKan would be proud of our music," Molly said on the early morning ride back home.

"Yes," Lulu said. "And I think that old Civil War soldier turned preacher-man would be proud of people getting along even after a bell has been rung."

"A bell can be unrung," said Winch.

"Yes sir," said Lulu.

Golden Amnesia

The man woke face down. His head rested on a rock, and he could smell damp earth. He groaned and rolled over onto his back. When he lifted himself up by his elbows, his head spun; there was blood on the rock. Rubbing his forehead, he felt a painful bump, and his hand came away bloody. His long johns had soaked up the moisture from the ground. A dog sat beside him, offering a paw and whimpering. Feeling nauseous, he leaned over to one side and vomited.

When he looked around, all he saw was bush. He didn't know where he was, what he was doing or why he was lying here. He struggled to his feet, but dizziness overcame him, and he fell over. He tried to think. The coolness of the soil felt good on his face.

He cried out loud, "What is this? Where am I?"

But there was no answer, and the sound of his question faded into the wilderness.

The sun was setting, and the air was cooling. He didn't understand what he was supposed to do; he was paralyzed by his ignorance. Not remembering confused him.

Hesitantly he walked into the bush, and the dog followed. Before he realized it, he'd lost his way back to his belongings.

"Where are we?" he asked the dog.

The dog sat, tongue out, panting, and offered his paw again.

He needed to rest. He found shelter under a wide spruce tree and covered himself with a mound of fallen needles for warmth. He was unable to sleep, and the sounds in the night made him anxious. The dog curled up and slept peacefully. Other than an occasional woof and growl, he didn't seem concerned.

When dawn broke, dew covered the ground, and he shivered uncontrollably. Hours later the sun rose, and he stood in its rays until the warmth revived him. He drank water from the creek, but there was nothing to eat.

The first day he picked rosehips and his stomach churned and growled after he'd eaten them. The black and white husky had two canvas saddlebags strapped to his back. Dried rice and beans stuffed one bag, and the other held tins of sardines and butter. He dumped the tins and dry food on the ground. The dog sniffed and licked at the pile of rice and decided it wasn't for him. The man kept the smaller bags that the beans and rice came in. He left the satchels strapped on the dog.

As days went by, he included roots and ant larvae in his diet. He was hungry and cold all the time. He bent saplings to the ground and tied willow branches together for a shelter.

As he wandered, the dog followed. The woods were full of grouse and squirrels, and he hunted them with rocks and sticks. He caught grayling in the shallow of the streams. He ate the meat raw.

The man lost his body fat, and his ribs started to show. His hair and beard grew, and his long johns tore and went black with dirt. His stocking feet were cut and bruised and the nails torn and cracked. Rain poured from the sky, soaking him, and his fingers and toes lost their feeling from the cold. He would lie in a shelter, rubbing his sore limbs, and on occasion he would curl up and not move for days.

On a hillside, he found the carcass of a moose that wolves had brought down. A lone fox ran off as he approached. The dog chased him, but the fox disappeared into the woods.

The wolves had stripped the carcass clean, but there was still flesh on the head and neck. He found a sharp rock and sawed the meat off. The dog clamped down on mouthfuls of hide and pulled hungrily to chew them off.

The man salvaged a piece of hide and draped it over his shoulders; it shed the rain and gave him warmth. At another kill he took more hide and tied it around his feet. He camped near the kill, and that night the wolf pack returned. They caught his scent and circled where he lay. The dog stood as close as possible, and the man threw rocks to protect himself.

In the far distance he saw a billowing column of grey smoke and ash. Curiosity drew him closer. The trees and floor of the forest were ablaze, and he could feel the heat. He sought out smaller fires along the perimeter. The fire burned his hand when he touched it; this was a strange animal, and it fascinated him. As he poked with a stick, the wind began to howl and the flames picked up, forcing him back. It's alive like the wolves, he thought. He couldn't control the wolves, but he could control fire.

He camped near the blaze. Its warmth and light gave him comfort, and staring into the flickering flames relaxed him. When he had fire, the wolves wouldn't come near. Feeling confident he answered the wolves' howls with screaming bellows of his own. The wolves went silent.

Around this time he spotted two men who called out loudly to each other and looked around, pointing to a sheet of paper covered in lines. He never considered that there might be others; he'd thought he was alone. He grabbed the dog and hid in the bush, and the men walked past. At the same time he saw a noisy thing drone across the sky and heard other sounds that weren't forest noises.

The leaves were full on the trees, and the berries were ripe. He built a more permanent shelter and foraged for food. He walked into a narrow valley blanketed in dense willow. On one side was an overgrown cabin with a caved-in roof and trees growing inside it, and on the other side a creek flowed.

He cautiously approached the cabin. A broken table was on its side, and rusted pots lay scattered about. Fastened to the wall was a bed frame, and on the frame lay a skeleton, its bones bleached white and its skull grinning a toothy smile. He backed out. He comprehended death and recognized his own mortality.

Bright yellow rocks of different sizes had spilled from a tin on the cabin floor. They looked like good throwing rocks, so he put these in his rice bag. He built a ring of stones and made a fire. He sat beside it until midnight, singing to himself and calling out to the one who lay in the cabin.

In the morning he found more of the yellow stones in the creek. He filled his sack and the dog's satchel with them.

On the way back to his camp the dog disappeared. Although he looked everywhere, he couldn't find him. He thought the other animals had taken him away. The loss saddened him, and he slept more fitfully without the dog to protect him.

A few days later he spotted the wolves in a clearing. They held their tails high in the air and ran waving them like flags. They were chasing something into the trees; they were on the hunt.

The arrival of cooler weather drew the man to the lower part of the valley, where it was warmer. What was that sound? He turned his head to listen, and his spine snapped noisily near his neck.

Again he heard the sound in the distance and said out loud, "Gun shots. Hunters."

He was back. He remembered.

The Forgettable Gold

My living at Rock Creek after Missy and I got married helped Zak and me become better friends. We drank coffee and talked about his life and my life back in New Mexico, where I was born. I asked him how he'd met his Halloo nephews.

"How I met them is a good story, and I will tell it to you and another one I think you will find interesting. Why don't you call your friend Tobias and have him sit in? He's always interested in Klondike history, and I'll tell these stories only once."

Next time I got to town, I phoned Tobias. When his mother answered, I said, "Hello, Mrs. Godwit, it's Joshua. Is Tobias around?"

"Yes, he is, dear, but I'm afraid he has had some bad news."

"What's that?"

"Flora, his girlfriend from university, wrote telling him she has a new boyfriend. He's locked himself in his room for two days and won't come out. He won't eat, not even the cobbler I made especially for him. It's his favourite."

"Do you want me to come over?"

"He might not want to talk, but you can try. His father has no idea what to say to him."

"No father in history has known what to say to a broken-hearted son. Why would Mr. Godwit be any different?"

As soon as I'd picked up Missy's dry cleaning at Shrinky Luc's and put gas in the truck, I went over and Mrs. Godwit let me in. I knocked on the bedroom door and called, "Tobias, it's me, Joshua."

"Come in," a weary voice said.

His room was airless and dark; it took my eyes a few seconds to adjust. Tobias lay on the bed covered with a blanket and facing the wall. He didn't move.

I pulled up the blind and opened the window, trying not to cough. "It's a little stale in here, Tobias."

Stinky was more like it. I removed a sock with the tips of my fingers to sit on a chair by the desk.

"I heard you had some bad news."

"Good news, bad news, whatever it is. She took up with another fellow, a classmate of mine."

He rolled over and faced me.

"That's too bad."

"What really burns me is that I should have seen it coming. Flora and my so-called friend were spending too much time studying together."

I couldn't think of anything else to say so I told him about Zak's invitation to try to cheer him up.

"Zak is telling his life history, and you're invited to listen in. He doesn't mind if you take notes. We start tomorrow evening out at Rock Creek," I said.

"I'll try to make it by seven."

He rolled over to face the wall again.

On the way out I told his mom, "I think he'll be okay. He just needs a little time."

"Oh, I hope so," she said. "Sit down Joshua, and I'll get you a bowl of cobbler and a glass of milk."

It was pretty good cobbler.

The next evening Tobias arrived at seven o'clock. He was pale and not in a good mood, but at least he was out of that smelly room.

We filled our coffee cups and claimed a quiet corner of the living room.

"Joshua," Zak said, "you asked me how I met my nephews. I didn't know the Halloos were my relatives when I first heard about an obnoxious family of bullies living at Rock Creek. It was a few days later that we had a personal encounter outside the old federal administration building. Three men were walking abreast down the boardwalk, daring anyone to step out in front of them. They tried to force me onto the muddy street. I'm less than half the size of any of them, but I stopped them dead in their tracks and gave my best steely glare. I looked them up and down and said, 'Well, then, what have we here, a spate of rudeness?'

"'We aren't rude,' OP said, towering over me.

"'I only call them as I see them,' I said.

"'Move, runt, or we'll move you,' Winch said.

"'I'll have your guts for garters if you talk to me once more like that,' I snarled back. I could tell by their shifty eyes they were bullies and wanted no part of me."

"I saw you that day," I said. "I looked up the street from the garage and thought, that little guy is going to get crushed. I was surprised when they stepped aside and let you pass between them."

"Walking between their bellies was like walking through the Khyber Pass, but they knew I meant business," Zak said.

"That's the truth," Clutch shouted from the kitchen, listening in.

"A month later their mother, my niece Alice, wrote me a letter saying, 'My boys have left for the Yukon and not on the best of terms with their father and me. If you see them, please give them my love and tell them to write or phone collect. And please watch out for them.'

"I laughed all the way out to Rock Creek. How the hell did I wind up with these numbskulls for relations?"

Clutch called from the kitchen, "Please don't call us numbskulls."

"OP recognized me as I drove up and ran into the house to get his brothers, who were eating lunch. As I got out of the car, I could hear them shouting, 'That guy is here!'

"'What guy is that?'

"'You know, the one you thought was the kung fu master, the one who wanted our guts for garters.'

"I could hear someone choking on his food. Then the screen door flew open, and out walked the three of them into the yard. They looked like linebackers for the Hamilton Tiger Cats. Their women stood back on the step and peered over their shoulders. I leaned on the front of my truck, real casual-like.

"'Look, we don't want any trouble,' Winch said, taking the checkered cloth tucked into the front of his bib overalls to wipe bits of a corncob from his face and beard.

"'I'm not looking for trouble,' I said in my quietest calming voice."

"You sounded like a cowboy hero from a classic western movie," OP said.

"'I've come out to see my dumb-ass nephews as per their mother Alice's instructions,' I said.

"'Uncle Zak!' the women screamed, rushing past their men to smother me in hugs and kisses.

"That was how we met. The brothers apologized profusely the entire time I was there. I told them about their mother's letter, and they said, 'We'll phone.'

"A year later Dawson City flooded in the spring, and my cabin was damaged. Lulu invited me to live with them at Rock Creek. I've been here ever since."

"Did you ever have any luck finding gold?" I asked.

"It's funny you should ask that, because I did and I didn't. I'll tell you the story. You might not believe it, but it's as true as the day I was born."

Zak pointed to his forehead. "See this scar? That's what it's all about."

Tobias was writing so fast I thought his paper would tear. He seemed in a better mood.

"Spring came early to the Yukon in 1959, and the river ice moved out sooner than usual. I built a sixteen-foot clinker boat in my yard and bought a nine-horse outboard kicker. Then I went up the Yukon past the mouth of the Stewart River, carrying two months' worth of supplies—flour, raisins, sugar, rice and lard—with a dog named Big Bopper that I'd borrowed from Dot and Nat Duffy for protection and packing."

"Big Bopper as in the song 'Chantilly Lace?'" Tobias asked.

"One and the same. He was a pup of Nat's black husky, Piedoe, and a female lead dog owned by the famous dogsled mail carrier Percy de Wolfe. He was the biggest dog I'd ever seen, with ears as thick as a phone book, but he was good-natured. That dog epitomized the saying 'man's best friend.' And smart! When it was high noon, he would stop whatever he was doing, sit down and wait to be fed. I could set my watch by him. In fact I did set my watch by him a couple of times. Half the year the dog was wrong because he didn't figure in the time change, but everyone adjusted anyway.

"At first Nat didn't want to loan him and said, 'Big Bopper goes every-where with Dot and me. Who will sit between us when we go for a drive?'

"I said, 'Look, Nat, I only want to borrow him, not keep him. I'll be back in a few months.'

"He finally agreed, but the day we left, Nat looked so upset that I thought he was going to jump into the boat and come with us.

"'Look after him for me, will you, Zak,' he shouted from the shore.

"I waved to reassure him. Big Bopper barked happily then we rounded the bend and Dawson disappeared from sight."

"Nat loves his dogs," Tobias said. "When he lived across the street from us, he got his ear bitten off defending Piedoe."

"Is that right?" I said, looking a little skeptically at Tobias.

"Damn right, it's right," Zak said.

"Okay, that confirms it. I'm sorry to doubt anyone."

Zak went on. "Big Bopper and I travelled upriver to Coffee Creek, where I pulled the boat onto the shore and secured it with rope. I was careful, because it wouldn't be the first time a boat was untied by the movement of the water."

Tobias nodded. "I had friends whose boat did that. They couldn't figure out how anyone could steal it because they were so deep in the bush, but a pilot reported seeing a freighter canoe drifting empty down the river. They got help fetching it. Tied it tight after that."

"I strapped the canvas packs on Bopper. He carried fifty pounds of dried food with ease. I shouldered my pack, and we hiked east into the Wellesley Lake area. Whenever I came to a creek, I stripped down and held my gear above my head to wade across. After I crossed one deep creek, I got out and was standing on wet rocks getting dressed when I slipped and fell. I saw the ground coming up and everything went black."

"Knocked you out cold?" I asked.

"It did more than that. When I came to, I was standing in a different place at a different time of day. Hell, the whole damn world was different. I couldn't understand why I was hungry, because Bopper and I had eaten breakfast. I stared down at my clothes, trying to comprehend why my long johns were so raggedy and dirty, why I wore moose hide on my feet and why I was covered from head to foot in bug bites, scratches and tree sap. I had a beard, and my hair was matted. My forehead had a raised, closed wound that hurt when I touched it. I felt scared. It was as though I'd been transmitted to another world. I gathered my wits, and my army commando training kicked in. I assessed the situation, and then I realized I must have had an accident. I remembered slipping and falling on the stones beside the creek."

"So that's how you got that nasty scar," Tobias said. "I'll take a picture of that to help document your story."

"We'll get it framed so you can hang it on your wall to remember what you forgot," I said.

Zak continued his story. I think he did not appreciate our humour.

"I'd been fit and muscular, but now my ribs stood out so I could count each one. My legs were skin and bone, but my feet were in the worst shape of all. Obviously I'd done a lot of walking. That knock on the head had put me out for some time, and my memory was blank from the moment I fell to the moment I woke up. I had no idea where I'd been or what I'd done."

"Sounds like amnesia," Tobias said.

"It was amnesia. To make matters worse, I had a satchel hanging from my shoulder, and when I sat down and opened it, gold nuggets tumbled out. The smallest was the size of an apricot pit, and the largest the size of an apricot. I held them in my hand and wondered where in hell they came from."

"You had a satchel of large gold nuggets but no idea how you got them?" Tobias asked, scribbling and turning pages without looking up. "Wow."

"That's right. Next I called for Big Bopper, but he was gone."

"Probably headed into town to register your claim," I joked.

"I wish," he said. He went on, "I started a fire with friction. The salmon were still spawning in the shallow streams and were easy to whack with a stick. After I ate, I lashed drift logs together with willows, and using a pole, I pushed off and drifted downstream toward Dawson. I placed the satchel behind me and kneeled to paddle. When I looked back, the satchel had slipped into the river. The only record I have is what I wrote in my diary after I got back."

"Do you still have the diary?" Tobias asked.

"Sure do."

"Can we see it?" I asked.

"Maybe. Just past the Stewart River I met a party of moose hunters. Ruth and Ben Naylor and their son Jerry took me on board, looking at me like they'd seen a ghost.

"'Everyone has been looking for you, Zak. The RCMP, and every trapper and prospector from here to Carmacks. What happened? We thought you were dead.'

"I told them I'd had an accident in the spring and knocked myself out for the summer, and for the life of me I couldn't remember a thing until a few days ago.

"They took me into Dawson, where I convalesced in the hospital. Everyone was glad to see I was alive.

"People said, 'We were going to have a memorial for you, but we waited. We figured if anyone could survive it would be you.'

"Saint Mary's hospital at the north end of Dawson City had burned to a crisp some time before, so the courthouse had been turned into a thirty-five-bed hospital with an operating room. When I arrived, the place was crowded because of a flu epidemic. A bed was made up in the men's ward, and the doctor and nurses gave me medical attention.

"My stay dragged into weeks. The doctor refused to let me leave, saying, 'You've been through a rough ordeal and suffered a nasty bump on the head. Amnesia is something to take seriously.'

"I was in bad shape and still suffered from dizziness. A specialist from Vancouver, tending patients in Whitehorse, took an interest in my case. He caught the next plane and arrived in Dawson City two days later.

"I was annoyed by the attention. 'I'm not a specimen in a bottle, so don't think you can prod and question me all day long,' I told them.

"After consulting with the local doctor and his colleagues in Vancouver, the specialist said, 'It appears you have a case of post-traumatic amnesia, which resulted from a traumatic brain injury, i.e., your bump on the head.'

"I wondered what 'i.e.' meant but I was too tired to ask."

"I.e. stands for the Latin for 'that is,'" Tobias said, writing and not looking up.

"The doc said, 'You were unable to remember events after the injury, and while the amnesia lasted, you could not store new memories. It appears you have no islands of memory during your amnesia.'

"'Yeah, yeah,' I said.

"Taffy brought a bottle of overproof rum from Alaska that he'd been saving for a special occasion.

"'No time like the present, Zak, my friend!' He broke the seal and poured two generous glasses.

"When Taffy started to sing ditties the nuns confiscated the bottle and manhandled him out the back door.

"'If you darken our doorstep again, Mr. Taffy, we'll beat you with a broom until your britches are on fire.'

"After that the nuns scrutinized my visitors closely.

"'Zachariah needs his rest, and you're disturbing the other patients with your loud card playing and smelly cigar smoke. And don't think we can't see what you're hiding under your coat!'

"Wilfred Durant was allowed to visit because he was a 'gentleman,' not like the rest of the rabble.

"When Wilfred visited I drew him close and whispered, 'I've got to tell you, Wilf, though it's crazy as hell. I had all this gold, but for the life of me, I can't remember a thing about where I found it.'

"Wilfred looked back and forth between the scar on my forehead and my eyes, trying to make a connection between the two.

"He said, 'Okay. You found gold and now you don't know where it is.'

"'That's exactly it,' I said, holding onto his upper arms and shaking them.

"'Zak, you're an honest man and wouldn't make things up, but I've heard of men hallucinating from hunger and hypothermia.'

"'I'm not talking about things I hallucinated. I'm telling the truth,' I said.

"A reporter from the *Whitehorse Star*, having gotten his hands on a copy of the *Dawson City Weekly News*, travelled up to interview me. I was reluctant to tell anyone of my adventure.

"I asked Wilf, 'Why would I confide in someone I don't know? Who does he think he is, my friend?'

"I gave the reporter no details, but he persisted.

"'This is very interesting, Mr. Zak. You lost your memory but still survived in the woods. How did you manage that?'

"'My name's not Mr. Zak, and how the hell am I going to tell you what I don't remember?'

"'Excuse me. What is your last name, then?' the reporter asked politely, holding his pencil over his notebook, ready to record this fascinating story for the history books.

"I'd had enough. 'Get the hell out, or I'll call one of those nuns to throw you out.' He picked up his bag and left as quickly as he could.

"Eventually the doctor let me go home. The hospital staff gave a going-away party with a candle in a carrot cake; I'd grown very fond of carrot cake in the hospital.

"After the goodbyes I joked, 'Do any of you nurses want to come home and be my new cook?'

"They called a taxi and sent me packing.

"'We'll beat you with a broom same as Taffy if you come back here and bother us again, Mr. Zachariah Funny Man.'

"Lovely women, those nuns. 'Angels, every one,' I told the taxi driver.

"My neighbours Nat and Dot lit a fire in my cabin to chase out the dampness and let the mice know the owner was back. Dot baked an apple pie and left it on the table, covered with a red and white tea towel.

"The minute the taxi pulled up, Nat came over to help carry my bag into the house.

"'Where do you think Big Bopper is?'

"'I'm sorry to say I don't know.'

"'Tell me the worst that could happen to him.'

"'My amnesia won't let me tell you anything, Nat. Honestly, I don't know where he is. I'm sorry.'

"'You mean he might be gone?'

"'I don't know. He's a smart dog. Let's wait and see. Maybe he's okay and will make his own way home.'

"Nat still looked worried sick, but he seemed happier with that answer.

"'Okay, that's fine. We'll wait and see. Good to have you home, Zak.'

"'Thanks.'

"A week later Big Bopper swam across the Yukon River at Dawson City and sat dripping wet on Nat's porch. It was twelve noon and he wanted his lunch. He was the worse for wear—underweight, with bite marks on his neck—but otherwise okay. Nat was never so happy in all his life.

"I wrote and drew maps of every single detail I could remember, but I couldn't pinpoint the gold.

"Wilfred didn't stop thinking about the gold either. He would show up on my doorstep at all hours to discuss it. It was good to have a friend; I was still concerned about my memory loss.

"'Do you think I'm losing my mind?' I asked Wilf.

"'No, believe me, I've come across people who have lost their minds, and you're not one of them. But I think you should take better care of yourself. You're still recovering from what would have killed other men,' he said.

"I tried to remember, but however much I pondered, nothing came to mind. I dreamed of wolves and long shadows in the forest. I hiked up the Dome Road and sat looking out over the town, trying to clear my mind. I rubbed the scar on my forehead as though it were a magic lamp, hoping a genie would appear to answer all my questions. The Dawson City library had a limited supply of books on amnesia; I read everything I could find. The nurses at the hospital supplied medical texts.

"'If you can understand these, you're welcome to them, Zak,' the nurses said.

"All this helped me understand the condition but didn't bring back memories.

"'I don't think it will return, Zak,' Wilfred said. 'You're locked up like a clamshell, and that area you were in is just too large to search. Without more information it would take years to find the gold.'

"When it seemed nothing else could be done, I wrapped the diary in canvas and dropped it into a trunk. I would wait for the day when medical science could find the gold that my mind had lost.

"'It's the Lost Mind Mine,' I joked."

"Did you tell anyone else besides Wilfred about the gold?" I asked.

"I did tell a few people, but they didn't believe me. They said, 'You must have been hallucinating as well as suffering from amnesia.'"

"I believe you," I said.

"I believe you too," Winch shouted from the kitchen. He and Clutch had been listening the whole time.

"Maybe we should go see if we can find it again," Clutch said, coming into the room with his coffee.

"I think so too," Zak said, "I told Mimosa Nightingale. I trust her intuition. She took both my hands across the table and told me, 'Zak, I can see everything you say is true, but your memory will never lead you back to your gold. It will take a lot of hard-working people, and the ending will not be so good. Also, buy an Irish Sweepstakes ticket on May 19, 1999, if you're still around.'"

"That confirms it," Winch said. "If Mimosa says it's true, then it's true."

A moment later, Buster, the eldest McKan, walked in. He said, "I heard someone talking about gold."

Buster always got a glint in his eye when anyone mentioned gold. I tried to remember where I'd seen that before, and then it struck me. Billy Beers! Buster had the same look in his eye as my friend Billy Beers, the delusional gold prospector who had gold fever so badly he convinced himself that ordinary rocks were nuggets.

"Naw, no one's talking about anything like that," Zak said. He didn't trust the McKans and didn't want them to be involved in his business.

"Okay," Buster said and left.

When Buster was out of earshot, OP jumped from the couch into the air shouting, "Yahoo! We're going after the motherlode."

"Hullabaloo!" Clutch yelled. "The motherlode!"

"Halloo! Halloo!" Winch joined in.

The three big men linked arms and danced in a circle, turning one way and then the other like Hasidic Jews as everyone clapped. The brothers shouted, "Yahoo, hullabaloo, Halloo! Yahoo, hullabaloo, Halloo!" over and over again.

The floor bounced under their half ton, and dishes rattled in their hutches. The rest of the household, hearing the ruckus, came running to join in.

Over the noise Missy yelled, "Joshua, what's happening? What's going on?"

"Gold fever!" I yelled. "It's gold fever!"

The Rock Creek Gold Bottom Company

The Halloo brothers were good fathers, providers, musicians and mechanics but poor businessmen. Zak eventually gave his nephews the diary that recorded where he thought a rich gold-bearing creek might be.

"I'll give it to them, Joshua, but I want you to keep an eye on it. They might use it for fire starter."

The brothers and I studied information and drawings until the binding came loose and pages started falling out. Everything was hush-hush. Our wives and children watched as we hunched over the kitchen table, our heads together, talking in whispers.

"What are Uncle Joshua and Dad doing, Mom? Are they learning their ABCs?" OP's youngest wanted to know.

"We won a pony and we're filling out the paperwork," OP said.

The kids were ecstatic and ran off to tell their friends.

Lulu didn't like to lie to the children and made us promise to get a pony. "Get it soon. I'd hate to see those kids disappointed."

"You're right, Lulu," Clutch said, "OP shouldn't joke with the kids like that."

OP nodded in agreement, since he could do nothing less. "Sorry, Lulu."

Eventually he did buy a pony, and the kids called her Uncle OP. They were developing a keen sense of humour.

We studied and speculated on the diary for a few hours three or four times a week. Tobias, who was always looking for a story, would join us, but we told him not to publicize anything until we had the gold in our hands.

OP sharpened pencils until they were stubs and left graphite smears on the oilcloth tablecloth. We drew maps and burned them after each meeting.

"Just like the FBI," Clutch said.

Lulu, Stella, Missy and Olive knew what we were doing and didn't interfere. They figured that if we found gold, they would be on easy street. They plied us with coffee and cake to keep us focused. Sometimes it had the opposite effect as OP liked a snooze after a meal, and he ate so much baking it was like a meal. He napped on the table with his head on his arm. We were too engrossed in what we were doing to pay any attention.

Zak sat in if we asked. "You guys figure it out, but I want royalties, lots of them, and all cash. I'm going to buy the longest, blackest Cadillac that General Motors ever built, with flaming red leather interior with white piping, an egg-crate grille, dual-stacked headlights and rear seat cigarette lighters." He usually left after making his demands known.

The brothers would eat an entire two-layer chocolate cake while Tobias and I nibbled at another one.

"You guys going to eat the rest of that cake?" they would ask, shaking the crumbs out of their beards.

"No, go right ahead," we said, knowing they would take it anyway.

"Lulu, honey, is there any more ice cream to go with this?" Winch asked.

The diary accumulated strawberry and chocolate colouring.

"Joshua, you're an experienced bushman. What do you think we need to find this gold?" OP asked.

"You're going to need thousands of dollars and a base camp to start from." Noticing that Zak had prospected near the same area that Billy Beers staked before he went bonkers, I added, "This might be a wild goose chase. The prospector Billy Beers lost his mind in that area."

"Zak did wander around for about three months. Almost anything could have happened," Winch said.

"Naw, couldn't be. Zak would never get gold fever. He's too savvy for that," Tobias said.

We called Zak in for about the hundredth time.

"Zak, do you remember finding anyone else's diggings?" I asked.

"Nope," said Zak.

"Do you remember finding supplies and maybe a helicopter landing pad with a windsock?"

"Nope."

"Do you remember ever bumping into a guy all dressed up like a Hollywood sourdough, wearing a ten-gallon hat and speaking with a funny accent?"

"Why the hell would I remember that? I was in the bush, not at a circus!"

"For God's sake, Zak," Clutch burst in, "do you remember what you had for lunch?"

"Lulu made me soup and a tuna fish sandwich for lunch, and change your tone or you'll be having a knuckle sandwich for yours," Zak said.

With that, Zak left the room, shouting over his shoulder, "Don't ask for my help again!"

"We need a grubstake," OP said.

"Let's all get jobs and save," Clutch said.

Olive walked out of the kitchen, wiping her hands on her apron. "Why not ask the McKans? They have lots of money. Tammy and Holly told me."

"We can't ask them to trust us now, after that Ruby thing," Winch said.

"Yeah, thanks, Clutch. See how things come back and bite you in the butt? Now we can't ask the McKans for help," OP said, throwing a couch pillow at his brother.

"I'll go ask them," I said. "Maybe they want to prospect for gold as much as you want their money."

I went over that evening and found the McKans so eager that they wanted to send a cheque back with me.

"A sign of goodwill, a sort of down payment to start negotiations," Jack said.

I remembered what my dad said: "Always take the money, Joshua." So I asked for a thousand dollars, and they paid it.

"We'll come over tomorrow after lunch, take a look at the diary and see if we can seal this deal," Chipper said.

The Halloos couldn't believe the money came that easily. They passed the cheque around, holding it up to the light like currency to see the watermark.

"I think you should be careful," Lulu said. "My instincts tell me these are good neighbours but also good businessmen who know how to make a buck and keep it for themselves."

Mid-afternoon the McKans walked over, and Missy ushered them into the living room. Jack stayed home. After coffee and small talk we got down to business. In light of Lulu's caution, Winch had the three McKans stand in the middle of the living room, raise their left hands and recite an oath that OP made up.

"You write this down and be a witness to all this, Joshua," Winch said. He began, "I swear that I will keep secret that which I'm about to hear and see."

"I swear that I will keep secret that which I'm about to hear and see," the men repeated.

"And to uphold the spirit of true Klondike sourdough justice," Winch continued.

"And to uphold the spirit of true Klondike sourdough justice," the men said.

"And to never forget to save a piece of dough to raise the next sourdough loaf," Winch said. He'd explained to Lulu that the sourdough thing was akin to other organizations' secret symbols.

"And to never forget to save a piece of dough to raise the next sourdough loaf," the men said.

Just then Zak walked in. "What the hell is going on, a Boy Scout meeting? Is someone getting a new badge?"

"We're taking an oath," Chipper said.

"You're all nuts," Zak said with a wave of his hand and left again.

"You're all nuts," the McKan brothers repeated.

"No, no," said Winch, "you ruined the oath." He made them repeat the last lines over.

Once the McKans read the diary and heard Zak's story, they were convinced they were on the path to the motherlode.

"I always wanted to do this," Buster said.

"I know we'll strike it rich," Chipper said.

The Halloos estimated prospecting that summer would cost twenty thousand dollars.

"We want Joshua in on this. He's the best bushman we have," Clutch said.

"That's okay with us, but his share comes out of yours and not ours," Moe said.

"Fine," said Winch.

The McKans slept on it. The next morning they happily agreed to join the company. We sealed the deal with handshakes.

Chipper made it clear that Jack wouldn't be in the bush but had him written in for a full share because he put up five thousand dollars. The Halloos agreed. Ruby made a big show of hugging and congratulating Jack on his inclusion in the deal.

Lulu warned Winch, Clutch and OP again, "I don't have a good feeling about this."

"This could be the deal of the century. What could possibly go wrong?" Winch said. He would later recall his words and answer that question himself.

We decided on the company's name more easily than we'd decided on a name for the band. After a short meeting the Rock Creek Gold Bottom Company was born. It was Clutch's suggestion, and he was pleased he'd finally got to name something.

"I know when we find Zak's creek, the bottom of it's going to be solid gold," Clutch said to Buster, whose eyes looked like they were going to shine right out of his head.

A week later Buster, Winch and I drove into Dawson City to interview Jerry Naylor, the last living member of the group that rescued Zachariah on the Yukon River. Jerry lived at the north end of town in a cabin he had inherited from his parents. The front yard was covered with a thick layer of sawdust and wood chips, the remains of last winter's ten cords of wood. Someone had made an attempt to gather it into piles but the sawdust insulated layers of snow making it difficult to rake. It would be easier once the sun melted it loose. The porch deck was worn enough that the nail heads were shiny. Winch knocked on the door and Jerry opened it.

"Hi Winch, Joshua," he said.

He was thin and less than five feet tall, with black hair cut below his ears and low on his forehead. He had a sparse goatee and a bright smile.

"Hi, Jerry. This is Buster," Winch said.

"Hi Buster," Jerry said, shaking his hand. "Come in. I'll make coffee."

We filed in and sat on the worn couch and around the Arborite stainless steel kitchen table. Jerry took down four cups from a sagging shelf and put a tablespoon of instant coffee in each. He turned on the tap, tested the water with his finger until it was steaming hot, then filled each cup to the brim.

"Coffee-Mate and sugar?" he asked.

"No, this is fine," Chipper said.

Winch nodded in agreement.

I reached for both.

Jerry's house was from the gold rush era: small and sparsely furnished. The windows were covered in poly and snapped in and out when the wind blew or the front door opened. The plastic had been on for more than a year and the sunlight had clouded it like a cataract. An airtight wood stove stood against a wall and radiated a comfortable, even heat throughout the room.

Jerry sat on a legless armchair that matched the couch and rolled a cigarette from a can of Player's tobacco.

"I keep a slice of apple in here, keeps it moist," he said as he closed the lid.

He seemed unmindful that this unexpected visit had a purpose.

One of his children ran into the room and jumped onto his lap. With his head to one side so as not to burn the child he lit the cigarette, took a draw and blew the smoke above his head.

"So what's up? What brings you gentlemen out to visit today?"

"We want to ask you about the time you and your folks rescued Zachariah on the river," Winch said.

Picking a piece of tobacco off his lip Jerry said, "Oh yeah, that. I thought you guys had something on your mind but I never would have thought it was finding Zak.

"My mom and dad were hunting moose in the fall when we saw this log coming downriver towards us. We were surprised to see a man hanging on to it, waving his arms like crazy. We were even more surprised to see it was Zachariah because everyone thought he was a goner. Some of us figured a grizzly got him or something. We hauled him into the boat. He was more dead than alive, all beat up, scratched, starving and bruised. He had a million bites on him. He was in rough shape and had a nasty wound on his head that had healed over—it should have been stitched so it didn't look too good."

"Do you remember where you found him?" Buster asked.

"I remember exactly where we found him," Jerry said. "It was near our traditional camp. My family has used it for years."

"Good," said Winch.

"We made land for a few hours, fed and bandaged him up as best we could. Mom had some ointment which eased his pain a little. He could hardly move and didn't talk but shivered and slept in the bottom of the boat all the way back to town. He must have been strong because what he went through would have killed other men. Being lost in the bush is no easy thing.

We tied up just below the hospital but he was delirious and crawling around, so we got help and a stretcher."

"Did he say anything about finding gold?" Buster asked.

Jerry's eyebrows shot up: now he knew what we were looking for.

Winch thought Buster had shown too many of his cards and gave him a look.

Jerry said, "Zak said nothing. He was in no shape to talk."

"No, I guess not," Buster said.

Jerry had a Yukon map pinned to the wall and pointed to the spot where Zak was found.

He surprised us when he said, "A year later I discovered Zak's boat stashed in the bush. We towed it back to Dawson City and Zachariah gave us a small reward for finding it."

Jerry also marked this spot on the map.

"Did you see a dog?" I asked.

"We never saw any dog," Jerry said.

"Can I get you another cup of coffee?"

We graciously declined, thanked him and left.

The information Jerry gave was invaluable.

Winch remarked, "Jerry had a forty-gallon hot water coffee pot."

The McKans bought a forty-foot aluminum riverboat and trailer built in Whitehorse and outfitted it with two 90 hp Evinrude motors. The boat could carry two tons of men and equipment. It ferried us up the Yukon River to the spot where Zak's boat was found by the Taylor family who rescued him.

We made rough calculations and hiked in to where Zak might have bumped his head. We split up and covered every creek, valley and hill we came across. We slogged through swamps, thick willows and dense overgrown spruce forests that nature should have burned off years ago. The mosquitoes and blackflies feasted on every part of our bodies. We used so much repellent our skin peeled off as if sunburnt, and if we didn't have nets over our heads I'm sure our eyes would swell shut.

By the middle of summer the seven of us had spent six exhausting weeks hiking up and down. It was then we decided to draw another line from the estimated accident site to where Zak figured he came out on the Yukon River.

We split into three parties. OP went alone and took the boat to meet Clutch, Chipper and Moe when they came out of the bush.

The three men found the going grueling, with days of rain-soaked clothing, cold meals and nights huddled under tarps hastily thrown over crude tent frames. The party camped for a night five miles from the Yukon River.

Moe was clearing the bush for the tent when he called the others over. "Chipper! Clutch! Come see! Look at this!"

Chipper and Clutch peered into the underbrush. There among the willows were two canvas saddlebags hooked on a branch.

Moe poked at one, and gold nuggets spilled out. The three of them stood bent over with hands resting on knees and their heads together and shouted in unison, "Pack sacks!"

They were the Big Bopper's saddle bags.

It was all true, everything Zak had told us. He had found gold, he did have amnesia and he did lose the nuggets. The size and quantity of gold made it evident that incredible wealth was just waiting somewhere to be picked up off the ground.

Chipper and Moe remained at the site and prospected in the immediate area. Clutch headed back to the river to meet OP and wait for Buster, Winch and me. Within four days we were back at the camp we called Big Bopper or BB.

We now knew where Zak hit his head, the boat's location, the canvas bags' location, and where he might have come out on the river. This area formed a rough triangle with the river as its baseline.

The question now was whether to look inside or outside the triangle.

"Let's flip a coin. Fortunes have been made on a coin flip," Buster said.

I flipped a coin. It landed on the ground and stuck on its edge in the mud.

"Well, that's a strange answer if I ever saw one," said OP.

We stood in a circle. Not one of us dared to tempt fate by making a decision.

"If we wait long enough, it's sure to fall over," Moe said.

"In about ten years," Winch said. We had only about another six weeks before winter would make it difficult to travel on the river or dig the frozen ground.

"I think it says we should look everywhere," I said.

"Right you are, Joshua," Winch said quickly.

Moe, Winch, Buster and I travelled west and found a small creek meandering back and forth across a narrow valley. We hiked up it, broke into a clearing and found the remains of a cabin. The roof had caved in, logs had shifted out of place and a makeshift chair stood alone. The remains of a collapsed bed leaned against the other wall. Scattered on the crumbling floor planks was a human skeleton. The skull was bleached white, and green moss grew on the frontal bone like a toupee. A tibia lay near the bed; its compound fracture explained the demise of the cabin's owner.

Winch picked up the skull. The teeth were intact and perfect. He stared at it for the longest time and then placed it back amongst the other bones.

Buster and I watched him. Hamlet came to my mind: "That skull had a tongue in it and could sing once."

Buster went over to the wall and brushed away one hundred years of dust and vegetation and read, "To Rebecca, Love never ends, it will always be something God-given, and heavenly free."

He took a step back and said quietly, "That's nice."

We knew what had happened. It was sad.

Later I cut out the log with the poem and kept it.

Winch picked up an empty whiskey bottle with the rusted cap still on it. Something jingled inside and he emptied the contents into his hand. "Well, look at that: ten dimes and six pennies, all American and all dated from the last century. This fellow must have been from the States."

"Let's bury him decently," Buster said.

The cabin and body were probably seventy years old. We saw signs that someone had built a ring of stones and a fire more recently.

"It's a law of the Yukon to give a decent burial. Why did someone camp here and not take care of the body?" Winch asked.

"Could have been Zak," I said.

No one had an answer but it got us thinking.

We made camp and cooked dinner, and afterward Moe went to wash dishes. We had all been distracted by the skeleton, so when he bent down to scoop up sand to scrub the pots and tin plates, he didn't see the gold right away. When he did, his yells brought us running.

Moe yelled "Eureka!" over and over again until he went hoarse. The men threw themselves into the creek, scooped up handfuls of gold, sand and gravel and tossed them into the air. They hugged and danced until they were exhausted, then dropped laughing onto the creek's bank. The gold was everywhere.

"Billions," Moe said.

"Yeah," Winch said. "We found it, we finally found it, and we're rich."

We called Clutch, OP and Chipper on the radio and gave them instructions in code (other prospectors would be listening in) for where to meet up.

"Uncle Albert is reaching hands across the ocean and the grass is green," were Winch's cryptic words.

"I sure hope they remember what they meant," I said.

Two days later they arrived. When they saw the gold, Clutch emptied his side arm into the air, and Chipper blasted off the shotgun. They linked arms and danced until they had to sit down and rest. They couldn't stop laughing.

We called the creek Bump on the Head Creek after Zak's now-famous bump on the head, but soon shortened this to Bump Creek. Some people misheard the name, and it ended up being called Bum Creek.

We staked miles of claims and established legal posts for registering at the Dawson City mining recorder's office.

Chipper, Moe and Buster volunteered to take the paperwork into town. The rest of us would stay behind and continue staking and assessing the ground. In hindsight, if I'd gone with them, things would have turned out differently.

The McKans returned to Rock Creek Saturday night to a warm greeting. Buster made a quick visit to the Halloos to bring them up to date on the latest developments and deliver letters.

When he returned home trouble had entered the room. That night and all of Sunday Ruby argued that the gold belonged to the McKans alone and they should keep it for themselves.

"Without your money, boat, brains and business experience those knuckleheads would never have found anything," she said.

"Hold on there, Ruby. We did shake on this," Buster said.

"That's just it. You only shook hands. You signed nothing. Think how stupid that is! What's wrong with you guys? Are you too weak and afraid of those men to take what is yours?"

The brothers thought it over. Ruby's argument was convincing; they had invested and worked hard to find the gold. The argument dragged on for hours.

"Let's take a vote," Jack said. "We'll vote whether to stake the claims ourselves or file the claims jointly with the Halloos."

The women insisted on having a vote.

"Okay, all those in favour of sharing with the Halloos, raise your hand," Buster said.

Buster and his wife, Tammy, were the only ones to raise their hands.

The men hugged their wives and celebrated with cheers and slaps on the back.

"After all," Moe shouted, "back home we were business leaders in the community. There is no reason why we shouldn't be that here."

"And that will teach Clutch to take our Ruby away," Chipper said.

Missy drove the kids to school that Monday morning and saw the McKans at the mining recorder's office bright and early.

Miles away, OP, Winch, Clutch and I were eating a late lunch, digging the last of the butter out of a can and spreading it on pilot biscuits to dip in tea. Unannounced, the carpenter brothers Orville and Peter Buttery-Byrds walked into camp. OP stopped telling us how happy he'd be to take a hot shower and eat a decent meal. At first we said nothing. We were surprised because only the McKans knew we were here.

"Chipper paid us to come out and take you back to town with their boat," Orville said.

Winch stood up, instantly suspicious. "The McKans should have come back themselves. What's going on?"

"We have no idea. We were given a map and paid to deliver this note," Orville said, and held out an envelope.

"We thought we were sent here to help you," Peter said.

Winch took the note and read it. His face went white and then red, and he clasped his fist to his head.

"What does it say?" I asked.

"It says, get off our land," Winch snarled between clenched teeth. He crumpled the note and threw it on the ground.

I picked it up, straightened it out and kept it for further legal reference. I had never seen Winch so mad.

"We've been jumped," Clutch yelled. "Damn McKans jumped our claims!"

"This is a joke," I said, and looked down the trail over Peter's shoulder, expecting Buster and his brothers to come walking up, laughing their fool heads off.

Orville followed my gaze and looked down the path. Turning back, he said, "No, it's not a joke, Joshua. We came alone."

Winch barked, "Come on, let's go."

We grabbed half our belongings, leaving things behind, and raced to the boat. We sped back to Dawson City. The only thing that stopped the Halloos from going over to the McKans was their wives, who physically dragged OP to the floor and held him down when he tried to leave.

"OP, stop it. You'll only cause more problems if you go over there," Olive said. She sat on his chest as he lay on the ground.

"But they took the oath," OP groaned.

"We have to keep our heads about this. The McKans would love to have the RCMP throw you in the clink," I said.

The McKans had no idea what law they'd broken and how much trouble they were in.

Word spread quickly around town. The greatest sin of all in the Klondike Valley had been committed: claims had been robbed. Soon the McKans were denied service at the hardware and grocery stores and restaurants. The gas attendants wouldn't turn on the pumps or even come out of the garage office.

"Get the hell out of here," the usually mild Brian told them when they tried to fill up at Huey Ford's Chevrolet Automotive Garage in downtown Dawson.

The cashiers at the grocery store checkouts refused to put their groceries through, and when the manager ordered them to do so, they threatened to quit. The Flora Dora Café staff refused to serve them a cup of coffee. When they inquired about heavy equipment or tradespeople to work for them, the door was shut in their faces.

The McKans had become pariahs. Breaking a law of the Yukon was weighing heavily upon their shoulders. People shunned and ostracized them.

But the McKans had deep pockets. When the legal battle began, there was no end to the lawyers they could hire and there was no end to the lawyers who offered their services.

Two suits, as the Halloos called them, arrived from the prestigious Vancouver law firm of Louis, Dempsey and Spinks.

"This is a slam dunk case," they told the McKans. "These people don't have a chance. It's all in your names, and that is 100 percent of the law."

On the other hand, the Halloos had limited resources. The good citizens of Dawson City recognized that the playing field was not level and gave them their support. The Halloos played two fundraisers. The town turned out to dance until the wee hours of the morning and raised over twenty thousand dollars.

Lulu was able to hire the help her family needed. She employed two hungry young brothers, Derrick and Craig Mossheart of the Vancouver firm of Briemon, Selnes and Tanner. They were as bright and capable as anyone the McKans could throw at them.

"Don't worry, Lulu, we're going to jam these guys up real good," Derrick said.

"Well, don't hurt them too badly," Lulu said.

The Halloos and their lawyers met upstairs in the post office building above the mining recorder's office and across the street from the Robert Service School.

"The way I see it, the McKans used your maps, information and bush expertise to find the gold. To exclude you from the benefits of that effort is criminal," said Derrick, the younger of the two.

"Derrick is right. The oath and the handshake are enforceable, but we will have to interview all who were present," Craig said.

"Well, I was there," Zak said, "and my word is worth double. I'm a veteran, you know."

The McKans had never envisioned the pain and stress of being shunned. They began to realize what their dishonesty had brought down upon their shoulders. They worried about their kids at school and the treatment of their wives in town, especially Ruby.

"There have been some unkind words," Holly said.

"In the old days we shunned criminals if they broke our laws. They couldn't survive alone in the bush—too lonely—and other people wouldn't take them in either," Chief Daniel told me when I ran into him at the grocery store. "Some died pretty quick."

The next day the McKans asked for a meeting in the same room above the post office. The meeting was tense. The McKans had brought their lawyers with them.

Winch stood up, and not looking at the lawyers, said in no uncertain terms, "The lawyers go or we go. We are not going to get into negotiations. We do the original deal we shook on or we go to court."

The McKans huddled, nodded their heads in agreement and instructed the lawyers to leave.

They didn't protest, but one said, "We'll be right outside if you need us."

"No one is going to need you. If they do, we go home," Winch repeated.

The Halloos had the upper hand; all the miners and townspeople were on their side. The McKans would perish in the Yukon without the help of others. Finally they'd realized this.

"We want to apologize," said Buster.

"Save it," Winch said, flipping his hand in the air. "We're not interested; the only thing we're going to do is go back to square one and do what we first decided."

"That's only fair," OP said.

"Yes, it is," Buster said. "I want you to know that I was against this from the start but I was outvoted."

It took only an hour to agree again on the original deal. The McKans offered to have their lawyer draw up the papers.

"No papers," said Winch. "We shook on this before, and that's all we need. This meeting is over."

The four McKans stood across the table with weak smiles on their faces and offered their hands to shake. We filed out, ignoring them.

That ended the relationship between the Halloos and the McKans. A relationship that had started out with so much promise of friendship and support was now gone, and in its place was nothing.

"For all their reading and trying, the McKans never caught the true spirit of the Klondike," I said.

"We learned it," Winch said. "We had to. This isn't downtown Vancouver, you know."

The band was gone forever, but the Bum Creek Band was born out of all the turmoil.

Clutch loved the name. "It's better than Crazy War," he said, remembering his first suggestion for a name.

The kids thought it was hilarious. "You said 'bum'!"

The McKans stayed in Dawson City for many generations and over time things changed and improved but they never lived down the dishonesty of jumping the claims. For many years merchants would deal with them only in cash, and some wouldn't even do that.

The name McKan became a byword for dishonesty in the Klondike.

"I like that," said Victor the Gypsy. "People not saying 'gyp' any more."

"Don't be a McKan" and "don't McKan me" were common expressions. The Halloos never missed a chance to use them. They also mentioned that Bum Creek was named after the McKans.

"Bunch of bums, that's all they are," OP said.

The gold on Bum Creek turned out not to be as rich as Bonanza or

Hunker, but it was rich enough, and the families worked it for many years and made a comfortable living.

In the summer the entire Halloo and McKan families moved to the claims and in the fall they moved back to Rock Creek. The Buttery-Byrds brothers, Arnold and I kept busy building homes, workshops and bunkhouses. It was a good life.

Billy Beers showed up at the placer mine. He looked longingly up and down Bum Creek and said casually, "This gold should have been mine, Joshua."

No one gave it much attention. Billy was invited to have lunch in the kitchen, where the Halloo women cooked for the large crew of miners and Zak had a permanent seat at a table. There he drank coffee and talked to anyone who would swap stories with him.

Zak's jet-black Cadillac Coupe de Ville with the red leather interior and white piping was parked outside his bunkhouse door. He polished it and sat in it almost every day. The odometer read five hundred miles when he passed away years later. Clutch inherited the car in Zak's will: "I called Clutch too many names too many times. I really didn't mean them. Here's the Caddy to make it up."

Clutch drove it for over half a million miles until his oldest daughter was learning to drive and drove it into a dredge pond.

"That thing floated around like a boat for half an hour before it sank," she said. "We had to climb out the windows and swim for it."

"Too bad. Nicest ride I ever had," Clutch said. "And that interior! We'll never see the likes of that again."

When Billy asked the Halloos for a job, they hired him. "I promise I won't start thinking gold nuggets are rocks."

Billy was a good catskinner, stripping the overburden to get down to bedrock. He was honest, and everyone appreciated that, since there was an opportunity to pinch nuggets from the sluice box. He insisted on having his wages paid in gold; he put it in a poke and slept with it under his pillow. "I have the sweetest dreams of striking it rich," he said.

The mine at Bum Creek cured the Halloos' and McKans' gold fever. The pursuit was more exciting than the discovery.

"It seems everyone is searching for something," Billy said. "Some of us search for gold."

"I searched for religion up on Hunker," Winch said.

"And I searched for aliens for the longest time," sighed Brian, who was visiting with his wife, Maude.

Late in the evening, after the day's work was done, the brothers and I would sit in the cook trailer reminiscing about our life together. Zak loved these times and told enough stories to fill a book. I regretted that Tobias was off at university because Zak told stories only once. Occasionally a McKan would wander in to get a cup of coffee and then leave. They never joined us.

We were richer than ever, but the cost of the gold was losing our friendship with the McKans. We all regretted it.

"Life in the Yukon should be full of friendships," Zak said, "but everything has its cost."

The story of Zak's diary and the discovery of the gold became well known throughout the Yukon. David Watts, a well-known and respected writer and journalist living in Dawson City, wrote articles for national publications. Tobias later wrote the book *Bum Creek Gold*.

The Whitehorse city councils, ever wise to the tourist industry, commissioned a bronze statue of Zak and the Big Bopper.

Today that statue stands outside the Chief Elijah Federal Building on Main Street in Whitehorse. Zak is a young, handsome prospector—Zak liked that best of all—confidently peering into the future. Big Bopper was cast half his size because the budget wouldn't allow him to be the size he really was.

Visitors from all over the world come to the Yukon to make love under the aurora borealis, believing the ribbons of light would increase the intelligence of their offspring. They also rub the pack dog's nose for prosperity and happiness. In a land as great and generous as the Yukon, surely all their wishes will come true.

Acknowledgements

I would like to acknowledge the readers from across Canada who have given me encouragement. It's a pleasure to know my work has brought humour and enjoyment into people's lives. Thank you.

Touted as the Yukon's Stuart McLean by author Laurie Glenn Norris, David Thompson is a writer and general building contractor who has lived in the Yukon Territory since 1962. His love for the land and its people inspires him to write fiction describing life in the Yukon. He has twice won Dawson City's "Authors on Eighth" writing contest for short fiction and has had stories published in local newspapers. David lives in Whitehorse with his wife, Wendy, who is a Montessori teacher, two children, Adam and Shawna, son-in-law Gary and two wonderful grandsons, Cameron and Jordan. His first book, *Talking at the Woodpile*, was published by Caitlin Press in 2011.